Beauty and the Beast

by
Sarah Winter

This is a work of fiction. Names, characters, businesses, places, events and incidents are either the products of the author's imagination or used in a fictitious manner. Any resemblance to actual persons, living or dead, or actual events is purely coincidental.

First Printing, February 2016

Printed in the United States of America

ISBN-13: 978-1519681669

Also by Sarah Winter

<u>Novels</u>

Snowbound
Over the Line
Beauty and the Beast
The Cottage

<u>Short Stories</u>

The Journal

<u>Anthologies</u>

Somewhere Out There

This book is dedicated to all of us who have felt judged by the way we look, the way we love, or the way we feel.

You are not alone, and things will get better.

I promise.

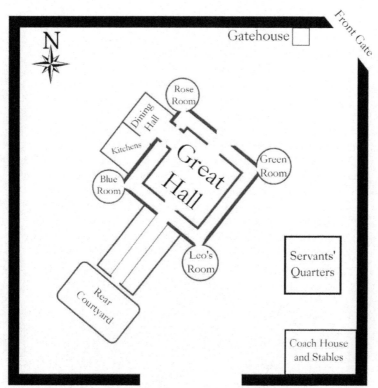

N

Gatehouse ☐

Front Gate

Rose Room

Dining Hall

Kitchens

Great Hall

Blue Room

Green Room

Leo's Room

Rear Courtyard

Servants' Quarters

Coach House and Stables

To the Tremonde Road

Prologue

A cold night in early spring, many years ago...

It all started with a promise.

A promise that led the old woman to run through the bare branches of the hawthorn and the rowan on an early winter's night.

A promise that led the old woman to question her actions as the frigid wind berated her for waiting so long.

A promise that brought the old woman near to death as icy slush slopped over her thin leather slippers.

The old woman needed to stop. Numbness was getting all too comfortable in her feet and all she was asking for was a moment to catch her breath and check her feet. That moment could also mean that her promise would be broken forever. She was living on borrowed time as it was— —her heavy breathing and the crunching of the frozen ground beneath her stiff old feet were evidence of that.

The temperature was dropping by the minute. The long, threadbare cloak she wore tied around her neck did little to block the bite of the wind, leaving her exposed skin feeling fragile and stiff. The old cloak was once a pale pink and was dotted with holes and tears from years of use and many travels. It was stained a shade of dirty grey except on her hunched back. There lay a swath of pink in the shape of a bird's extended wing.

As the old woman ran along the path she felt her arthritic knuckles about to lock up on her. She shook her gnarled hands and blew what heat she could into them, hoping it would suffice. In her left claw was a walking stick as crooked as a dog's hind leg and as full of gristle as its owner. She leaned on it heavily as she trudged on, her sunken and rheumy blue eyes swiveling left and right over everything in her path to search for any source of warmth. The road was little more than a goat trail, winding around large obstacles but full of sharp rocks and deep wagon ruts full of freezing water and ice. The road led her up a gentle, uphill grade away from the village of Fontainbleu. Soft lights glowed from the windows of the small homes and farms there, but she would not return to the town tonight.

The path wound around the hill as it went up, draping back and forth over the side of the hill like a sash. The old woman felt relief as she caught sight of the torches lining the final quarter of a mile, lighting

1

the path that led to the towering oak doors of a great white stone château. They would offer little warmth, but they would be better than nothing. As she neared the building, she saw the brass nail heads that decorated the gigantic doors. Only then did she allow a toothless smile to split her face, a grotesque display of her maw.

She heard music playing somewhere inside the hulking structure, the happy sound setting countless toes to tapping and hearts to lightness. The chorus of a birthday song came to her through the many windows, a jangling chorus for the prince that lived inside.

With what little strength she had left, she wrapped her hand around the round brass knocker. She tried as hard as she could, but she was so weak, a person standing on the other side of the door with an ear to the wood wouldn't hear it. The old woman drew up to try again. The noise was still soft and small, but louder than the first.

After waiting several minutes, she realized no one had heard her second attempt any better than the first. She fell back and raised her arms up over her head, her old joints cracking with the effort. Putting her hands together in a loose fist, she was just bringing them forward to pound on the door when it opened.

A liveried man stood on the other side, staring at her weary face full of deep wrinkles. He let out a silent *humph* when he widened the door opening and got a better look at her. Even this man, no more than a servant, felt himself better than her.

The old woman spoke, her voice so clear and musical it took the servant by surprise.

"I'm a weary traveler seeking shelter this night. Might the masters of the château have a room for an old woman to hide away and warm her bones?" she asked, her blue eyes swimming with hope.

The butler could see her thin body shivering beneath the ragged cloak. His breath and the warmth coming through the doors had created a fog of thick steam that obscured his vision beyond where she stood. If he didn't let her in, she would perish in this weather. If the servant were to allow this poor creature in the door, he could guarantee himself a return trip out of it before morning. Freezing to death on the long walk to Fontainbleu was not on his schedule for tonight.

It was Prince Leopold de Villeneuve's birthday —and the year of his majority. He had been abominable all day long, throwing childish tantrums over unwanted guests and demanding more gifts than any eighteen-year-old boy deserved. Prince Leopold still had the impatience

of a child. That, in combination with the temper of a large man, often
caused the destruction of half the royal family's possessions when he
was in one of his black moods.

After much consideration, the butler responded.

"I am sorry Madame, but we are unable to take in drifters."

He started to close the door when her craggy arm snaked into the
gap, stopping him.

"Prithee, sir," she pleaded in that beautiful voice. A stab of regret
clutched at his heart and he paused. "I have but this rose to give thee
for thy masters' kindness."

From within the ancient cloak she drew a single rose. The petals
were a pale ivory edged with a deep pink and its leaves a dark glossy
green. As she held it in the steamy air the flower began to glow with a
soft light from within the delicate bowl formed by its petals. So gentle
were her fingers on the stem that it appeared to be floating in midair
with no support. Unamused, the butler hung his head and pushed
against the door. She heard him mutter a soft apology before the door
closed on her.

Deterred for only a moment, the old woman placed the rose back
into her cloak and again set herself back, preparing to knock on the
door again. Her journey and her waiting would not be in vain. A
different servant answered this time, a taller and much older man than
the first. His eyes were less kind and his countenance severe in its
distaste at the sight of the old woman. His powdered hair was in a
queue so tight that when he spoke, the old woman was sure the hairs at
his hairline would pull free from his scalp in one painful rip.

"Oui, Madame?" he said, his voice sniveling and shrill. His nose
pointed upward at such an angle he had to look down his cheeks to see
her.

"Prithee, sir," she said, again earning surprise at the softness and
beauty of her voice. "I will perish in this weather. All I request is
lodgings for the night. A warm place to rest until morning." Her eyes
shone bright in the melancholy blue moonlight and flickering torch
flame.

The footman's nose wrinkled in disgust at her request. "Have you
money to pay for the room?" he asked, his voice telling her he already
knew the answer to his question.

"I can give but this rose," she said, her careful fingers bringing
forth the simple bloom. One of the petals had begun to droop, its edge

puckered. It still gave off a faint glow when she held it out. "I know 'tis a humble offering, but heed mine warning: if thou dost not accept what I tender, which is everything I have in this world, thy decision will endue great misfortune to thy household."

Her eyes glowed blue, lit from within as if the force that drove lightning grew inside her. The footman stood mesmerized. He shook his head, forcing his eyes from hers and stepping back a few paces. When he lifted his head, the eerie light from her eyes was gone and he was sure he had imagined the whole thing. The old woman still held the rose in her crooked fingers, the bloom lit with the same inner light as she.

"Away with you, witch!" he cried, his voice carrying over the distance between them, and slammed the door as hard as his body would allow.

"Be thou warned," she hissed, knowing he could hear her, "I will not turn away thrice."

A gust of wind kicked up dead leaves and a grit of hard snow pellets from the ground, whipping them around the old woman. She gave herself a harsh shake and a film of snow and ice that crusted her body fell away. No sooner did the ice clatter to the ground than loud yelling and a woman's weak voice called out. The old woman heard booming footsteps approach the door. She grinned when the doors opened wide, putting her in plain view of King Alaric and Queen Adele de Villeneuve. The old woman knew they had hoped this day would not come, or that she would forget about it in the intervening years, but they were the reason she was at their door.

The old woman's smile widened when she saw tears gather in Queen Adele's eyes, and the slight tremor in King Alaric's hands as he grasped his wife's shoulders. She saw the shock and recognition, all the memories flooding back to the king and queen from all those years ago. She smiled as tears fell from Adele's pretty green eyes and her hand flew to her mouth, muffling the sharp cry she couldn't quite hold back.

King Alaric's hair had gone to grey and his middle had gone to fat. His eyes closed, the lids dropping at such a pace their movement was almost imperceptible.

Part of the old woman rejoiced at the chance to prove that someone of such a rank was fallible. A larger part of her, the one that knew that with their failure came her own, hung its head. After tonight, there would be no more charms, no more curses, and no more magic.

After this night, the last of the old woman's kind would die on the doorstep of a palace.

And still, the tiny part of her that held out hope for herself and for Prince Leopold, smiled. She reached her gnarled claws inside the cloak one last time and drew the blossom from its rotten folds.

"Prince Leopold," the old woman began. "I will perish without shelter and warmth for the night. Prithee accept all I hast, this rose, as payment for thy ado."

A soft glow emanated from the bloom, reflecting how the boy had grown into a fine specimen of a man. He'd grown tall and broad, with long dark hair and rich brown eyes in a fine boned face not unlike his father's before him. But when he raised his hand, he proved that he still held only the feckless cruelty of his youth. Her body sagged when he chopped his big hand through the air, dashing the rose onto the stones of the walk.

The old woman lifted her eyes to his and realized that it was his cruelty that was causing the coldness in the stone walls.

"Begone, witch!" Prince Leopold ordered, but his voice held no conviction.

The old woman resigned herself to her own fate even as she condemned him to his.

Lifting her hands skyward, she called forth all the magic she had left in a slippery language none of the royal family recognized. It was an ancient tongue, one that had not been spoken for hundreds of years. A ball of light formed against her palms, its warmth slipping into her old veins. The light erased all the signs of her age and turned her into a beautiful young woman. Her skin was milky white, her eyes a brilliant blue, lips painted a succulent red. Her dress was no longer moth-eaten and falling apart. It was now a stunning confection of emerald silk, trimmed in gold braid and panels of fine ivory on the bodice and sleeves. Her tattered cloak was now a sleek riding habit of emerald silk so fine the whole kingdom could never afford cloth so rich. The Queen herself had never looked so stunning.

Leopold's eyes widened and his mouth fell open. Alaric and Adele moved to stand beside him, each putting a hand on one of their son's arms. The last glimmer of the magic fell away. The old woman, now a beautiful woman at the peak of youth, stood before the three of them and their stunned servants.

"Ten years ago, we met at the bank of the River Chaud, Prince

Leopold. Thou insulted me, and threw stones, and made me feel like a low creature. For thy failure to see what lies within a person despite what they wear on their outsides, I cursed thee. I see the man thou hast become, Beast-child. I promised that day that thou would learn what 'twas to be a beast. Because thou couldst not see what lay within this haggard woman 'ere thou made thy judgments, thou shall wot the beast very well, indeed." She stepped back, weakness taking over her body.

"Thou hast until the end thy twenty-seventh year to make this right. Thou shall isolate thyself in thy château. Thou shall find nay relief to thy suffering until thou love and art loved in return."

The woman lifted her hand and the pink and ivory rose drifted up off the ground. One petal fell and her eyes closed on the importance of that small piece. "This rose, which thou cast aside, will count thy time from this moment forth. When the last petal from this rose falls, thou shall stay a Beast forever."

Leopold smirked at the woman, his expression arrogant and self-assured. The look on his face angered her and she screeched, closing the distance between them in three steps. He stumbled back, forcing his parents along behind him. The rose floated in the air beside her, bobbing and turning.

The siren continued. "Thy mother and father have failed thee thus far in thy life, but no more. Both shall perish by the strike of twelve tonight and thou will suffer alone in this place. The life thou hast enjoyed thus far will fall apart from thou. Thou will not make shift looketh at thy own image in the looking glass. Thou servants will fear thee for the rest of thy days. So shall ye be until the day thou can learn to see others for what they are rather than what they appear to be. Fail this, and thou will die in this place a monster. Succeed, and you may yet find happiness, Beast-child."

Her face was inches from Leopold's, and he saw in her crystalline blue eyes a truth such as he had never known.

He glanced back at his parents. "Is this true?" His voice cracked on the words and he hated it for making him sound like a child.

Neither the King nor the Queen said a word. The bleak look in their eyes— the fear and resignation— told him everything he needed to know. Tears filled his eyes and he turned back to the beautiful woman outside. She looked exhausted, her skin thinning, stretching over her bones as he watched. She lifted her hands up once more, chanting those odd words again. A revolving ball of light grew before them and within it, a silver hand mirror formed. It fell free and he caught it before it could shatter on the frozen ground. Another, smaller ball forged a ring of silver that fell at Leopold's feet.

She took a long look at him and cackled a harsh laugh. A gust of wind shot the air full of hard pellets of ice and Leopold had to close his eyes. When he opened them, the beautiful woman was gone. The only sign she'd ever been there at all was the frayed cloak which lay in a crumpled heap on the stone floor.

Chapter 1

An early morning, more than nine years later...

If that baby didn't stop screaming, Jolie Babineaux would smother him with her pillow. Her older sister, Mireille, had been visiting for about a week and every morning Mireille's youngest son woke at sunrise and commenced his favorite activity: testing the limits of his lung capacity and vocal volume. Mireille and her husband Malcolm tried to silence their son, with little success. Their other children— Jacques, Aimee, and Olivier—did as they pleased, and baby Gaspard would be another child cut from the same cloth.

Jolie dragged herself out of the bed and threw on a green jacket over her chemise. She wandered into the hall toward the kitchen, where she spotted the boy and his father.

Malcolm paced with the baby, who seemed content to keep up the noise until the Rapture.

"If that child doesn't learn to sleep past sunrise, I'll feed him to the Grey Man myself," she muttered.

Malcolm chuckled as she passed. If Mireille had heard her speak ill of her children, there would be hell to pay. But Jolie's brother-in-law was much more inclined to just laugh at her grumpy morning attitude.

"The Grey Man would spit him right back out. The one child the beast wouldn't be able to choke down," he whispered, bobbing the baby in his arms. "Besides, he's too young to understand that folk tale anyway."

"Well, I'm not," Jolie said. She smiled over her shoulder and wound her way through the halls to the kitchen. Her father Armand's strong tea was already brewing.

The Grey Man was a creature the village children swore stalked the valley at night. They told stories of the creature eating naughty kids and spitting their bones into the River Chaud. There were people who claimed to see this shadowy figure, but no one knew who or what he could be. The latest sighting had been just last Thursday and had all the village gossips in a dither. Jolie didn't believe the stories for a minute but when a woman awoke before sunrise, anything was just punishment for the person doing the waking.

There were too many people in her father's home. Even with five large bedrooms, there were children everywhere, and not enough room in any of the hallways. The house was still in good condition, despite its many years as the Babineaux family home. It had been in the family for eight generations, and had served its purpose well. But when there were four children under the age of seven and four adults crammed into it, it felt much too small to Jolie.

There were also not enough people in the household to help. The maid Henrietta and valet Desmond helped, but two servants weren't enough. One look at Henrietta this morning told Jolie the older woman was far out of her depth. Her apron already bore a stain from Gaspard's breakfast, and there was some unidentifiable filth smeared on her cheek. Jolie met her watery eyes and knew Henrietta wanted to go home for the day, but neither of them could afford it.

Jolie looked out of the window and saw Desmond leaning against their carriage, a bottle of brown liquor in one hand. When he saw her looking, the old valet tossed the bottle onto the seat and smiled sheepishly.

Armand had released all the other household help when Mireille married. With only two people living in the house there was no need for all the people they'd been paying all these years. Most of the time that was true, but this was not most of the time. Six extra people in the house was overwhelming everyone.

If she didn't get a full night's sleep soon, Jolie would dispose of social convention altogether and find her own home to live in. At twenty, she still hadn't married. There had been two proposals since she'd turned sixteen, but she felt no urgency in the matter. Both men who had made offers for her hand had been less than ideal. Jolie knew she was young and still had time for marriage.

Rather than spend all her time trying to find a husband, she preferred to stay at home and help her father in any way she could. She had ulterior motives for helping him, but he didn't know that, of course.

Armand was a merchant who dealt in spices and tea from India, sending his wares on ships to the French islands in the Caribbean. Jolie inspected the goods as they arrived from India, readied them for shipment, and even loaded the freight onto the ships with the men if needed. She'd always enjoyed activities expected of a boy more than those of a girl.

One of her greatest hopes was that someday he would let her travel on one of his ships. All she'd ever known was Fontainbleu and

Port Lucerne, where their last remaining ship was docked. Village life was familiar but boring. Books taught her much about the outside world, but not enough. She wanted to see the islands she'd read so much about, feel the oppressive heat and breathe the sea air.

Jolie and Mireille's mother, Grace, died of birthing fever a few days after giving birth to Jolie. That was the reason she and her father were so close as she grew up. Mireille, who was several years older than Jolie, learned feminine ways from their mother. Jolie spent all her time shut up in a room with Papa reading about trade routes.

Jolie wasn't just different from Mireille in her mind. They were different physically, as well. Mireille was the image of their mother. Tall and willowy, with soft brown eyes and thick and fashionable blonde hair, the older girl had drawn the stares of the most eligible young men in the kingdom.

Jolie had taken after Papa. With her wild, curly red-blonde hair, deep green eyes and rampant freckles, she had never been one to draw attention like her sister. She hadn't inherited Grace's figure, either. Short and tending toward chubby, it felt like she'd gotten a body no young man in Fontainbleu desired in a wife. As a wealthy merchant's daughter, though, she had high value as a bride. Her father's wealth and connections could provide a substantial income, if a man was willing to look past Jolie's unfashionable appearance.

Marriage aside, Jolie had long since learned to accept herself and her body for what it was rather than wishing it was something it wasn't. She didn't have time to worry about a stylish dress she'd never be able to squeeze into.

Jolie knew a typical life would never satisfy her. Mireille had found a husband and was on her own by Jolie's age. While she had always been kind and friendly to her suitors, Jolie had never felt any real interest in any of them. Armand hadn't helped matters. He had never insisted that his youngest child take any of the offers that came to her. That wouldn't last much longer, though, and Jolie knew it. Armand wasn't getting any younger, and neither was she.

Just yesterday Quentin Garamonde had come to call. Jolie was out at the time, shopping for ribbon at one of the village shops with Mireille. When the women had returned home, Armand had expressed his surprise at Quentin's presence, but made it clear he thought the boy would be a good match for Jolie.

Papa described him as tall, but a little narrow through the

shoulders and soft in the hands. He looked like someone who'd never done a day's honest work in his life. The old man launched into a whole conversation about this new beau. According to Armand, his hair was the color of a wheat field and his eyes were as grey as a stormy sea. Villagers spoke well of him, praising his ability as a hunter. He didn't need to work because of his family's wealth so his only real pursuits were women, a hobby which some villagers said he was as skilled at as hunting. Every eligible young woman in the village was hoping for him to knock on their door, so when the boy showed up to call on Jolie, Armand was surprised and more than a little discomfited.

Quentin was by far the wealthiest young man who had asked for an audience with Jolie. Armand knew how important that was, and it was only growing moreso by the day. More important now than ever because Armand was holding back the greatest secret he'd ever had to keep. With war breaking out in the Americas and piracy and privateering more and more common on the Atlantic, freight wasn't going out the way it used to. Even if it went out, there was no guarantee it would arrive at its destination. A journey that had always been perilous was becoming next to impossible.

Armand had sold off his entire fleet of ships save one, the *Lisette*, to cover debts he could no longer pay with profits from his trade. Shipments from India only came a few times a year now. Armand spent most of his time waiting for news from each trip the *Lisette* took across the sea.

He had told his family nothing of these troubles, trying to protect them from the knowledge of his failure.

Times were getting desperate and Armand didn't know if he could keep his secret much longer. He no longer earned money like he had in years past and Armand was worried. He saw how much Mireille's unchecked spending had cost him through her youth. It was now clear that he spent far too much on Jolie and his grandchildren. He'd taken more chances than he liked in recent years just to stay solvent.

The *Lisette* had left port three months ago, and before it sailed, the captain had expressed his fear that she would never see the shores of Martinique. As he'd heard no word since it sailed away from port Armand had begun to wonder, albeit only to himself, if it had sunk or been taken.

Without the money the goods would bring him, Armand would

be bankrupt. He would have to sell their home and everything in it to have enough money for his own survival. Mireille had a husband to support her but with no income, what would become of his Jolie?

A knock on the door interrupted Armand's thoughts. Desmond announced the visitor and let him in. Armand's solicitor, Pierre LeBoeuf, slid through the doorway looking disheveled and rail-thin. His eyes were wild and his cravat hung loose around his throat. He held a thick missive covered in water spots and sloppy handwriting in his fist.

Pierre and Armand had known each other for many years. Their friendship and working relationship went back to before Armand had married his late wife, Grace. Pierre was the one person outside the family who knew how dire the Babineauxs' situation was. There was no need for him to mince words, and he didn't now. "The *Lisette* was taken a month ago by pirates off the coast of Barbados."

Armand's hands fell limp at his sides in disbelief. "All is lost?"

"Perhaps not, my friend," Pierre said, and let the paper in his hand fall onto the desk. "I received this letter this morning, along with the news. Something must have delayed the message telling of the *Lisette's* capture. It would appear that your ship has returned to port. I don't know how, but this is a letter from the harbormaster reporting that she's docked in slip seventeen, waiting for you to claim her."

Armand could have danced a reel on his desk, so light his heart became at this news. "How fares the crew?"

"No word of them in the letter, which hopefully means they all returned and are accounted for," Pierre said, but he sounded puzzled that their condition wasn't mentioned.

"And the freight?"

"Your ship returned heavily laden, and none the worse for its long time at sea," Pierre smiled, his black eyes all but disappearing into his cheeks. "Read the letter."

Armand read the letter, his head flicking to and fro hard enough to make the wisps of his grey-streaked red hair wobble. "My old friend, you bring me the greatest relief with your news. This could not come at a time when I needed it more." His eyes sparkled with tears as he clapped Pierre on the back. "I will leave for Port Lucerne at once."

"Would you like me to keep an eye on your home while you are away, or will Jolie be accompanying you?" Pierre asked.

"I have been diligent in leaving her and Mireille in the dark,"

Armand said, lowering his voice in case of eavesdroppers. "And you are to tell them nothing. I do not wish for either of them to find out this way. I will sell the goods from the *Lisette* in Port Lucerne and release the crew from their contracts so they might find work elsewhere. If I can find a buyer, I will sell the ship herself as well. The city has always been kind to me, and when I return I will once again be solvent. With a few smart decisions, I need never tell the girls about all this bad luck."

Pierre smiled and shook hands with Armand. "I hope all is well. I will leave you to your preparations, then. It is a long journey to Port Lucerne, and I believe you will be making it on horseback?"

"Yes. Why hire a carriage when I can more than make it there and back? I'll be home before you realize I'm gone."

Pierre smiled and excused himself.

Smiling, Armand felt as if he were floating around the house rather than walking. He told Mireille and Jolie of the *Lisette*'s strange journey, then began preparing for his own.

"Papa," Mireille squealed, squeezing her father in a hug. "I am happy to hear of the ship's return. Buy me something in Port Lucerne?" Her blue eyes dazzled him, as her mother's had so long ago.

"Of course, darling." He knew if he didn't agree she would pout and beg until he relented.

She squealed again, rubbing her hands together. Ticking items off on her fingers, she launched into a list of things she wanted from the city. Fabrics and buttons, jars of gold leaf. As he tallied the amount of money all these things would cost, his head swam. Of course, he wouldn't buy *all* the things she wanted but he would have to spend some money to mollify her.

And to hide your secret, he reminded himself. *Mustn't forget that.*

Armand would spend more time agonizing over just what to buy his oldest child as he did flogging the wares from the ship. And if his gift wasn't expensive enough, she wouldn't be happy. There never seemed to be enough money spent to please her. Armand worried she would pass her greed down to her own children and Malcolm would never be able to meet all their demands.

The grandchildren were small enough he could pick up a bag of sweets for them to share. Malcolm wouldn't expect anything, but Armand would pick something out for him just the same. He was a good man and deserved a little gift from his old father-in-law once in a while.

Through all the listing and grousing and pleading, Jolie waited. As patient as a parish priest, she listened to her sister until the older woman ran out of air.

Jolie felt like her sister always asked for more than necessary. She believed simplicity was the key to happiness. While Mireille demanded hundreds of francs' worth of presents, Jolie preferred the joy she felt when their father smiled to the happiness she got from a gift.

"Papa, I would like a rose," she said, settling her teacup on its saucer. "I have always loved them."

Armand smiled and touched his daughter's hand, his head bowing in a little nod.

"Antoine's flower shop always has such beautiful flowers, no matter what time of year it is."

Mireille's glare could have melted brie. Armand didn't notice as he passed out of the kitchen and into the library. "Always have to make yourself look better than me, don't you?" she hissed.

They could hear Armand rummaging around for clothes and other necessities for his journey. Jolie rolled her eyes, begging whatever forces she could muster to help her to not slap her sister. "I don't want him to spend all the money he is going to make on me, that's all. Why do you always think ill of me?"

"You're forever making me look like a spoiled brat, even though you're the one who has everything. Papa always took you along on his trips to port. He spent money on you while you were away, then spent all his time with you when we were home." Mireille slumped in her chair, folding her arms over her chest. "Bad enough you took Maman away from us, but then Papa had to go and love you more."

For a moment all Jolie could do was stare. Tears rose in her eyes at the barb. It was always the one Mireille used when she was feeling most hateful. Which, when it came to Jolie, was all the time.

"And now you've caught the interest of the Garamonde boy. The one whose older brother Alphonse rejected me," the older woman whispered. Her lower lip puffed out in a most unattractive way and she picked at a splinter in the table's surface.

"I suppose that's my fault, as well," Jolie said. She blinked against the sting in her eyes. "You like to blame me for all your other misfortunes, why not that as well, even thought I was just a child. Everyone knows the reason he had to reject you was he got caught with Elise LeGrande in her father's hayloft."

15

Mireille had no response for that. She tore the splinter away from the table with more force than necessary, taking a long strand of wood veneer with it. "It doesn't matter anymore, I suppose. Once Quentin gets to know you he won't want you anyway. No man wants a wife who thinks she's smarter than everyone else."

Mireille flicked the strand of wood away, sitting up straight. "Actually, I doubt he'll want you once he gets a good look at you. You've a fortune to lure him in but you don't have the beauty to keep him interested." She smiled at her younger sister, then stood and left. Jolie watched as she walked toward the nursery where all but one of her children still slept.

Her older sister knew which parts of herself Jolie hated. She paid attention whenever Jolie thought no one was looking, which is always when a person reveals their weaknesses. If Mireille couldn't use the information right away, she'd store it away for times like now. Then she would unleash whatever she thought would hurt her younger sister the most.

It took Jolie a moment to collect herself but when she did she got up from the table, set her cup in the wash basin for Henrietta, and headed for the library.

Papa came by the library about an hour later, dressed and ready to leave for port. Jolie wished him well, then watched him ride away toward Port Lucerne with a heavy heart. This journey would not end well, she was almost certain, but didn't know why she felt that way. She tied on a white cap and took a few steps out the front door to watch him ride away, pulling her cloak tighter around her shoulders in the chill wind.

Dread rose up in her as he rode out of sight, filling her stomach with lead and burning at the back of her throat. He passed into the dense woods at the base of Château Hill and was gone. As soon as she lost sight of the man and his horse, she wanted to call out to bring him back. She even opened her mouth to do so, but forced herself to stop.

A brisk wind blew across the valley and smoke billowed from several chimneys. Dead leaves rolled down the street in a roiling wave. The sky darkened and Jolie couldn't tamp down the apprehension she felt.

In the house, Gaspard let out a long wail and Jolie closed her eyes. Between worrying about Armand and the baby's constant crying and carrying on, it was going to be a long few days cooped up in the house.

16

She would do well to find herself a hole in a wall somewhere. If she started the search now, perhaps she could find a few hours of peace before Papa came back.

Chapter 2

Armand's journey wasn't terrible, but it wasn't pleasant either. The roads between the two cities wound in and out of thick forest land. With the exception of the wind and the leaves rustling, the forest was unnervingly silent. Armand listened for any signs of life and gave Garnet a gentle nudge with his heel to increase his pace as they neared the edge of the forest. Armand gave a sigh of relief and patted Garnet's neck, "We made it boy, Port Lucerne is only a few miles away now."

The wind picked up and the temperate dropped as Armand neared the city limits of Port Lucerne. Armand was unfazed by the change in temperate as the excitement of seeing his ship kept his heartbeat up.

When he reached the docks, he looked at his slip and felt his heart sink. This ship was not the *Lisette*. It was much too small and made of inferior materials. The harbormaster, one Charles O'Leary, could only apologize for the mistake as Armand pulled on Garnet's reins to turn him around.

Armand dragged himself away from the city as empty-handed as he'd arrived. He didn't even have enough coin to get himself a room to sleep in for the night. As darkness settled in, clouds blanketed the night sky. The temperature dropped even lower and frost bloomed over everything that wasn't moving.

Opting to find somewhere warm to feed himself, Armand climbed off of Garnet and tied him to a post at an inn without bothering to look at the sign. He walked inside, then sat down near the fireplace and he bought himself a bowl of lumpy lamb stew. The hunk of bread they served him tasted almost as old as the barkeep that served it to him.

"Haven't seen weather like this in years," Armand heard a crooked old man down the bar mutter. "My old knees haven't stopped screechin' 'bout it nigh on three days."

"Bound to be like the night when our king and queen died, bless their souls," the barkeep said. Armand let his eyes wander from under the brim of his hat. The barkeep was a sloppy, plump woman with a wart on the end of her nose. She had more grease in her tuft of black hair than there was in the stew pot. She set to mopping up a clot of spilled stew with one hand and crossed herself with the other. Judging by the grime of the inn and the length of time it took her to get the congealed mess to move, someone had spilled it last week.

"Think you they was poisoned?" the old patron asked. He scratched at his yellowed grey beard with a hand blackened by dirt.

She leaned over the bar and said, "I think they was into some bad business and got themselves 'et up by the Grey Man."

The patron scoffed, slapping the bar with his filthy hand. "Just a story."

"Look at the windows late at night, sometimes you'll see a light on. Someone's havin' that wall built 'round the castle. A senate elected from the noble families within a fortnight of their deaths," she said, ticking off the oddities on fingers the size of sausages. "The young prince disappeared that night. We all heard the screams. And worst of all, a creature what no one ever seen before showed up right after?"

The old man waved her off and she backed away. Before she could turn her attention to him, Armand spooned the last bit of stew into his mouth. He tossed a few coins on the bar, not bothering to look at how much he'd just paid for stew that he was sure would eat a hole in his innards by sunrise.

He gathered up the knapsack from the floor and pulled it on, then headed out to where he'd tethered Garnet. He mounted the trusty roan, preparing for the return journey and knowing it would be longer and even less pleasant than the ride into Port Lucerne.

Snow started to fall less than a mile outside the city, and along with it came a howling wind from the north. Garnet's hooves crunched in the crusted snow, and steam blew from his nose with every breath.

Armand covered his whole face save for his eyes, wishing he'd had the foresight to bring heavier clothes for the journey. His breeches and hose did little to protect his legs from the stinging pellets of sleet and frigid temperature. His cloak kept his torso warm right up until his feet got cold, then he started shivering.

"What were you thinking, you old fool?" he asked himself. The chances of freezing to death on a night like this were high, especially at his age.

Hunkering down in his cloak, he urged Garnet on. He didn't realize just how cold he was, or how quickly it had happened, until he caught himself falling asleep. Twice his head bobbed forward, bouncing his chin against his chest, jarring him awake. He couldn't feel his hands or feet, and the numbness was creeping up his calves and forearms.

Knowing just how much trouble he was in, he looked around for any kind of shelter. He had a flint and steel in his pack to create a spark,

19

all he needed was somewhere to settle in to build a fire. Numb as he was, it would be a miracle if he could even gather the kindling he'd need. It would just be his luck to freeze to death trying to find shelter he needed to survive.

In his search for shelter, he lost track of where he was on the road and missed the intersection that would lead him to Fontainbleu. The woods grew denser as he rode along. The trees crept closer to the old road, now not made of even cobbles but rough dirt. Heavy boulders that blocked parts of the path. He guided Garnet around them, not registering that the road to his village was well-maintained and the one he was on was far from it.

A crossing came into view and pulled the reins to turn right. Within a few hundred yards, the road narrowed to little more than a goat trail. By then, Armand was coming close to falling off the animal altogether.

A part of his mind knew he was on the wrong road, going farther from home. That small part of him was struggling to survive, screaming for him to wake up. The rest of him, the part that was crystallizing in the cold, was tamping down its alarm. By the time he lost consciousness, the part of his brain trying to keep him alive had silenced.

Armand woke with a jolt, his body using its last defense: a shot of adrenaline to his heart. Jerking straight up in the saddle, a searing spasm bloomed in all his frozen extremities and he yelled.

Garnet had stopped. Eyes watering from the rush, Armand looked around. They were standing at an eight-foot-wide gap in a high stone wall. The wall was at least fifteen feet tall and made of huge grey bricks.

Drawing his feet out of the stirrups made him cry out again, then he dropped to the ground, another bright shot of pain spearing through his legs and arms. He felt millions of needles in his skin as warm blood started reaching those parts again.

It was hard work but he managed to get inside the wall. Torches made of wrought iron stood cold and unlit along a path, ghostly sentinels in their dusting of frost. The path led around the perimeter of the wall and from where he stood to a great pair of wooden doors mounted in the stone walls of a castle.

Armand's brain, hysterical from the combination of cold and adrenaline, was able to process that he'd made it all the way up

Château Hill. The south tower stood to his right, the north tower to his left, with the castle proper looming between them.

He'd been looking for shelter and could hardly do worse. Pulling Garnet along with him, he led the way up the walk to the huge doors.

Light flickered in a south tower window so briefly he thought he'd imagined it. Everyone knew, even the crazy people at that inn in Port Lucerne, no one lived here. If anyone did, it was the Grey Man. If he lived here, Armand would be dead by sunup so it no longer mattered.

The doors slid open before he got to them. In his frozen state, he didn't find it at all odd and went inside without pause. Garnet balked but after a little sweet talking Armand got the horse to come inside. The warmth was too much to bear and once the doors closed behind them, Armand collapsed at the agony in his body as it warmed.

Shivering and screaming on someone else's floor in a well-lit hall in a fortress that legend said only a monster lived in, Armand slipped away into sleep, still in his riding clothes.

****

The warbling of a mourning dove woke Armand from his deep slumber hours later. Thinking he was still on the hall floor, he felt around beneath him and instead of hard stones he felt a thick feather tick. Instead of his own riding clothes, he wore a nightgown of finest linen. The sheets and blankets were made of silk and cotton, of such rich colors he had no doubt he was in the castle.

Armand rubbed the fog of sleep from his eyes, then looked around. As everything slowly came into focus, he saw the walls of the room were covered in ivory wallpaper with quaint village scenes flocked on the paper in Delft blue. Armand got up and walked around the room, letting his eyes roam over the beautiful covering. Mahogany wainscoting covered the bottom half of the walls. It matched the glossy wood of the bedstead and furniture. The floor was covered in thick carpet woven in ivory and the same bright blue as the flocking on the wallpaper.

Armand curled his toes into the carpet and closed his eyes. As prosperous as he'd been in life, he'd never before stood on a rug so sumptuous, nor seen such fine furnishings as these. Then again, he'd never been in a home that had once housed the royal family. Whoever it was that lived here was beyond generous to let him stay, and he wished to express his gratitude. He walked to the wardrobe and donned a thick blue velvet robe he found there. He slid on a pair of matching slippers from under a cushioned bench at the foot of the bed, then left the room.

As Armand walked through the door he found himself in a great, wide hallway. The moment he stepped across the threshold, he heard a soft voice call out to him. "Monsieur," he heard. "Our Master would like to invite you to break your fast this morning in the formal dining hall."

A man stood just beside the doorway, hands behind his back and nose in the air. He looked just as Armand had always imagined a royal servant would. His uniform was starched so it looked as if the fabric would shatter if he moved. The uniform was black and white with big gold buttons on the jacket, polished to a mirror shine. The buckles on his shoes had more gold in them than a jeweler's inventory, and the black leather shone like the surface of a still lake.

"My name is Willard LeChance. I will be your valet during your visit, and I will lead you to the dining hall," the footman said, holding out a white-gloved hand to show which direction they were headed. "You must be famished after your journey."

Armand's stomach did feel rather hollow, now that he thought about it. He nodded and followed as Willard led.

"Thank you, Willard. Who do I have to thank for this gracious hospitality?"

"The master of this château," Willard said, his voice rising on the last word like he was asking a question. His hands fluttered a bit at his sides. Armand thought he wasn't accustomed to answering questions. "You need know no more of him than that he wishes you to be comfortable and well-fed while you are in this keep."

Willard gave a little nod and Armand thought it was a nod of satisfaction for what he'd said. He wondered how often the so-called Master entertained if his servants didn't know how to answer simple questions about him. And what kind of host was he if he didn't show himself? Maybe he really was the Grey Man.

The valet didn't offer any more information and as the smell of hot food drifted down the hall from the dining room, any questions he might have had faded from his mind. When they entered the dining room, Willard led him to a chair at the head of the table. Another servant, this one a plump woman in a maid's black and white uniform, set down a tin platter of breakfast foods.

A porcelain plate for him to eat from went next to that, and he stacked it full. He chose two shirred eggs topped with a crust of cheese, a half dozen rashers of crisp bacon, fresh bread still hot from the oven, butter, and a tin cup of buttermilk. There were no servants that he could see other than the plump woman and Willard, which seemed odd considering the large meal laid out before him.

As he finished eating his breakfast, Willard stepped beside him, ready to lead him back to his room. The whole experience—being in a palace, eating the highest quality food he'd ever had in his life—was strange, to say the least. When he stood, Willard took a step back to allow him room, then moved back to stand directly to his left.

As they walked back down the hallway toward the bedroom, Armand looked around, his eyes wide as he took in the heavy tapestries that hung on either side of the hall, their tails dripping with gold braid. Portraits of the royal family, dating back a thousand years, fit in between each tapestry. He was captivated by the faces on the beautiful paintings.

Women of the family were on the right hand side, men on the left. Here, halfway between the dining hall and his chamber, was Charles de Villeneuve, great-great-grandfather to the missing Prince Leopold. Charles had caused a scandal in his day by marrying commoner Portia Cheveux. They had ruled after his father's death for over sixty years and brought the country to such prosperity that no one batted an eye when his son Leland followed suit by marrying Marcheline Ormille, daughter of a penniless dairy farmer.

Their son, Alaric, had married Adele Lagerschmidt, the fourth daughter of a German crown prince. Adele had had little aspiration for the crown herself but when she caught the eye of the French prince, she got a throne anyway. After waiting many years for an heir, when Leopold was finally born the country rejoiced. Doted on by all who met him, it was no surprise when rumors ran rampant of the prince's terrible behavior. It would have been more surprising if the boy had turned out any other way.

And now, no one had seen hide nor hair of the boy in nearly ten years. When Armand got to the place where Leopold's portrait should hang, there was nothing but a blank space on the wall.

"There was a portrait of Prince Leopold made, of course. It was meant to hang in this spot," Willard said, folding his hands at his waist while Armand stopped to look. A thick spike stuck out of the wall as if it were waiting for something to jump up there.

"What happened to the portrait?" Armand asked, turning to Willard. What he really wanted to ask was what had happened to the prince, but knew he would get no answer.

The servant looked nervous, his eyes darting around as if he was looking for the answer. "It has been...in storage for several years." Armand didn't miss the pause and wondered what it meant. Willard's eyes met Armand's and, seeing that this response wasn't good enough, he elaborated. "Almost ten years, actually."

"When your master took over the château?"

Willard didn't flinch, but his eyes dropped from Armand's for a moment.

"Who is your master, Willard?" Armand took the lead once again and with one last glance at the empty space where a portrait should be, headed toward the bedroom. Now that he'd seen one, he saw all of the spikes protruding from the stones. They stuck out every few meters down the hall, waiting for their important cargo to arrive.

Willard ignored his question outright this time. "Our master wishes you to spend as much time as you like here as you recover. You may explore all that you wish. I must warn against the South Tower, though. It is in a sad state of disrepair and is unsafe for exploration."

Armand couldn't remember much about the exterior of the building, but had no recollection of any of it looking as if it were poorly maintained. He had seen many a tumbledown building in his day, but this castle was as far from that as he'd ever seen. It didn't matter anyway, because he wouldn't be staying long enough to see such a thing for himself.

"I would like to depart soon. Perhaps this afternoon. I must return home. My daughters will worry," he said with a smile. "I would like to thank our master for his generosity, if such an opportunity should arise?"

"I will forward your regards to him, Monsieur." Willard's tone was firm, and he did not return Armand's friendly grin.

They came to the bedroom door and Armand saw that while he'd broken his fast, someone had changed the linens and tidied the room. Part of him wanted to stay here one more night so he could do all that exploring Willard had mentioned, but he thought of Jolie, who no doubt was worried sick about him by now.

"Thank you, Willard. I will prepare for my journey."

"I will ready your horse and bring it to the front doors. Will you be able to find your way home from there?" There was a wry smile on the valet's face now and Armand thought he was poking fun at Armand's unorthodox arrival.

"I shall be fine, thank you," the old man said, shaking his head at Willard's amusement.

"I will leave you, then. If you should need anything else, please ring the bell." Willard cut a gallant bow and left.

Readying himself was slow going today. He still felt the cold in every bone, and his chest felt hot and tight, like the frigid wind had gone inside him on a breath and frozen his lungs. A few days at home would serve him well. A little spoiling from Jolie couldn't hurt, either, and he'd be sure to get plenty of that.

With his thoughts on his daughter, he remembered that he'd not been able to get any of the gifts his girls had asked for. Mireille would have to do without, because there was just no way he could bring her even one of the gifts she so desired. Jolie, though, and her simple request of a rose, lingered with him as he dressed and gathered his knapsack.

Through the bedroom window, he saw rose bushes in the rear courtyard. He could slip back there and see if even one of those beautiful flowers lingered in the cold before he left. With no one but his horse waiting on him, he had time.

The great hall made up the central square of the stronghold, with a wide corridor wrapped around it and the four towers coming off each corner. More rooms came off one hall that extended off the southwest wall. Armand found the door to the south courtyard without trouble and let himself out. The sun was warmer this morning than it had been last evening, but the air still held an awful chill. Ice crystals floated in the air, spinning and falling on the rose bushes.

The vines were blackened, barren and dry, but Armand was determined to do his best to find a rose for Jolie. As he set out among the roses, he got a chill up his spine that had nothing to do with the weather. Hairs on the back of his neck stood up and the muscles of his back tightened. Just a few feet from the palace's back door he stopped dead in his tracks, sure that someone was watching him. He could feel eyes on him, making his scalp prickle and his heart pound.

His eyes darted all around searching for the onlooker but found

25

no one in the courtyard with him. There was no one standing in any of the narrow arrow-slit windows. The back door stood ajar as he'd left it, and no one waited for him there.

Shrugging off the eerie feeling, he wound his way through the plants, holding his coat away from the thorns as he looked at every leaf and hip for a bloom. It didn't take long for his old body to start shivering and he gave up on his foolish endeavor. Disappointed, more in himself than anything else, he stepped over a low-lying bush and as he looked down to make sure his breeches didn't get caught, there it was.

As red as the skin of an apple, and as big as a man's fist, was the most beautiful rose Armand had ever seen. Even before he bent down to cut the stem away from the bush, its fragrance teased his nostrils. Once he had it freed, he lifted it to his face, brushing the velvety petals over his skin and breathing deep of the flower's perfume.

Warmed by the excitement of this small treasure, anticipating seeing his daughter's pleasure at his gift, he tucked the rose into an inner pocket of his long coat and hurried to the door. His happiness put a bounce into his step and he couldn't hold back a laugh.

Armand had just put a foot across the threshold when a great force slammed into him from behind, spinning him around on the spot and pulling him up off the floor, forcing him up to eye level with a hideous monster.

Chapter 3

"Jolie, if you keep looking out the window, someone will think Papa has hired more help," Mireille whined. "Especially in that dress." She fanned herself with a sheet of Papa's expensive vellum, even though it was freezing outside and not much warmer inside. Jolie wondered if her sister was with child again, the way she carried on and overheated all the time.

"I don't care what the neighbors think," Jolie said. She had to force herself not to smooth the skirt of the simple muslin day dress she wore. It was plainer than anything else she had, in a monotone pale grey, but that didn't excuse Mireille's rude remark. "Why should it bother me what they think when you make sure yours is the only opinion I hear?"

"My opinion is the one you should listen to," Mireille said.

"You've always made it quite clear your opinion is the only one that matters, Mireille. It must slay you that I disagree." Jolie did move away from the window, taking a seat at Papa's desk. A sheet of paper was spread out on its surface, an order for goods from India she may have no occasion to send. If something happened to Papa on his trip, there was no reason to get fresh stock in.

Twiddling a pen between her fingers didn't help ease her anxiety, and neither did trying to decipher the order. Her eyes refused to focus on the numbers, straying again and again out that blasted window.

Malcolm dragged his feet on his way into the study and the moment he sat down on the padded bench before the fire, Gaspard screeched in an unholy one-child chorus. Mireille got up this time. As she passed, the two touched hands, their fingers pulling apart not by choice but only as the distance between them grew too far to maintain the grip.

Malcolm was a good-looking man, always had been, with his deep auburn hair and sparkling green eyes. He was a master cabinet maker, one whose skill drew the attention of royalty all through Europe. More than that, he adored Mireille, and was a loving and attentive father to their brood.

"I'll be glad to get back to our own home, where I can let a nanny take over. It was nice to let Gertrude have a few weeks to spend with her own family, though." His thick Scots brogue lilted through the words. His smile was genuine even through his bleary-eyed exhaustion. "Is my wife giving you a hard time?"

"As usual," Jolie sighed. How that woman had found a man to tolerate her was beyond Jolie's ability to understand.

"Business as usual, then?" Malcolm laughed and she joined him. "What's this I hear about a suitor?"

"I know nothing of him," Jolie said, which was the truth. "We've never even met."

"I hear this Garamonde chap is quite wealthy." He lowered his voice and crossed the room to take a chair closer to Jolie. "A man of his sort could be just what you need to get out of here."

"He'll take one look at me and change his mind," she said, allowing herself to mope a little for once. "They all do."

Malcolm looked skeptical but didn't interrupt. The best thing about him was he listened rather than injecting his own opinion. He made himself comfortable, keeping an ear cocked toward the nursery in case Mireille called for help.

"They come here expecting someone who resembles my sister and when they realize all they'll get is me, it's never enough. I don't live up to their expectations." She straightened, tossing Papa's pen on the desk. "Or we talk and they figure out I have thoughts of my own and they run screaming out the door."

"What about Phillipe Marchant? I hear he's a very level headed lad, not out for a fortune or title in a wife. Your father told me he'd called on you a few times and that you got on well." A tireless gossip, he leaned forward, elbows on the desk.

"Everything seemed fine for a while. He had dinner here and we went for a walk through the valley. He made me laugh," she admitted with a blush. "And he is handsome. But..." she paused, looking at her hands as she wrung them together in her lap.

"What happened?" Malcolm asked, his brogue deepening.

"My school friend Roslyn overheard him in La Fleur Rouge talking to his friends about me," Jolie said, the bright red of her blush spreading over her cheeks and inflaming her scalp. "He wasn't saying nice things."

Malcolm shook his head and sat back in his chair. "What did he say, lass?"

Jolie glanced at him, then back at her hands. "He said I have hands like a longshoreman." When Malcolm raised his eyebrows at her she knew that wouldn't be enough. "He called me fat and said I was too smart for a girl. He said he didn't want a wife who would make him

28

look stupid."

"Bastard," he said. Such language wasn't acceptable in mixed company but Jolie was an exception, as she'd been around men more than she had women. Men she was familiar with didn't see her as a woman at all, just another of their friends.

"I sometimes wish Papa had remarried," she said. "Maybe if I'd been around women more, men wouldn't find me so horrible."

"I don't find you horrible," Malcolm said, his tone aggravated. "Far from it, lass. And I guarantee I'm not the only one. Maybe this Garamonde pup will be the right sort."

Even though she doubted it, after all the past disappointments, she nodded. "Why is it bad that I'm smart? Or that I know things that men usually teach their sons?"

"Men are afraid of women like you," he said. "You intimidate them, that's all. They don't know how to justify a woman that proves they can be more."

"That's why I need to get out of here," Jolie groaned, exasperated. "Antiquated ideas and the people who adhere to them like they're law. I shouldn't have to marry to leave home."

Malcolm nodded. "Just you wait. You'll get out, I know it. You're going to change the world, little girl." He winked at her, then stood and headed to the kitchen.

Bolstered by the chat with her brother-in-law, she smiled and checked out the window for the hundredth time. Little feet pattered down the hall toward the formal dining room. Jacques, Aimee, and Olivier were all chattering, full of stories and last night's dreams.

Mireille carried Gaspard to the study door. For once, the cherubic little boy was quiet, mollified by a wooden horse. He drooled all over the toy as his mother bounced him on her hip.

"Aren't you going to eat with us?" Mireille asked, her voice sweet but her eyes darting over Jolie's body as if trying to find a weakness she hadn't exploited yet.

"I had tea and a pair of boiled eggs when I woke." Staring out the window again, she saw a horse and rider approaching. She jumped to her feet and ran to the window, her heart in her throat until she realized they weren't the ones she was looking for. The horse was a gigantic black and the rider's clothes were all wrong. Papa never wore green.

"And biscuits and cheese after a while, I'm sure," Mireille said and Jolie could feel her sister's critical eyes on her stomach and thighs.

"Not all of us skip meals to keep thin, Mireille." Jolie was worried and didn't have the patience to hold her tongue anymore. "There's nothing wrong with being thin, but you look like you haven't eaten in weeks."

"It's hard to fit into the latest fashions with a behind that won't fit through a doorway, Jolie," Mireille said, screwing up her face. "Not that you would know. There's no way you'd ever fit into them, no matter how much you starved yourself."

"I'd rather be fat than cruel." Jolie didn't yell, didn't raise her voice at all, but she skewered her sister with a look, her green eyes flashing in anger. "At least there are people who like me."

"Not men, God knows." The older woman squared her shoulders as much as she could with a baby on her hip. "Papa will see his grave before he sees you married."

Jolie came around the desk, her hands shaking in her anger. As she spoke, her voice rose and her halo of red curls shook on her words. "That would please you, wouldn't it? To see me, the ugly sister, die a lonely spinster with nothing for company but a few dozen cats?"

Mireille's eyes narrowed to slits. "Papa won't be able to pay any young man enough to marry you. No man wants his children to come out looking like you." She looked her younger sister up and down once more, then turned and flounced down the hall to the dining room.

Jolie stood frozen in the study, still shaking, the words echoing in her mind. Over and over, she heard her sister's slights coming back to her. Every woman has insecurities about her looks, but to have someone spell them out where anyone walking by could hear was beyond horrible.

Jolie would have given many years off her life to be able to leave the house and never look back. Without Papa there as a buffer, Mireille said whatever she wanted without fear of repercussion. Until he came home, nothing would improve. Malcolm had little power over his wife's words, and rarely heard the horrible things she said to Jolie anyway.

Tears fell on her dress, dotting the fabric with dark splotches. She pressed the heels of her hands into her eye sockets, trying to stanch the flow. Letting a deep breath out through her mouth, she willed her heart to slow.

When she dropped her hands to her sides, she tipped her head back, breathing deep. *Just a few more weeks.* She kept repeating these words to herself, over and again, until she calmed.

Through the window she saw there was still no one coming and decided to take a walk. She grabbed a shawl from the back of Papa's desk chair, tied a cap over her curls, and left through the French doors that led from the study to the side garden.

Once outside, she wrapped herself in the thick woolen shawl and set a brisk pace toward the road. Her father had disappeared down this route yesterday morning. Maybe she could do the same. For now, she could pretend.

Cold as it was, the outdoors always calmed her. Like a compass needle, she needed natural forces to get herself pointed in the right direction. Even so, while her walk served to revive her spirit, it still left her wanting. More than wanting to get away from her sister's poor treatment, Jolie wasn't satisfied with the life she had led so far.

The older she got and the closer she got to that institution that felt so like a prison, marriage, the more she felt the need to get away from everything she'd ever known. She wanted to walk down this road until she found another. And another. This one small corner of the world wasn't big enough to hold all the things she wanted to do and see. Getting married meant starting a family, putting down roots. Roots held you down, kept you in one place. The right husband would indulge her desire to travel, but she had never known a man to bend to what his wife wanted. Even Papa and Malcolm, both of them good and supportive men, believed that a woman's place was home. Papa might encourage her need to learn and entertain the idea of letting her travel without a husband, but he ultimately wanted her to marry and start a family.

Which meant she would marry, whether she wanted to or not.

Life didn't end with marriage and children; she wasn't silly enough to think that. But it wasn't as easy to travel the world the way she wanted to with a gaggle of toddlers to worry over, though. She wanted a family someday but there were other things she wanted to accomplish first. At just twenty years old, she feared she'd already run out of time.

****

Quentin Garamonde pulled on the lapels of his coat to straighten them and checked his attire in the full-length mirror. This was a very big day, and he hoped that by the end of it, he would secure himself a bride that would bring him both wealth and sons.

His mother, Odette, poked her head in the door, most likely to say goodbye before she and his father Antoine set off for Paris. When she saw how he was dressed, she straightened herself, a confused look on her face.

"Where are you off to?" she asked in her usual imperious tone.

"I plan on calling on Jolie Babineaux while you and Father are away," he said, giving himself one last look in the mirror. "I called there yesterday, but she was not home."

"Why on Earth would you want to call on her? Her strumpet sister broke Alphonse's heart, if you recall," she said, her face screwed up in disgust.

"Well, Mother, after the incident with the Tremaine girl in Nice last summer, I feel I have very few options for a good marriage. Her father is still reasonably wealthy, and has good connections," he said. "And if you will remember *correctly*, Alphonse threw her over for Sophie."

Quentin didn't think it possible, but his mother's face screwed up even tighter at that. He could tell she also didn't appreciate being reminded of what had happened the last time they'd gone to her husband's ancestral home. Antoine had caught his son with the local magistrate's daughter in a very delicate situation, and it had taken a great deal of money and all of their considerable influence to keep the news from getting out. When the girl had fallen pregnant, Antoine had nearly blown the roof off the house with his rage.

"If you were more careful, I wouldn't have to ask so many questions," Odette growled. "And if you bring up that bastard child again, I will have you disinherited. It's no more than you deserve."

"I could have married her, then it wouldn't be a bastard child to be ashamed of," Quentin snarled right back.

"No son of mine will ever stoop so low as to marry the child of a magistrate!" Odette was furious now, her face purple in her anger, and Quentin backed away a few steps. "So go on and marry the Babineaux girl, whatever will keep you from dragging our family name through the mud again. You almost killed your father, you little ingrate."

"Oh, did Mireille kill off that Scottish husband of hers?" Antoine picked that moment to join his wife at the door, coming to stand next to her.

"No, Antoine," Odette snarled, rolling her eyes. "The *younger* one."

Antoine pulled a face. "I would wait for the older one to find a way to widow herself. That younger girl looks too much like Armand, all red hair and freckles. You'll never be able to take her to Paris."

"I have no plans to show her off," Quentin said. "I plan on marrying the wench, getting a son off her, and shutting her up in the house with the brat while I go live my life as I see fit."

"You'll have a hard time getting a son off that girl," Antoine said. "You should at least like the look of your wife, son."

"I can consummate my marriage with the lights doused, Father," Quentin said and grinned as his mother groaned and walked away.

"Yes, I suppose you could," Antoine said, and Quentin knew his father didn't see the humor in his joke.

Antoine walked up to his son until he towered over him and grabbed the boy's shoulder, putting their faces just inches apart. "If you can't secure a marriage to this Babineaux girl by the time your mother and I return, I shall make arrangements to send you to work our sugar plantation on Barbados. Your life here, and all of your finery, will be gone in a heartbeat. You will have to work for everything you will ever have, and to provide for whatever family you wind up with. I will disinherit you so quickly you will feel the wind from my pen rewriting the will from there."

Quentin tried to staunch the trembling of his body but couldn't, and felt a bone-deep shame for his weakness. He nodded his assent and his father backed away, patting him on the shoulder as if they were old chums.

"You have embarrassed me for the last time, Quentin. If you cannot prove your ability to be an upstanding member of this family, you will not be a part of it at all any longer," Antoine said, his voice just audible enough to send a shiver up his young son's spine. "Do I make myself understood?"

"Perfectly, Father," Quentin said, his voice cracking. "I will secure my marriage to Jolie by the time you return."

Antoine gave his son one last lingering look of disbelief, then turned and left the room. Moments later, Quentin heard the front door open and close, then the carriage left the drive.

Chapter 4

It was late afternoon when Armand came in the front door. For a moment no one said a word, then Jolie was on him, hugging and squeezing.

He could read her worry in her hair, bigger and wilder even than usual, like she'd been pulling on it all day. Her clear green eyes were rimmed with red. "Pet, what is the matter?"

"You were gone so long, Papa! I thought you were lost," she said, pulling away from him. Mireille wound her way between them and gave him her usual perfunctory hug.

"Truth be told, I did get lost," he said, scrubbing at his beard stubble with his knuckles.

The sheepish gesture made Jolie feel better, but then she saw a ring on his right middle finger, a silver one polished so smooth it had to be new. "Your new ring, Papa. It's lovely."

He tucked his hand into the pocket of his coat. When he brought it back out, he held the blood-red rose he'd taken from the garden. He tucked it into Jolie's hand, then turned to Mireille.

"What did you bring me, Papa?" Mireille asked. "If you could buy yourself a ring, you must have been able to sell the whole ship's worth of freight in Port Lucerne." She held her hands together in front of her as if in prayer. Jolie knew better; the only thing her sister prayed for was for her own benefit.

Armand's face fell and Jolie understood. "The ship is lost, isn't it?"

"Lost at sea," he lied. It wouldn't help Armand or his girls to tell them the whole story. "The harbormaster made a mistake. The ship in our slip was not the *Lisette*."

Mireille crinkled her nose and screwed up her mouth like she'd tasted something foul. She'd not gotten what she'd come into the room for, and by the time she walked back toward the room she was sharing with Malcolm, she'd forgotten all about her father's new jewelry.

"I'm sorry about the ship, was there no news at all from the harbormaster?" Jolie asked, resting her hand on her father's arm as he closed the door behind him.

"None to speak of. Pierre told me when she didn't arrive back home in a timely manner she'd likely been taken by privateers, and that's what I believe to be true," he said, working the heavy cloak off his shoulders.

She helped him take the cloak off, still wondering where the ring came from when his satchel fell to the floor. The bag landed with a heavy thud and fell open, spilling its contents on the woven rug that lined the hall. One object, an ornate silver hand mirror, fell from the bag and landed, spinning, on its handle end, flashing and flickering in the light from the windows.

It spun on end for what felt like minutes, and in the glass she saw flashes of trees and a great stone château. Jolie blinked and shook her head, dispelling the images. The mirror stopped spinning, the glass facing her, then fell to the floor. The glass flickered a few times, then went blank. Jolie and Armand watched it as it lay there, waiting for it to do something more.

Jolie looked up first and when Armand's eyes met hers, they laughed at how ridiculous they were being. She picked the mirror up and looked into the glass. It was like no other looking glass she'd ever seen, no black around the edges, its surface smooth and perfect.

Jolie looked at her reflection and was shocked by the haggard woman looking back at her. She looked like an old woman, bags under her eyes from worry and lack of sleep. Her skin looked thinner, her hair standing on end.

"I look like a witch. Why hasn't Mireille told me?" Patting and combing with her fingers to try and tame her hair, she didn't notice when the mirror began to glow in her hand.

Armand plucked it away, stuffed it back in the knapsack, and began to gather up the rest of his things. "Your sister wouldn't tell you if your hair was on fire."

Jolie stopped her primping and looked at her father. "Papa, I'm surprised at you. You never speak ill of anyone, least of all us." She kept her voice low, wanting Mireille to remain ignorant. "Is something wrong?"

"Not at all, Pet. I'm just a tired old man whose journey is not yet done," he said. He heaved the bag onto his shoulder and swept off to his bedroom.

Jolie watched him walk away, wondering what this had all meant. The ring, the mirror she was sure had shown her strange images, his insult of Mireille. What he'd said about her wasn't kind but it *was* true. There was no love lost between the two girls, especially after spending this last week in the same house without benefit of his interference. But what he'd said left Jolie wondering what had happened on his trip.

Whatever it was, he didn't want to tell her and that made her afraid.

****

Desmond let in a guest later that evening after suppertime. Armand was both surprised and disheartened to see Quentin Garamonde walking behind the old valet. There was no better time than now to suss out the man's intentions toward Jolie. With all of his secrets about to spill forth like water from a bucket, he needed to secure his daughter's future sooner rather than later. More's the pity.

"Monsieur Babineaux, I would like to speak to you as to my intentions," Quentin said with a pleasant smile.

There was something in the boy's eyes, a sort of emptiness, and Armand thought for the first time that Quentin might not be a good match for not just Jolie, but any girl. There was no evidence to lead him to such a conclusion, of course. Nor had he seen anything from Garamonde or his kin that would suggest any sort of danger. Antoine and his wife Odette had produced four sons and three daughters, all of whom had married well and been successful since their majority. There was no reason their youngest child should be any different.

Still, Armand got the feeling that he was making a mistake as he held the study door for Quentin to enter. The young man's eyes were avid as they darted around the room, taking in the surroundings. Armand felt naked, as if the wealthy youngster wasn't seeing his property but his skin.

Quentin joined their father in the study and through the glass in the wide double doors between them, Mireille and Jolie watched the two men.

Mireille turned to her sister. "You could certainly do worse, sister," she breathed into Jolie's ear.

"My question is why he's interested in me?" Jolie let her eyes wander over the younger man's face and body. "There are prettier girls in town."

"I will never say this again so listen well, little one. You are not as ugly as you think you are. You look *different* from me, not worse."

Jolie was so surprised by her sister's compliment she turned away from Quentin's beautiful face to look her sister in the eye. Mireille ran her fingers through Jolie's unruly hair and smiled. "Besides, it's Papa's fortune and connections he's after, not your looks."

And there was the jab she'd expected the first time around. Jolie started to skewer her sister with a retort, but Gaspard chose that moment to unleash an unearthly scream from the nursery, letting Mireille off the hook. The older woman scampered off to tend to her child and Jolie was left with no other option but to turn and wait and see if she would be brought into the conversation her father was having with Quentin.

****

"I'm sure, sir, that I've made my affections toward Jolie quite clear." Quentin seated himself across from Armand's desk and pulled off his fine kidskin gloves one finger at a time.

"Please, by all means, take a seat," Armand grumbled as he rounded the desk.

To his credit, Quentin shot back up from his chair, his hands up in apology. "I'm sorry, that was rude of me," he said, that vapid smile still on his lips.

"Yes it was," Armand agreed. Past the age where he felt the need to defer to his betters and out of time for niceties, he carried on with no intention of letting Quentin sit again. "I have been informed of no such affections. I have heard nothing of any intentions on your part. If you have any, please let us dispense with them and have done with it." He couldn't stop the impatient clip of his voice any more than he could stop the clock from ticking away what little time he had left with his daughters while he was stuck in this room.

"But you must agree that your daughter and I would make an excellent match," Quentin said. He looked unhappy with being forced to stand through this meeting. "I, the wellborn son of a Baron…"

"Youngest son of a minor Baron, let's not forget," Armand pointed out, an edgy feeling of uncertainty creeping up his spine. He didn't miss the flare of anger in the widening of the boy's nostrils, nor the way his hand clenched into a fist, squeezing the life out of his expensive gloves. "While your eldest brother will hold a high title, you will not. I figure you're about sixteenth in line for your father's barony. Behind your paternal uncles and your own brothers."

"Be that as it may, Monsieur, a merchant's daughter could hardly do worse as marriages go," Quentin said after a deep breath. He hadn't

37

meant to bring up her lower status, hoping to make her father believe it didn't matter to him. "I have a large trust which I can claim upon my marriage to care for her with."

That was true. The Garamonde family could trace their roots as distant cousins of the Plantagenets of England, and they were favored in both the French and English courts. Their wealth was both old and vast.

"What else would you offer her as a husband?" Armand asked, making a mental note of Quentin's outburst and slick recovery.

"A lifetime of comfort and protection," Quentin said, fiddling with an antique sextant on Armand's desk. When the older man didn't respond he flicked a glance to him and saw his disappointment. That was not the answer he'd been looking for. "What more could you ask for? War in the Americas and talk of revolution right here in our own dooryard, and I can provide her with safety."

Considering the aristocracy was the reason for those 'talks of revolution,' marriage to the son of a wealthy baron wasn't enough, not by half. Much less than Jolie deserved but just what she would need. A wealthy husband could get her out of France and away from danger if revolution became a real threat. He wouldn't be here to protect her anymore.

Whatever part of him felt such apprehension toward this young man refused to let him make it easy for Quentin. "Where did you meet my Jolie, Monsieur Garamonde?"

A blush worked its way up Quentin's cheeks to his hairline and he let out a tiny cough. "I have yet to make her acquaintance."

Their meeting wasn't going well. Jolie could tell by her father's brusque reception and Quentin's discomfort. When her suitor admitted he'd never met her, she suffered a sense of vicarious embarrassment for the young man. If he didn't handle the rest of the conversation well, whatever his intentions were toward her would be dashed on the top of that massive mahogany desk.

She was looking around the room, trying to come up with an excuse to interrupt, and in turn, introduce herself to her potential fiancée when Mireille burst into the study, taking away her chance. Gaspard was happily babbling on her hip and she curtsied before Quentin with such grace Jolie felt a pang of jealousy.

Quentin cut an elegant bow and introduced himself to her. As they conversed, Armand watched over his spectacles, his eyes expectant. It was then that Jolie realized he didn't like the young man one bit. He was watching for something specific, something he'd seen but needed confirmation of.

Everyone turned toward her as she entered the room and she froze two steps inside the door. There was an awkward pause, a moment when no one was sure what to do or say now that the subject of their conversation had entered the room.

Quentin handled it best, sketching another bow and introducing himself. "Mademoiselle Babineaux, I am Quentin Michel Garamonde, son of Antoine and Odette Garamonde, Baron and Baroness of Nice."

"Monsieur Garamonde, I am Jolie Lisette Babineaux. It is a pleasure to make your acquaintance."

When she straightened she shot a look at her father and saw an expression on his face that she'd ever seen there before. He looked like an old man, tired and resigned.

That strange silver band on his hand glinted in the lamplight and he looked at the hand mirror on his desk. Jolie wondered again if he'd found them on the journey to Port Lucerne. He'd told none of them where he'd gotten them, and since the *Lisette* was lost at sea he hadn't had the money to buy them. Where had they come from? Papa was hiding something; she was sure of it now.

The silence in the study was crushing, no one moving or saying anything. Then Quentin smiled and took a step closer to Jolie. They looked each other full in the face for the first time and where she found him arrogant but good-looking he seemed to find her lacking, his mouth turning down at the corners and his eyes dropping to the floor on a heavy sigh. His lips pressed together and he ducked his chin as if trying to hide his disappointment.

After a moment he recovered, at least on the surface, and his smile was bright. "I am pleased as well to make your acquaintance, Mademoiselle. I came tonight to speak to your father on important matters regarding you and I."

"I heard," she said, wary after his assessment of her. "I was in there." She pointed at the library and furrowed her brow as Quentin looked into the other room as if he'd never noticed it was there.

He smiled and she saw the same emptiness Armand had, the lack of emotion in the rest of his face even as the corners of his mouth lifted. "Whatever were you doing in the library?"

"Reading," she said, slowing the word as if she were talking to a child. "What else would I be doing in there?"

"I've never known any woman to spend time in the library for any reason other than getting lost," Quentin said with that same vapid smile.

There was an aloof light in his eyes, a prejudicial air to his words that made Jolie's skin crawl. With a glance at her father, she quirked up a cheek hoping he read the question in her eyes.

Armand stood with a cough meant to draw attention. Everyone turned to him, including Gaspard, still perched on his mother's hip. "If you will all excuse me and Monsieur Garamonde, we have important matters to discuss and we require privacy to accomplish the task." His expression brooked no argument, and everyone began to disperse, leaving the men to their business.

As she left the study after her sister and nephew, Jolie threw a look over her shoulder at her father. His green eyes met hers across the distance and the look in them scared her.

The look in her father's eyes told her that he felt he had no choice but to accept Quentin as her suitor, which was scary enough. But what frightened her more was not knowing why her father felt like this man, who neither of them had gotten a good first impression of, was to be the one she would marry. Her father looked desperate, which only made her more certain that there were things he wasn't telling her.

****

Jolie was settled on a settee in front of the fire in the sitting room when Armand followed Quentin out of the study. She stood, looking from one to the other, trying to figure out how their talk had gone. The younger man shot her a satisfied smile and pulled his gloves back on before he slipped out the front door. Looking from him to her father as the door closed with a click, she saw Armand's face fall as her eyes met his.

He sat on the settee next to her, his eyes far away and his expression stern. He kept fumbling with the silver ring on his right hand. The way he drew a breath in then let it out on a sigh, over and over again, told her that he had something important to say but didn't know how to begin.

Armand stood and faced Jolie, then dropped to one knee in front of her, his joints popping on the way down. He looked like he'd aged ten years in just a matter of days. Her pulse quickened, her heart beating a tune on the insides of her ribs.

"We have lost everything, Jolie," Armand said, deciding to keep his words plain. "The *Lisette* returning to port was my last hope to give you a good life to live as you desired. But that will never happen."

Jolie took a moment to absorb her father's words, turning them over and over in her mind. Trying to find any way she could have misinterpreted what he was saying.

"I can sell this house and all our things. It will only give me enough money to support one of us. You will live much longer than I, and you will need more than the sale can provide just to get by." He stood again, walking away from her with his hands in his hair, clutching at the thinning grey-red strands as if his life depended upon it.

"I must marry Quentin, then?" she asked, understanding the meeting in the study with an awful clarity. "I am left with no choice?"

"I could give you the money from the sale but it would only provide for you for a short time." He thought for a moment and when he spoke again his eyes wouldn't quite meet hers. "And it would leave me with nothing."

"Out of the question, Papa. But must I marry *him*? I know he is a good match, especially now, but there is something about him—"

"--iit is as good as done," he interrupted, dropping his hands to his waist as he turned to face her again. "His solicitor and Pierre will meet Quentin and I here tomorrow and draw up the contract, but I have agreed that you will marry Quentin as soon as possible. I will write a letter and have it delivered to Pierre before I retire."

Anger flared, her eyes turning to flint and straightening her spine. "All my life I have worked beside you, made decisions with you, and now after all this time you make the most important decision of all without me?"

"This is the way it is done. I did the same with your sister—"

"--Wedding her to a man of their own choosing!" She said, blood rushing to her face.

All she could see stretching out before her was a life of babies and coming-out parties and boring normalcy. A reality, one she'd never believed would be hers, was setting in of never leaving Fontainbleu. If she went through with this marriage, she was guaranteed to never fulfill her dreams of exploring the world. Muscles in her legs and arms

41

shuddered and she thought her knees wouldn't hold her up. She shook her head, sending her curls bouncing around her face.

Armand turned toward the front window, looking out over the village, the few people still out after dark now heading home.

"How long have you known we were insolvent, Papa?" Jolie asked, letting her knees give out and sitting on the settee with a thud. "How long have you been keeping secrets?"

"Close to a year," he admitted, hanging his head and leaning on the windowsill. "You already know I started selling things then. I was trying to cut my losses with the proceeds of those sales. I sold all my sources in India to Hammersmith Shipping last week, which leaves me with nothing left to sell. We were about to fail." He slammed his palms into the sill in a show of anger so rare Jolie jumped. "How could I have let this happen?"

She wanted to comfort him, come to his defense, but she was facing as uncertain a future as she ever had and wasn't inclined to make him feel better. It was his fault, as much as she would like to believe otherwise. His hands went to his sides and he fiddled with the ring again.

"No more secrets, Papa. Where did you get the ring? You've never worn one before."

Despite his casual position leaning on the windowsill, she saw his hands trembling. She'd seen her Papa go toe-to-toe with men half again his size, and had always thought he was afraid of nothing and no one. But now, his face paled and when he spoke his voice was higher than usual.

"Château Villeneuve," he said. "The rose I brought you was from the rose garden there."

"The château was abandoned after the King and Queen died," she said, disbelieving. She flicked her eyes through the library doors, as if she could see the red rose on the table from here. "The villagers----"

"Are wrong," he interrupted, his eyes wild on hers. "It is no longer home to a prince but a monster. I was freezing, thought I'd die. I passed out in the courtyard. When I woke the next morning, I was in an exquisite bedchamber. There was a valet who took me to tables filled with things for me to eat. Whoever owns that castle saved my life, and I felt well enough to make my way home. As I was leaving I searched the whole garden. None of the other plants has a single bloom on them, but then I saw it. One perfect flower in the whole wasted garden, and I plucked that rose for you."

Jolie glanced toward the kitchen again and felt a pang of guilt tear through her chest. Papa wasn't done talking though, his words slurring together as they all fought to get out of his mouth at once.

"I took it and hid it away, and when I got inside, someone grabbed me from behind. It was—" he paused, his voice breaking. He shook his head as if to clear it, then continued. "He dragged me back into the castle before I could scream. He's so big, Jolie!"

Armand crossed the room, his legs stiff, his eyes wide. He grabbed her by the shoulders and shook her as if to emphasize his words. "He must stand three heads taller than me, and broad! His shoulders wouldn't fit through the doorways in this house. His hands were huge, like the paws of a bear, and his face!" His eyes closed as if he couldn't stand to conjure the image in his mind. "His *horrible* face!"

"Papa…"

"The Grey Man, Jolie! The monster the children speak of, and he's real!" His voice was an urgent, shrill whisper, and he gave her shoulders another shake. "The ring will take me back tomorrow and I must remain there for the rest of my life for the theft of the rose."

"Papa!" she cried, trying to wriggle out of her father's hands. "You're talking like a crazy person!" Pulling free with a great effort, she tumbled off the settee and backed across the room to the doors of the study.

"The mirror will show you what you wish to see, if you think I'm lying." He put his right hand in his left and yanked the ring free from his middle finger, then tossed the band across the room toward her. "Tomorrow night, I will be out of your life forever, whether you believe me or not."

The ring landed flat on the floor a few feet away but as she watched, it turned itself onto its edge and rolled to her feet. Eyes wide, she looked at her father with a thousand questions in her eyes. She squatted and picked it up, cupping the cool metal in her palm.

"How does it work?" she asked, slipping the ring onto her own finger. Before her eyes, the ring shrunk itself to fit her finger. Her heart leapt, she was sure it wouldn't come off but when she pulled on it, it slid off her finger as easily as it had gone on.

"I don't know, little one," Armand said, and all at once exhaustion settled on him like a mantle made of lead. His shoulders drooped and he bent at the waist, his hands on his thighs the only things keeping him from collapsing. "I just know that if I turn the ring on my finger three times it will take me to the palace."

"What if you do not return?" Jolie asked, defiance in her tone, but as soon as she saw her father's defeated expression all of the fight went out of her.

"My children will die and I will live the rest of my life knowing it is my fault." His breath shuddered and he clutched his stomach. "The Grey Man said he would kill you and your sister."

Tears built in Jolie's eyes and she closed them against a heavy feeling in her chest. "What if someone else went in your place?"

"Now who's talking like a crazy person?" Armand asked. "Look at the life you will have once you marry Quentin. You will have a good home here in Fontainbleu, and lots of fat babies." He looked his daughter in the eye.

There was something in Armand's eyes, like he was trying to tell her something he couldn't bring himself to say out loud, or wasn't supposed to. She felt like he was offering her a choice but she couldn't see the options clearly enough.

"None of those things are what I want, Papa. Not yet. You know I wish to see other parts of the world before I marry. And no matter what you say, I will not be happy with Quentin. There is nothing in his eyes when he smiles," she said, slipping the ring back on her finger. "I am afraid of him, Papa."

"I, too, noticed his empty expressions," Armand admitted. "But if anyone can warm a man's heart, it's you." For some reason, Jolie didn't think he was talking about Quentin anymore. Her father was still keeping secrets. What had happened while he was away?

"What will he do when he finds out that I have no fortune or connections for him to take advantage of?" Jolie asked, and a realization struck her. Without her father's fortune she wouldn't be able to travel as she wanted to so badly. She might be more trapped into this engagement than she thought.

Heaving a sigh, Armand straightened and walked away, again turning to look out the window. "You will already be married and there will be nothing he can do. I have enough money to offer him a handsome dowry to secure the marriage, so he will understand nothing until after you are already his wife."

Desperate for her to understand, he took her face in his hands and stared into her bright green eyes. "I was a foolish old man trying to keep his baby with him as long as he could. The choices I made with your other suitors were rash. If I had chosen one of them for you, we wouldn't be in the situation we're in tonight. If you were secure, I could go back to the castle without worry, but I can't to leave you here alone."

"I do not want to marry a man I don't know," Jolie said, her tears falling in earnest now.

Armand pulled her to him and clutched her to his chest for what he knew could be the last time. If he opened his mouth to speak of this anymore, he'd be on his knees begging for her to take his place. He had no right to ask her to go, it had to be her decision.

"This may be your last chance for a good match. If we anger the Garamonde family by backing out now, you will have to settle for even less. He is already less than you deserve."

Her sobs subsided and she pulled away. "Pierre will be here in the morning and the marriage contract will be written?"

He took her face in his hands again, hating how her pretty green eyes, so like his own, swam in her tears. "Yes. Tomorrow morning, it will be done."

Armand walked back into the office, and through the French doors she saw him scribble the letter to Pierre. He yanked the bell pull on the wall and Desmond trudged down the stairs, his old joints refusing to let him do it at any great speed. He took the letter in his hand, bowed to her father, then was gone.

Without another word or even a glance at her through the doors, Papa walked down the hall to his bedroom. As soon as the door to his bedroom closed, she fiddled with the ring that was still wrapped around her finger, the weight of it on her hand making it impossible to ignore.

Armand's words repeated over and over as she stared into the fire. "Turn it three times," she said, her voice low. "Tomorrow morning it will be done." Over and over, she heard how her father had emphasized 'tomorrow morning.'

"Tomorrow morning, I will be obligated to marry Quentin," she said, starting to pace across the room. "What difference does that make, when tonight— "

She stopped dead in her tracks, the breath leaving her body in a whoosh. "Tonight, I'm not."

Armand was asleep already, his snores rattling the windowpanes in the hall between them. If she waited until tomorrow her plan, such as it was, would be foiled. Whatever his intention had been, she knew what she had to do.

She crossed into the study and drew a sheet of paper from under her father's blotter, then picked up one of his pens. When she pulled the inkwell closer, her shaking hands tipped it over with a clatter and she froze. She kept her eyes on the hall, sure Papa or Mireille would come out and ruin her idea.

Nothing happened and the snoring continued, so she pulled the stopper out of the little bottle and set it far enough away she didn't need to worry about spilling it. She dipped the nib of the pen in the ink and started writing.

Papa,
I understand now. Someday we will meet again. Even the Grey Man can't live forever.
Jolie

She added a flourish to her name, then stoppered the inkwell and put everything back where it belonged. Her traveling cloak and cap were across the room, draped over the back of a wing-back chair near the big window. As she crossed the room to retrieve them, she looked through the window at Château Hill in the distance.

The old palace stood at the top, no light visible through the windows. A chill stole over her as she thought of the stories village children told.

All anyone knew for sure was Prince Leopold hadn't been seen since the night his parents died. Some said the Grey Man had appeared that night and killed all three of them. Others said the creature, being very old himself, raised the prince as his own to continue on as the Grey Man once he died.

Jolie shivered, then pulled herself away from the window. Ludicrous, a grown woman like herself frightened by a fairy story. She shook her head and grabbed her father's knapsack from where it hung off the right arm. She pulled it up into the seat and rummaged through it, pulling out the hand mirror. As she held it in front of her, the glass flickered like it had before, going black for a moment, then clearing again. She had the strange thought that the thing recognized her.

Gazing into the mirror, waiting for it to flicker again, she watched as the handle started to glow. The light emanating from the cool metal was faint white at first, then blinding as the glass changed. Images flashed across the glass at the speed of her thoughts. Cobbles on the street outside, the ring on her own hand, the tired look on Papa's face as he talked to Quentin.

"Show me the Grey Man," she said, then jumped at the sound of her own voice. She hadn't intended to speak her desire out loud.

The mirror blackened and at first she thought it hadn't worked, but then she saw in the glass a gigantic man moving through a room she'd never seen before. He strode over a deep blue rug down a hallway lined with fine tapestries, past windows curtained to little more than slits. As narrow bars of moonlight passed over his face, she had to bite down on the inside of her cheek to keep herself from screaming.

The Grey Man's arms were as thick as a cow's hind legs—long and heavy with muscle. His thick legs carried him swiftly up and down the halls. Thick black hair that covered his arms and huge hands thinned around his face. That face was a man's, only with features that were exaggerated, enlarged beyond recognition. Eyes as black as the night sky were trained on the path in front of him.

His expression wasn't angry, as she would have expected with the speed of his movements, but exhausted, the lids of his eyes heavy and drooping. His steps echoed on the stone floor he paced and Jolie wondered if he was awake not because he chose to be but because he didn't *have* a choice. He walked the hall like a man possessed and she wondered if he would just sleep wherever the energy boiling in him ran out.

Pitying a creature she wasn't even sure was human was ridiculous and she chastised herself for it in language more colorful than her father would have permitted. When she set the mirror down on the desk to ready herself for whatever this journey was going to be like, the glass flickered and the eerie glow faded out.

Jolie drew the traveling cloak about her shoulders, tied on her cap, and took one last glance out the window. Using her thumb to turn the ring against her middle finger, she counted its revolutions and as she got to three, she felt a tug behind her navel and a thunderclap sounded in her head, then all was dark.

There was a sensation of being pulled through a fibrous membrane like the skin on the inside of an egg, slow at first, then all at once. Then she went into freefall, floating along weightlessly, her body turning in the air.

When she landed, it was abrupt and violent. Her body hit a hard surface with a smack. The mirror clattered to the floor to her left, its landing imitating her own. Her ears rang and she pressed her eyes closed to try and dispel the darkness but when she opened them the world around her hadn't gotten any brighter. She'd landed face down on a stone floor and her joints were paying for it. She pushed herself up to sit, then fluttered her fingertips over her face, feeling for injury. Nothing felt broken, but she was sure she would have bruises everywhere come morning.

"Who are you?" Jolie heard a deep voice. It startled her and she gasped, coming to her feet so quickly her head swam. Something that felt like an enormous hand pressed against her ribs, preventing her from falling. On instinct, her hand shot out to grip the arm attached to that hand and fell on a mat of thick, springy hair.

Remembering the vision the mirror had shown her of the Grey Man, her thoughts ran wild. Her heart beat against her ribs, threatening to burst from her chest.

"Answer me," the voice came again, deeper than any she'd ever heard and so soft it was hard to hear over the pounding of her heart in her ears.

She had to answer him this time. He might not do anything awful to her, but no one's patience lasted forever. "I— "

"Look at me when you are speaking to me!" the deep voice roared, echoing off the stone walls.

Jolie looked up at him, trembling. "I am Jolie Lisette Babineaux," she said. "I have come in my father Armand's stead." She took a couple of deep breaths to calm herself and stood up straight, hoping good posture might make her look stronger than she felt.

"Do you come willingly?" This was the first time his voice showed any life, like this question was important.

"Yes," she said. She held a hand out to try and find where he was in front of her, but all she felt was air rushing past her fingers as he dodged them. "It's very dark in here. Can you see me?"

"I see very well at night," he said.

"I— "she cut herself off, nerves not letting her finish right away. "I would like to see you, too."

Heavy footsteps walked away from her. The room felt colder, like he'd been throwing off enough heat to warm them both. Far away, from around a corner, he returned. A cloak and hood covered him from head to foot now and he carried a torch over his head. His head hung low and she couldn't see his face under the rim of the hood.

At first glance she didn't think he looked like that large a creature. The hallway was long, though, and as he drew closer he got bigger and bigger until he was towering over her by at least three feet. He set the torch into a sconce on the wall, then pulled the hood back with a massive hand.

It wasn't easy but she managed not to gasp at his appearance. It was much easier to believe this was a creature that would make good on his threat to kill her family if Armand didn't return.

Just as the mirror had shown, he was a grotesquely large man. His nose was as broad as a garden spade, his brow projected low over his eyes, and his chin jutted forward. Hair covered every inch of skin she could see, sparse enough over his face she could see the skin beneath it, but thicker as it covered his neck and arms. The hair that grew from his head was thick and shiny, flowing down to his elbows.

The man's clothes were well made and Jolie guessed they were custom because of the amount of linen and wool. A white tunic with a drawstring neck was of an old fashion but more suited to his great size than the modern gathered-neck shirts men wore. Fawn pants covered his thick legs and his knee-high boots were made of so much leather it must have taken a whole cow to make them.

"What are you?" Jolie asked, then gasped as she realized her mistake. She covered her mouth with her hand, embarrassed at her own folly.

The man scoffed, his brow furrowing at her question.

The moment he'd seen her land on the hall floor, he hadn't been able to look away. He was captivated by her wild red curls that sprung out in every direction from under her cap. Her green eyes were the most beautiful he'd ever seen, her freckles like a map of the stars on every inch of skin he could see. He saw her strength in the way she'd spoken to him and hadn't run away when he showed himself. Hope flickered in his heart for the first time in almost ten years and he had to fight not to let it take over.

Jolie took a step forward and looked up at him, leaving him nowhere else to look but into her eyes. His heart swooped, making his stomach feel a little sick, but in a pleasant, warm way he didn't understand. Fighting against what he was feeling, trying to make his face look uninterested and impassive, he tried to step back but backed into the wall and could go no further.

A small scraping sound came from behind them, and a flicker of weak light. They both looked away at the same time to see the silver ring spinning on its edge a few feet away, faster and faster until it seemed to run out of energy and collapse. It hopped up once like a child finding that one last bit of gumption to move before dropping off to sleep.

"What magic is this?" she asked, her voice still unsteady.

He didn't answer her, and when she looked at him again, his expression hadn't changed.

He was not as deaf to gossip as his people would believe. All the odd stories people told about the creature that stalked these halls had made their way to the him on the lips of the servants. Ignorance and superstition led the villagers to believe him some mythical creature rather than the man he was. And although he held out little hope for the chance to regain his former form, he *was* still a man.

Soon enough, he would tell her the truth about how he'd wound up in this body, but for now she needed rest. And he needed her to be anywhere but where he was, or he knew he would do or say something stupid. "Follow me. I will show you to your chambers."

Leading her to the East Tower, he clenched his teeth together. This would all have been so much easier if Armand had come back instead of sending this girl. Something about her made him feel different than he ever had before and the absurdity of his wayward emotions was enough to make him question his own sanity. The old man would have changed nothing about his life, but at least he wouldn't have to deal with the pretty little woman behind him.

Every once in a while, he heard the ring rolling along the stones, turning a corner, following along like a faithful pet.

"You know that thing is following us?" Jolie asked.

"Yes," he said.

"Why is it doing that?" she asked and he could tell she was turned away, watching the ring.

They had arrived at the East Tower door and he held it open for her without answering her question.

Jolie sighed as she passed. Once inside the room, she looked around, taking in her new surroundings.

As he watched her, he said, "We called this the Rose Room. These were my mother's chambers."

Her eyes flew to his. "So it's true, then? You're Prince Leopold," she said, her voice shrill in surprise.

"Who else would be in this château?" His irritation was clear, his brow raised and his mouth a grimace telling her he thought she was about as smart as wallpaper paste.

"Highness," she said, her voice reverent despite his obvious disdain. She bowed her head and dropped into a curtsy. Rattled, it took her a moment to find the ability to speak.

"What would you like me to call you? Will Master be acceptable?" She folded her hands at her waist, holding her back ramrod straight and trying to look as respectful as possible.

"Of course," he said, his chest puffing and his nose tilting ever so much higher.

"What sentence will I be serving, Master?" Jolie was ruffled by his arrogant demeanor, but as there was nothing she could do about it, she tried not to grit her teeth as she waited for his response.

Leopold didn't want to be unkind, because the way she was looking at him right now brought back the swooping sensation in his belly. But no matter what else she was, she was a prisoner. Even if she could eventually be more to him than just that, he couldn't see yet how they would ever get there.

"You are mistress of this castle and grounds, and it shall be your home, but you are never to leave. The château is yours to explore and enjoy as you wish, but you are my prisoner and shall remain so for the rest of your life," he said, his voice cold and emotionless even as his words devastated her.

"I'm never to see my family again?" she asked, her voice cracking.

"You are to serve the sentence I condemned your father to."

Jolie backed away from him, her eyes closing. She drew in a shaky breath. "I'm only twenty," she said, more to herself than to him.

Leopold closed his eyes, his heart burning in his chest at the memory of losing his own family. Though it had been ten years, the grief was just a memory away. No one should suffer the loss of their family so young, or a lifetime of isolation for what amounted to a crime of ignorance. He couldn't stand the thought of showing any kindness to her, though, and kept his mouth shut before he did something like apologize to her. If her father had wanted to spare her this agony, he wouldn't have let her come here tonight.

Jolie opened her eyes on a new thought. "How did you know to clean a woman's chambers if you expected my father would come?"

"Your father told me the rose was for his daughter," Leopold said, his voice soft and rumbling. "The punishment was for him, but I suggested he could send a child of his own in his place. I left the choice up to him."

"All of his talk was so I would choose to take his place?" She remembered how Papa hadn't let the ring go when he got home, but how easily he'd walked away from it once she had it on her finger. Aghast, she sat on the bed. Jolie recalled something else her father had said and the pang of surprise turned into a painful riptide in her chest. "Did you tell him that you would kill all of us if he didn't return?"

A coldness stole over his grotesque features. "It is my right as the crown prince to punish those who trespass against me in any way I see fit. I offered my hospitality and generosity to your father in his hour of need, and he repaid my kindness by stealing from me— "

"—he took a flower, not the crown jewels!"

"Flower or diamond, it was my property and not his to take!" His voice echoed through the room and Jolie cowered, backing up to the bureau. He bent down, holding his face just inches from hers.

This was a creature confident in his right to rule with an iron fist. In the prince's eyes, all she could see was a cold, arrogant *thing* looking back at her.

"Your father took what was not his, and he must be punished for his crime. Or, as he chose, you must be punished in his stead. You, as my prisoner, have no right to question my decision." The prince's voice was deep and booming, echoing off the Rose Room walls.

"Your punishment doesn't fit the crime committed, *Prince Leopold*," she said, sneering his title and name in a way that only served to rankle him further. His petulant anger reminded her of Mireille and, despite her fear, she couldn't hold back for this monster any more than she could for her sister. "I must never leave this keep, and my duty shall be to serve you until one of us dies, all for want of a flower?"

Rage widened his eyes, the irises so black they looked like bottomless pits. He walked to the door and when he got there, he turned to her once more. She looked stricken and in a rare moment of compassion he wanted to comfort her. But the anger he'd felt at having his authority questioned was still simmering too close to the surface, so he stood his ground.

Jolie could feel his anger coming off him in waves like heat, and knew she was treading dangerous ground.

Pulling herself together, she stood with that perfect posture again and folded her hands at her waist. Serving a sentence would be a more pleasant experience if she would try to get along with her new master. "Forgive me, Master. I spoke out of turn and must apologize."

The dam of anger within him broke at her words and he felt stupid for feeling it in the first place. He'd gotten himself cursed for that same impotent rage and overblown sense of privilege, and if he wasn't careful he'd be stuck like this forever. Having a yelling match with a woman who had volunteered to be imprisoned for her father's crime would prove nothing, and there was her position to consider as well.

Prince Leopold pulled the door closed with a loud bang. With a heavy key from a ring in his trouser pocket, he locked the door before walking away down the hall. Willard was waiting at the foot of the steps to his south tower chamber, in his night robe.

"Master, is anything amiss? I heard yelling."

Leopold growled as he walked by his valet, but didn't answer. Willard followed behind him as he headed toward the South Tower.

"Did the Babineaux man return as promised?" The older man had to run to keep up with the prince's long strides and the prince slowed down so as not to wear him out.

"His daughter did," Leopold said. Willard was the man he trusted most in the world and if ever there was a time he needed a level-headed person's advice it was now.

"The man sent his daughter?" Willard stopped mid-stride and Leopold waited for him to collect himself. The old man looked as bewildered as Leopold had ever seen him.

"So it would appear."

"I thought I heard a woman's voice. But, why? How old is the girl?"

"I don't know why," Leopold said, and his confusion was obvious as his shoulders slumped and his hands went up. "She's twenty years old. I don't know why any father would condemn his daughter to prison in his stead."

Willard looked around in wonder, his cheeks lifting with a smile. "A young lady of marriageable age in our midst for the first time in years. Perhaps this is the girl who will break the curse?"

Leopold looked thoughtful for a moment but then shook his big head. "That curse will never be broken, Willard."

"Is she beautiful?"

Leopold's sheepish smile told him all he needed to know, but there was doubt in his eyes and tone when he spoke again. "She will be no different than the villagers. She'll never be able to see through all this." He raised his hands, letting the cloak's voluminous sleeves fall around his elbows.

"Why would she, if you insist on bellowing at her all the time? If you treat her poorly, you'll be lucky if she lasts a single night here."

The pair of men started walking toward the south tower again, one brooding and fuming, the other plotting and hoping.

At the foot of the tower steps, Leopold stopped again. Willard refused to follow him into the mess he made of his chamber. "What should I do?"

"It never hurts, when in pursuit of a young lady, to practice a little tenderness, Master." Willard met his eyes, raising his eyebrows so high they almost reached his hairline.

"I'm not in pursuit, you old sop," Leopold scoffed, tossing his head.

"The curse that old witch laid on you was in punishment of your charming attitude, was it not?"

"Yes," Leopold grumbled, starting to think that he allowed his valet too much leniency with his own attitude.

"And all these years it's never occurred to you to actually fix it?"

Sheepish again, knowing he was in the wrong, Leopold hung his head. "How do I do that, Willard?"

"I would wager that if you just try, you'll surprise yourself." Willard put his hand on Leopold's arm, his eyes encouraging on his master's. "Why don't you try by treating her as a guest rather than a prisoner? Make her feel at home, maybe give her a task to do that will keep her occupied."

"What about the crime she's meant to atone for?" Leopold felt the impotent anger again and fought hard to kill it before it colored his every thought.

Willard gave him a stern look, his mouth a tight moue of distaste. "She will remain here, as promised, but if you do not make her comfortable, how can you ever hope she will see more than this?" He plucked at the hair on Leopold's arm and the prince pulled away, his eyes full of shame.

"It also helps, Master, if one does not scare the living daylights out of the young woman he wishes to keep around. All that frightful yelling is not an attractant." Willard yawned, covering his mouth with his hand. "Perhaps you could give her a gift, as a way to atone for your behavior tonight?"

Leopold nodded. "What could I give her?"

Willard's head dropped back in exasperation, his eyes rolling. "Master, it is late and while you enjoy staying awake to all hours, some of us do not. May I please go to bed? Perhaps in the morning we shall speak of this some more."

"Of course, Willard. You are dismissed. I apologize," Leopold said, waving the old man away. He climbed the stairs to his chamber and when he reached the mess that lived on the landing, he tiptoed around it on the way to his bed.

Back in the Rose Room, Jolie slumped against the door, sliding down it and winding up on the floor. She curled into a ball and put her face in her hands. She'd tried to be strong in front of the man who had imprisoned her, but in this strange room, alone, there was no one to impress, not a single person she needed to hide her tears from.

On the floor, with no one to hear her, Jolie lay on the floor and cried as her heart shattered into a million pieces.

Chapter 5

"Papa!" Mireille shrieked. Her footsteps clacked and clomped all over the house, echoing off the walls. When she got close to a wall, the objects on it rattled and teetered. "Papa, I cannot find Jolie anywhere! Where could she have gone?"

There was panic in her voice, but since Armand knew where Jolie had gone and why, he took his time getting out of bed. Normally, he woke when it was still dark, which would have given him plenty of time to explain what had happened before the girl had a chance to fly into a fury. He'd caught his death on his journey from Port Lucerne, though, and slept past nine o'clock.

He pulled his robe on and tied the sash before he walked into the hall. Malcolm was slouched into a chair in the kitchen, a hot cup of tea in his big hand. "Father Armand," he greeted the older man. "You look terrible."

"I feel terrible, my boy, but I shall be fine. Once your wife stops that infernal tapping and yelling."

"Mireille, darling, please come in here and have breakfast before you wake the whole village." Malcolm grabbed her arm as she flew through the kitchen for the hundredth time.

"I haven't seen Jolie all morning. All of her things are here." She stopped when her father held up a hand.

"Jolie is at Château Villeneuve. She went there last night, and if you will sit still long enough, I will explain how and why."

A tickle was building in his throat and he tried to cough it away without making too much noise, but the feeling was persistent. By the time he got his coughing under control, he was in tears and there was a hot, burning sensation riding low in his chest. When he met eyes with Mireille and Malcolm over the table, his tears began to flow in earnest.

"My darling baby girl is lost to us forever," Armand said. "And it's all my fault."

Launching into his story, he told them everything. From the loss of the *Lisette* to the night at the château, to the stolen rose. When he was done, the two of them were looking at him in shock. He knew neither of them were sure they could believe this wild tale, but there were a good many obvious truths in his story, and they couldn't discount it.

"You must get her back, Papa." Mireille said.

"Why, for you to spend another twenty years tormenting her?"

Mireille looked surprised and hurt at his harsh tone, but his head hurt and his chest felt tight. He didn't have the time or patience to let her pretend to be heartbroken. "You're not upset by the loss of your sister. I know my daughters well enough to know you harbor no feelings for Jolie."

Even Malcolm drew back from him this time. "Armand, you're not well. Perhaps you should just go back to bed. With some more rest, you'll feel better."

"Jolie is serving my sentence. There will be no more getting better," Armand said, resting his elbows on the table.

"What can we do to get her out of there?" Malcolm trained his eyes on Armand's, not liking their feverish gloss. Beads of sweat stood out on the old man's forehead and his skin was pale.

"There is nothing you can do, and I don't want you to try. We have to trust that the Grey Man will care for her," Armand said, tears streaming down his cheeks.

Mireille whirled around, her eyes wide. "The Grey Man?" she asked, her voice shrill in surprise.

"Armand, make sense," Malcolm said, surprised at his father-in-law. "Surely you don't believe those stories?"

"You didn't see the monster," Armand said, his eyes wide.

"Papa, you have a fever, you're imagining things."

"Don't tell me about my own mind, woman!" Armand roared, coming out of his chair. His whole body shook and he looked crazed for a moment, then settled back into his seat, all the strength sapped from him by his outburst. "I know what I saw!"

Mireille and Malcolm exchanged a wary glance. "I'm sorry, Papa," she said, her tone earnest. "Perhaps you should go back to bed. I think a little rest would help you feel better."

"Put me in a more agreeable mood, more like," Armand grumbled. There was still fire in his eyes, but his shoulders slumped and he nodded in acquiescence. "I am tired, though. Malcolm, will you help me to my room?"

"Of course, Armand." As he guided the old man back down the hall, he shot a look over his shoulder at his wife.

Concern deepened the lines around Malcolm's eyes and Mireille knew whatever her father had brought home was serious. When he returned to the kitchen, he looked haunted.

"He's burning up, and his breathing is ragged. I'll ride to the village to fetch the physician," he said, leading her to the study. "I will post a letter to Pierre while I'm there, so we can be sure your father's affairs are in order. Just in case."

Following at his heels, she steered around Jacques and Olivier where they played in the hall. "Will he die?" she asked the moment the door closed behind them.

"Mireille, it's far too early to tell right now," he said, rifling through the desk for paper and pen. He scratched out a letter, the words large and slanting in his rough penmanship.

"Do you think what he said about the *Lisette* was true?" she asked. "Do you really think the ship was lost?"

Malcolm looked around the room and found Armand's knapsack. He dug through the contents, but found no ship's manifest or receipts of any kind. There was no evidence of goods exchanging hands. "If she'd been brought back, he'd have some record of the ship in here, but there's nothing."

Disappointment flashed across her face and Malcolm felt a pang of his own, but with his wife rather than the loss of the money. It was a personal affront that she didn't think he could keep her in the lifestyle she was accustomed to. Now was the wrong time to bring up the problem, though, and he returned to the letter, keeping it simple.

"I'll go into town and send the doctor, then post this letter to Pierre and return before you know I'm gone. I'll summon Henrietta to help with the children," he said.

Mireille nodded, letting him kiss her on the forehead as he headed for the door. It felt to her like everything in her life had fallen apart in just a few days. If even half of what Armand had said this morning were true, nothing would ever be the same.

****

Jolie didn't leave her room for days. The servants began to think that Jolie was not the one they all were waiting for to break the curse after all. For two long weeks, Jolie took her meals in her room. When Rosalie, the only maid, cleaned the room or offered help with a bath, Jolie sat and looked out the window while she did her work.

After so much time, Willard began to worry that the master had punished this young woman too harshly. If she truly was the woman who was meant to break the spell, he knew Leopold would have to find a way to make her happy again. Which seemed to be the prince's last concern. Instead, he spent his time as if nothing was different. He continued his long walks through the village every night, then haunted the halls like a ghost until sleep took him. The master acted as if nothing changed, but Willard knew that was because he was afraid. Afraid of everything the young lady in the Rose Room meant. But no one in this château had time for fear.

Time was running out, and while Mademoiselle Jolie was grieving everything she had lost, Willard was coming up with a plan. He headed for the south tower to roust his master. Two weeks was long enough. It was high time Prince Leopold showed Jolie what 'royal hospitality' truly meant.

****

Pierre and Malcolm put off the Garamonde boy as long as they could. With Armand's condition deteriorating over the last two weeks, they could hold the boy off no longer. The solicitor arrived at the Babineaux house at a quarter of noon. He looked harried already, and when Mireille delivered the news that Armand had worsened again over the last night, the old man looked fit to have an apoplexy.

"As we discussed after Armand first came home, he has had a will in place for many years, and has kept it updated regarding—" he paused, unsure of how much to divulge, given the circumstances.

Mireille looked away, disgusted, and left the room. Down the hall, the men heard the nursery door open and close.

Malcolm said, "We are aware of Armand's recent misfortune."

"I thought he may have told you when he returned, but I couldn't be sure," Pierre said, looking relieved. "Well, he made sure that proceeds from the sale of all of his earthly goods would be distributed between your wife and her sister in specific amounts depending on Jolie's marital and financial status at the time of his death. With her being unmarried, she stands to inherit seventy-five percent. Armand knew she would need more than Mireille did, given your income." Pierre spoke quickly, with his voice a near-whisper so the woman he spoke of wouldn't hear.

"Quite right," Malcolm said with a nod. "About this marriage contract—"

"—nothing was set in stone," Pierre interrupted. "He promised

59

her in marriage verbally, which is not a contract at all. Especially since there were no witnesses. The only proof we have that marriage was even discussed is his word."

"Which is no proof at all," Malcolm said with a nod.

"Exactly, and that means there is no way that Garamonde can press his case," Pierre said.

"Yes, and with Jolie at the château, she can't fulfill her duty to him. We must make that clear to him," Malcolm said, leaning against the desk. "He is due to arrive any moment."

"How much does he know about her whereabouts?" Pierre asked, jotting down a note on a piece of paper. "I trust you've kept him in the dark about where she's been these last weeks?"

"It hasn't been easy with the little cur being so persistent, but I have been able to hold him off with Armand being ill," Malcolm assured him. "I haven't let him in the door."

"And he hasn't made any mention of the engagement?" Pierre was giving him a hopeful look. Malcolm didn't know Armand's solicitor well, but knew when someone was forming a plan.

"Not a word," he said. "Armand told me about it, but Garamonde has made no mention of it whatsoever."

Pierre scratched at his chin with the pen, leaning back in his chair. "As her next oldest male relative, with her father incapacitated by illness, Jolie has to abide by and be subject to any decisions you make until her father recovers." An idea came to him and he chewed on it for a moment before bringing it up. "I have an idea that might save you a rather large headache, if you will play along when the time comes?"

Malcolm nodded his assent and Pierre chuckled. The knock they'd been waiting for came to the door and Desmond answered. As he walked their guest down the hall, Malcolm couldn't help but notice the smug, self-satisfied expression on the Quentin's face. They were all introduced and Desmond left them to their business.

"Where is Monsieur Babineaux? I assumed he would be in attendance today," Quentin asked, taking a seat across the desk as Pierre took the one behind it.

"I am afraid I don't know what you're talking about, Monsieur Garamonde," Pierre said, his face the picture of innocence. One good thing about being a solicitor, his skills at selling falsehoods were at their peak. "Malcolm's invitation was unbeknownst to me, as I am here on other matters. Armand has taken ill these past weeks, as I am sure you are aware. He has taken a grave turn in the last few days, and I met with Malcolm and Mireille today to discuss his estate should the worst come to pass."

"I have intentions to marry his daughter, Mademoiselle Jolie, and have been trying for two weeks to write and sign the marriage contract," Quentin said, a tight smile on his lips. "I have been visiting frequently in an attempt to speak to her and her father about this matter. I must admit that my solicitor is growing impatient with the inattention this matter has been given thus far."

"I am terribly sorry, my boy, but no such contract was discussed with me," Pierre said, sitting back in the chair. If the man had a tell, neither of the other two could see it. Quentin looked suspicious, just the same, and his eyes narrowed at the older man.

"Surely, as her brother-in-law, you could negotiate this contract in Monsieur Babineaux's stead?" Quentin's eyes darted between the two older men, not yet desperate but close.

Malcolm stepped in, standing next to Pierre on the other side of the desk. If they could present a united front, they could sell their story and get Garamonde to leave with none the worse for wear.

"I could, if I knew that such a marriage was desired by either Monsieur or Mademoiselle Babineaux. At present, I know nothing of this arrangement," Malcolm said, his burr thickening in an unconscious attempt at intimidation. It was working, and the boy squirmed in his seat. "Neither I nor my wife were witness to any such verbal agreement and Armand is in no condition to make these decisions."

"This can be cleared up easily. Bring Jolie here. She can confirm our engagement." Quentin leaned forward, elbows on knees, hands spread as if in supplication. His tone was clipped, tight. "I have not formally proposed, but surely her father made her aware of the arrangement."

"That is neither here nor there, and we cannot confirm it either way. Jolie Babineaux isn't here," Pierre said.

"Where is she? We are talking about my fiancée, here, and I demand she be brought forward to—"

"—to what?" Malcolm interrupted. He pulled himself up to his full height. "Prove your betrothal?"

"Of course!"

"Jolie has been detained," Pierre said, standing next to Malcolm. "For two weeks, she has been held prisoner for the crime of theft."

Quentin's eyes flew open and he sat back in his chair, shocked. His eyes darted between the two older men, flicking back and forth. Sweat shone on his upper lip and in beads on his forehead. A sour taste rose in the back of his throat and he nervously played with the queue of blonde hair at the back of his neck.

"She is serving the sentence in place of Armand, at her own insistence." Pierre gave him the news with an undertaker's calm, nothing in his countenance giving away the gravity of the situation.

Under Quentin's surprise, Malcolm saw anger in his grey eyes. Quentin had been expecting to walk out of here with the promise of a bride, but everything Pierre said had changed his plans. He smoothed his blonde hair back into its queue, then stood and straightened the lapels on his long brown coat.

"Where is she being held?" Quentin asked, recovering.

"She is at Château Villeneuve," Pierre said, meeting the kid's eyes, his own unwavering. There was no way this whelp would be able to get her out of a sentence served at the palace. The man who lived there was either a prince or a monster, and both were more powerful than Garamonde could ever dream of being.

Pierre continued, "Until further notice, she is a prisoner there. Between her imprisonment and the undeniable fact that you have no proof of an engagement between yourself and Jolie Babineaux, I would suggest that you give the Babineaux family privacy during this difficult time."

Quentin looked as if he was about to object, his mouth opening and closing like a fish on a dock. He pointed a finger at Pierre, but he was no fool. Both of the other men were larger than him. What's more, they were right, and anything he did now would only reflect poorly on him.

Instead of exploding the way he wanted to, he stood and bowed to Malcolm and Pierre. "Gentlemen, I am sorry for the misunderstanding, and will leave you alone. Please send my regards to Armand."

Quentin turned on his heel and walked down the hall toward the door, leaving Pierre and Malcolm watching his exit, their victory turning a dismal day just a bit brighter.

As Quentin exited the house, flinging the door open, he saw a small boy, no doubt one of Mireille's brats, sitting at a desk practicing his letters. Intent on ignoring him, he started to leave when the boy spoke.

"Grandpére said Aunt Jolie went to the Grey Man," the boy said.

That stopped Quentin in his tracks. He took a step back and looked at the child again. "What was that?"

"I heard my Grandpére talking right after he got home, and he told my Papa that the Grey Man took Aunt Jolie, and he's a monster. He's going to eat her, and we're never going to see her again." The child said it in a matter-of-fact way, but Quentin saw how his lip quivered.

Quentin didn't respond to the boy, but grinned as he left the Babineaux house, leaving the door standing open as he went. As he stomped his way down the road a short while later, he kept his head down. The reins to his horse were balled into one fist and the animal trailed behind. He could hear the sugar cane whooshing past his ears as if he were already on that island, feel the reeds cutting into his hands. He suffered no illusions that he would be given an easy job on his father's sugar plantation. He would be working himself to death like everyone else and that was no life for a man of his station. He had to fix this. Just two weeks ago, he'd not been happy, but he'd been satisfied. Then, he'd had what he wanted: a guarantee that he wouldn't have to work for the rest of his life. With his engagement to Jolie, he would receive his due from his father, which was less than it had been before his indiscretion in Nice, but still more than enough to live on for the rest of his life.

Now, though, there was nothing left. His inheritance had disappeared like dust in a wind. His fiancée was in a château while he would be on a boat to Barbados before the end of the month.

When he reached the end of the road, he mounted his horse. He drove the animal hard, pushing it to the limits of its endurance on their way home. There was work to do and he needed to come up with a plan. Time was not on his side, and with his parents' return in a few days came the end of his freedom. If the Grey Man had taken his fiancée, perhaps he should make preparations to remedy the situation.

<u>Chapter 6</u>

Jolie woke late on her fifteenth day of imprisonment with visions of the castle in her head. The images were fuzzy, unclear, and the only other person she saw in them was a tall man with thick dark hair. He was dressed in regal finery, wearing white breeches and gold braid on his blue velvet coat, glossy brown boots. Throughout the long night, she never saw his face. She remembered the prince telling her that she had free run of the castle, but she couldn't imagine treating this place like it was her home. She knew where her home was, and this was not it.

Before she got ready for the day, she threw open the curtains and looked around the Rose Room for the millionth time. Wallpaper covered the walls from floor to ceiling, expensive silk paper of a pale green with dusty pink roses all over it. The wood used in the room was oak, and everything in it coordinated, from the canopy bed she slept in to the armoire that stood near the window. One of its doors was open, a morning gown of pale pink muslin draped over the top. She hadn't opened the door, or noticed a servant doing it. Some strange things happened when she turned her back, and she entertained a fleeting thought that the castle was haunted. Logic told her she was being silly, but that didn't change the fact that a dress had appeared where none was before.

Dressing herself was difficult, but she managed every day. This morning, she managed to get the petticoats on without breaking a sweat, and the dress went on easily enough. When she turned around to the armoire again, a long ivory buttonhook was swinging from a nail on the inside of the door. She was certain it hadn't been there when she'd taken the dress down, but she needed it and didn't question its presence.

Her hair was a nightmare, as it was every morning, and she worked the worst of the knots out with her fingers. She washed her face at the dry sink and scrubbed a brush over her teeth, before going to her usual spot on a settee in front of the window.

Since her arrival, she'd seen no birds in the trees, no animals, no signs of life. The village below teemed with life, but here on Château Hill, it seemed that no more animals ventured near the keep than people. In two weeks, she hadn't seen so much as a sparrow.

Jolie knew she couldn't live the rest of her life like this. As much as they drove her crazy with their crying and screaming, she had begun to miss the noise of her nieces and nephews. A fight with Mireille would have at least broken up the monotony of sitting in this room.

The whole time she'd been here, she hadn't set foot outside the room, even to venture into the hall. Breakfast would be brought to her in about half an hour, more than enough time to find the dining room and see what it looked like. How hard could it be to find? If all else failed, she'd follow the scent of the food cooking. If she didn't find the dining hall, she was sure she'd find the kitchen. In the armoire, she found a pair of pink slippers that matched her gown and slipped them on.

Jolie poked her head into the hall and looked from left to right. She smelled pastries and tea, and breathed their aroma in deep. The hallway was dark as a tomb, the only light in it coming from the door to her room. Cobalt blue velvet curtains covered all the windows. A rug the same color as the curtains, the one she'd seen in the mirror on her first night here, covered the floor in one long strip.

As soon as she closed the door, darkness covered her and the hallway floor to ceiling. Turning to her right, she dragged her fingertips over the paneling to try and keep her bearings as she set off, hopefully to find the food that smelled so delightful this morning.

"You're going the wrong way," a deep voice rumbled behind her, making her jump. The prince was there, in the dark.

"The butler must have forgotten to give me the map," she snapped, twisting around to go the other way. She heard the prince chuckle and then heavy footsteps followed behind her as she made her way down the hall.

"I don't have a butler anymore, but I do have a valet named Willard who would be very offended to be called one," that deep voice said. "I thought you might get turned around in the palace, trying to navigate it for the first time, so I've been waiting outside your room until you awakened."

"Every morning?" Jolie asked, finding it unlikely he would waste his time in such a way.

"Of course," he said, as if it should have been a given.

The gesture was oddly touching, that he would wait for her to come out, but she had to wonder at how little he had to do that he could afford the time.

65

"Is it customary for a prisoner to be left alone in a room for weeks on end?" Jolie asked. "Not much of a warden, are you?"

Leopold chuckled and said, "You are going to spend a good many years in these halls. I wouldn't want to make you miserable the entire time. You needed time to grieve for your losses, so I allowed you that."

Surprised by the thoughtfulness of the time he'd allowed her, she mumbled thanks. She wondered who had been there for him when his parents had died and, shocked at herself for thinking of his feelings over her own, shook her head to dispel the thoughts.

"Well, it is not much of a hardship staying in the Rose Room, allowed to do whatever I please, or nothing at all, should I choose," Jolie said, then paused to think. "Although, with nothing to do it certainly feels like a punishment."

"Is the room satisfactory?" Leopold asked, wondering what she meant.

"Yes, of course, but the time passes so slowly. I have nothing to occupy my time, and there are a great many things I can do," she said, unsure of where she was going with this line of thought, but bored enough already that she couldn't imagine spending the rest of her life the way she'd passed the last two weeks.

Leopold thought to himself as they walked along, wondering what jobs she could do that weren't already being done. Small as his staff was, they were more than enough, but Jolie didn't know that yet. Rosalie was looking to lighten her workload as she got older. Perhaps she could assign some of her chores to Jolie for the time being. The older woman would need to retire before long and Leopold would have to train someone to replace her. The sooner, the better.

"I will inquire with the rest of the staff about jobs you could help with, or take over. I'm sure I can find something suitable," he said finally.

"That would be—oh!" she chirped as her fingers slipped from the wood and found open air. She flung her hands out in front of her, fanning out her fingers to feel anything she could find before she ran into it face-first.

Leopold could see her even in this near pitch black. She had gone through the doorway that led from the east corridor to the Great Hall. He stood back to watch as she tried to find her way through the cavernous room. She was smart, bending a little at the waist and putting her hands out before her so they were the first things to make contact rather than a shin or her forehead. She shuffled her feet so she didn't trip on the rugs that covered the floor.

"Damn!" she swore in frustration at their slow progress and heard the outburst of laughter behind her. "I know you can see me, so why don't you stop laughing and lend me a hand?"

Leopold's huge hand swallowed hers as he swept it from the air.

"Must be fun for you, watching from the shadows while others struggle. That was a cruel thing to do," she said. He walked alongside of her, his strides so long she had to run to keep up.

For answer, all she heard from the prince was a chuckle. It felt like a confirmation of everything she had heard about the prince from before whatever had happened to turn him into the creature he was now.

By the time they got to the dining room, she was out of breath. Candelabra lit the table from one end to the other, and she only saw one place setting. The hour being so late, she was the only member of the household who hadn't eaten, and Leopold led her to her seat. Without another word, he left the room, leaving her swathed in the dreary semi-darkness.

Jolie wasted no time tucking in. Flaky, fruit-filled pastries and fresh milk were served along with toast, poached eggs, and smoked ham. She was just finishing off a pastry when she heard soft footsteps approaching. A man she could only assume was Willard came in the room, carrying an oil lamp. He bowed and came to the end of the table to wait while she finished eating.

As soon as she pushed her chair back from the long table, he turned and offered her a gentle smile. "Mademoiselle Babineaux, I am Willard LeChance, valet to Prince Leopold. I welcome you to Château Villeneuve."

"I didn't realize I was a guest," she said, wiping her hands on a linen napkin. Odd that a valet, personal servant to the master of the château, would greet her like this.

"Regardless of what the master might say, you are to be treated with respect and dignity as long as I am still in charge of staff here," Willard said, his head cocked up at such an angle he had to look down his hooked nose at her.

She stood and took a few steps toward him, trying to get a clear look at his face through the wan light from the lantern. With his powdered hair and icy blue eyes set in a wrinkled, careworn face, he looked like a kindly father. His uniform was exactly as a royal valet's should be— stiff and starched. There was a kind light in his eyes that made her think of her father, though, and she had to smile.

"I thank you for your kindness, and your patience," she said, not surprised to feel the prickle of tears in her eyes again. "I did not expect it."

"You will always find it with me," he said, his voice warm. "There are only two other people on the staff aside from me, but they're all in the village at the moment."

"A staff of only three?" she asked as they left the dining room. There was a clatter of dishes behind her, but when she turned around, she saw no one there that could have made the noise. "If everyone's gone for the moment, who cleared the table?" The whole table was empty other than the candelabra. Their flames flickered as if in a wind, then settled.

Willard was smiling when she turned back to him, and he blew out the lantern as they crossed the threshold into the Great Hall again. With a whooshing sound that surrounded her in its cacophony, all the curtains in the room opened at once, with no help from human hands, bathing the whole room in natural light.

"This is not possible," Jolie whispered, her eyes wide. Looking around the room so quickly she was making herself dizzy, she pressed a hand to her chest as if to calm her pounding heart. "There has to be someone, a machine or something."

She was reminded of the odd things that had happened in the Rose Room. The pitcher that filled on its own just when she needed it, the buttonhook that appeared in the armoire after she donned her dress. Everything she'd ever known told her that what she was seeing, what she was experiencing, was impossible.

The room was enormous, much larger than she had expected. It formed a perfect square within the square formed by the outer hallway, with tall windows that opened the corridor to the light from the windows in the outer walls of the keep. The golden wood floor gleamed and not a single mote of dust twinkled in the air. The occasional tables against the walls shone as if their varnish was still wet. A ball could have been held in this room last night and it couldn't look cleaner or more ready to receive guests.

"This is more work than three people can perform," she said, awestruck.

"Yes it is," Willard said with a knowing smile.

Jolie walked by one of the windows and caught a flicker of movement out of the corner of her eye. When she turned her head, the tail of the curtain swept up from the floor and crossed over its own fabric body. At first she didn't understand, but then she took a second look and realized the thing was bowing. She looked around the room and saw that all the drapes were mimicking this one, cutting deep bows as if they were twin rows of blue-coated footmen.

"I struck my head," she said, backing away. Her voice grew shrill as she thought out loud, "I struck my head and I'm still in my own bed, at home, dreaming all of this. I can't be here, with curtains that bow and rings that jump, pitchers that fill on their own and armoires that help you dress."

Shaking her head, she kept backing away until she was in the breezeway between the dining room and the corridor again. The curtains straightened themselves, standing at attention.

Jolie thought back, remembering her meals over the last two weeks. A tray appeared outside her door, and an odd sort of sound that was more like something running into the door than a person knocking.

Willard could see her mind working overtime, her eyes flicking to and fro as she thought. He waited patiently until she was ready to speak again.

"The tray that brings me my meals?" Jolie asked, finally pulling herself out of her own mind.

"Yes, Mademoiselle," Willard said, that knowing smile still on his lips.

"Does the cart move on its own?" she asked, taking a step toward him.

Willard nodded and she shook her head in disbelief again.

"How does it work?" she asked and it was her turn to see surprise written on his face. No one had ever bothered to ask that question. She knew it had been years since there had been guests here, and his reaction to her curiosity made Jolie sure that those who had come after the curse hadn't stayed long enough to see any of the oddities she'd witnessed so far.

Jolie doubted many people saw any of the things she'd seen. She wondered if Willard was giving her some kind of test; showing her a few smaller tricks to see if she had the mental strength to deal with what this castle could do.

He gave her a shrewd look, his eyes flickering over hers as if trying to divine something in her. "That's a story Prince Leopold must tell you himself."

"Surely, you must know something," she said, hoping flattery would convince him to tell her what he knew.

"My lady, it is not my story to tell," he said, his tone firm, and she knew better than to press the matter. She blushed, knowing she had crossed a line.

"If you will follow me, I will give you a tour," he said, all hint of irritation gone from his tone as he took up the mantle of the professional once again. He led her back into the corridor. Every curtain in the keep was open, illuminating every square inch of the royal splendor before her.

"You already know, but the master wanted me to reiterate this: you are not to leave the grounds for any reason. This is your home now, and you are free to go anywhere you like aside from the south tower," he said, pointing in its direction as they approached the door. "It's not off-limits, per se, but it houses Prince Leopold's private chambers."

He led her around to the two towers she hadn't seen yet. Both the north and west towers housed private chambers with their furniture covered in white sheets. Both had been cleaned regularly and smelled a fresh as the one she was staying in. Jolie wondered to herself if the rooms took care of themselves as so many other things seemed to.

Willard then took her to a hallway that stretched straight off the southwest side of the keep. She saw several recreational rooms, including a drawing room, a music room with a huge pianoforte and a stunning golden harp. The last room he showed her was a library stocked with more books than any person could read in a hundred lifetimes.

"You are welcome to use any of these rooms whenever you wish," he said from the doorway. Every one of the rooms was spotless, fresh-smelling and every surface as shiny as it must have been when new.

"Our master is not very good at punishing people, is he?" she asked with a smile. Instead of laughing with her, Willard's face was pained, his eyes serious.

"The master has had no occasion to punish anyone with anything more than his own sunny disposition," the valet said. "His contact with the world outside these walls has been, shall we say, limited in recent years, as you can imagine. He also realizes, with a little help from myself, that you will be here for many years and doesn't want those years to be any more miserable for you than they have to be."

The prince had said as much as he'd led her to the dining room this morning. Jolie mulled that over as she walked through the shelves of books, dragging her fingers over sumptuous leather covers and stiff spines.

"He knows how it feels to be trapped here better than anyone," Willard said, surprising Jolie with his honesty.

"I always heard he was such a handsome young man. What happened to him to make him look like that?" Jolie wrapped her arms around herself and lowered her voice. These stone walls could carry a whisper all over the building.

Willard shuddered, his whole body racked in a shiver at the memory. "Once again, my lady, I must tell you it is not my story to tell." Her disappointment was clear, but he would elaborate no more on the matter.

"It will be lonely here," she said, looking out one of the big windows. All she could see for miles around were the tall trees that lined Château Hill. Stripped of their leaves, they looked like weary grey sentinels awaiting orders from a long-dead warlord.

"That is going to be my real punishment, to stay in the Castle of Great Mystery all my life with three servants and a monster of legend for company." Said mostly to herself, her words were tight with such sadness Willard once more felt a sense of secondhand shame for his master's decision to keep her here.

Willard knew Jolie was much too young to be shut away her whole life in a drafty fortress where the only person of her own age was a man she may never see as anything but monster. Of course, he had plans to change all that, but neither she nor the master need know of them. Yet.

Jolie spent the morning in the library, creating a pile of books in the corner. There were volumes of Greek and Roman mythology and Norse legends she'd never seen or heard of before. On high shelves, there were huge volumes by Plato and Marcus Aurelius, philosophers and leaders from worlds and times she knew nothing about.

On lower shelves were writers and scientists like Isaac Newton and Johnathon Swift. Jean Jacques Rousseau's *Social Contract* sat on top of a slim volume written by Voltaire. Many of these books were frowned upon by the aristocracy, so it was surprising to finding them

71

here. Books like these, and their subject matter, were the reason revolution had been the subject of the worst fever dreams of the members of the French court recently.

The pile grew higher and higher until she was sure she would never live long enough read all of the books she chose. If she'd thought her father's library was eclectic and well-stocked, this one was a treasure trove. Though not a large room, there were books everywhere she looked.

Jolie dropped a few more books onto the pile and turned toward a bookshelf near the room's only window. As she looked at the books on the shelf, something moved outside the window and she turned her attention to it. Through the gap in the unfinished wall she saw a stag, its coat a dull winter grey. The stag grazed outside the wall, nipping off what little dry grass it could get on its way. A pang of jealousy seized her heart, creating a sick feeling that bloomed in her stomach.

How was she going to cope with the years of confinement ahead of her? She could see them, day after endless day, stretching on and on into a future without change or end. All of a sudden, as if seeing that deer had sent her back two weeks into the past, the shock of what she'd done caught up with her and she fell to her knees. Her eyes stayed locked on the deer as it crossed the gap in the wall and disappeared. There was no one there to stop the animal from coming and going as it pleased. No master to hold it back from seeing the other deer in its herd. She missed her father terribly and wished she could walk through the front door of her childhood home more than she'd wished for anything in her life.

Tears prickled the corners of her eyes and her chest tightened. Her vision blurred as the deer went out of sight and she covered her face with her hands. She wanted to leave the way the deer had, to walk past these walls and go home. The force of her longing hitched her breath and shook her shoulders as her soft cries built to sobs. The sound reverberated off the wall, all the way up to the top of the south tower and the man that lived there.

Leopold woke with a start to the sound, sitting up bolt straight in his gigantic bed and nearly dumping himself onto the floor. At first, he was angry at being woken. But the sound that pulled him from his slumber was so pitiful, plaintive and full of raw anguish, that his own heart answered it, constricting so strongly it took him by surprise. He'd heard this emotion in his own voice often enough over the last few years to recognize it in someone else. Even if he understood it, though, he wasn't sure he could help Jolie. After all, he was the man who had put her in a position to feel it in the first place.

Perhaps it would be better if he just waited and let Willard take care of her. Or, better yet, Rosalie. A woman could take care of another woman better than he could. As he waited, though, her sobs didn't subside and while he knew he wasn't the best person for the job, it didn't seem as if anyone else was about to take up the mantle either. He washed and dressed, then headed down the long flight of stairs to the corridor.

He found Jolie collapsed on the floor of the library, a stack of books almost as tall as she was to her right side. She was stretched out on the floor by the window, lying on her side with her back to the door.

Uncertain of what to do to get her attention without alarming her, he rapped his knuckles on the doorjamb. "Girl?"

Startled at the sound and instantly annoyed with the prince's name for her, she pulled herself up to sit but didn't say anything. Sitting up put her at eye level with the window again and she watched for a moment to see if perhaps the stag had returned, but he was long gone by now. That twinge in her chest returned and she sucked in a deep breath through her nose, trying to fortify herself for what was going to be a difficult conversation.

"Yes, Master?" she asked, her voice thick. She dashed her hands over her cheeks. Over her shoulder, one of Leopold's huge hands appeared, a white handkerchief the size of a tablecloth dangling from his fingertips. She took the cloth from him and blew her nose into it, then crumpled it in her hands. "For such a large man, you really don't make much noise, do you?"

He stepped back, sliding his boots along the floor. "I could not help but hear that you're upset."

"Imagine that," she said, her tone caustic.

The flame of his anger, never really out, flared with its usual vigor. Hands shaking, he took a breath of his own, trying to calm himself, but he couldn't stop the words that flew out of his mouth any more than he could stop the rage that burned within him.

"You expected your sentence to be pleasant?" he barked, his voice a low growl.

"I am not a criminal, so I have no expectation of what this should be like," Jolie snapped. "I have spent every day of my life in my father's care. I have known no other life than the one I led in his home. I expected that if I ever did live outside that house, it would be in either marriage or travel of my own choosing."

"You wish to travel?" His words managed to sound both impressed and condescending, as if he admired her desire to travel but at the same time found it ridiculous. Only then did he notice how many of the books she had on her teetering stack were written about other parts of the world. Many of the titles were by authors who had lived abroad, some for decades.

"Try not to sound so disbelieving," she said.

"I have never known a woman to want anything more than a husband, a family, and a home of her own to care for," he said, opening one of the books to look at the first pages.

Jolie turned to him, her mouth open in shock. As upset as she was, she didn't watch her tongue as well as she should. She knew the creature before her could make her life miserable, or end it altogether, but she couldn't help herself.

"And so, because it is outside your experience, it must be impossible for a woman to want anything else?" she asked, her voice rising in volume. He flipped the book shut with a snap and turned to her.

"I see no reason for a woman to desire anything but what a husband can provide her," Leopold said, his eyes boring deep into hers in challenge.

Jolie rose to meet it, coming to within a foot of where he stood and glaring up at him with those beautiful green eyes, her wild crop of hair punctuating her movements as it undulated around her face.

"You disgust me, thinking that women are on this Earth just for what you have use for them for. Perhaps the fates convened to make your outsides match your insides. A job well done, I would say," she growled. Her words hit home, she could see it in the way he backed away from her and how his shoulders slumped.

That hurt, and he couldn't hide it from his expression. The anger exploded into rage and he had to fight to prevent himself from reaching out and shaking her by the shoulders. He took a step forward, his hand clamping around her upper arm, but that was as far as he got.

Willard chose that moment to sidle up to the library door, his eyebrows raised with concern. He placed his hand on Leopold's shoulder, distracting the big man from Jolie. Prince Leopold stepped back, letting her go so suddenly she had grab a bookshelf to right herself. Willard pulled Leopold out of the room and into the hall.

"Master," he said, his voice soft and soothing. "She meant no harm with what she said."

Jolie stepped into the doorway and watched the exchange with interest. The valet had whisked the prince away from her with the lightest touch and the anger she'd seen in his eyes had dissipated into a look of desperation, even despair. This quick change reminded her of Mireille's children and how, in the middle of a tantrum, their pique would end as quickly as it had started. It was as if Prince Leopold had never grown out of this phase, and she wondered if his parents had been as indulgent with him as her sister was with her children.

Seeing for herself why his personality was so flawed didn't make it any easier for her to condone or forgive his attitude. There was a chance that she might be able to convince him otherwise, though. She certainly had the time.

"Don't you see, Willard?" Leopold asked. "She is right, and nothing has changed."

Willard kept his words soft, so only his Master would hear. "Whether or not anything has changed is still up to you, my prince," Willard said.

"I don't know how," Leopold said. He brought his hands up to either side of his face and closed his eyes.

"We're running out of time," Willard whispered, drawing his face close to Leopold's. "You didn't know she would come, but she did. She could learn to like you, if you tried harder to control yourself."

Leopold dropped his hands to his sides and he took several deep breaths. Willard nodded in encouragement, a hand on the big man's and his eyes locked on Leopold's.

"I hope you're right, Willard," Leopold said.

Jolie had to strain to hear. She was as confused as she'd ever been and was hoping to find out what in the world they were talking about.

"I *know* I am, Highness." Willard was leading the prince down the hall away from the library. Leopold looked like a giant next to his valet, twice as wide and two heads taller. Jolie sank back into the library, burying herself in the stacks of books again, her mind filled with all they'd said.

Down the hall, Willard walked beside his master, guiding him away from Jolie so the rest of what he had to say wouldn't be overheard. It didn't look like it but the older man had orchestrated every moment of the conversation so she would hear just enough before they walked away.

He knew as soon as he'd heard the way she snapped back at Leopold for his rhetoric that she could be just what they had waited for. There were just weeks to go before the spell the old witch had cast became permanent, and it would take a strong, intelligent woman to see the prince inside the monster walking beside him. If Jolie was brave enough to stand up to him, maybe she was brave enough to understand him.

"This château can only do so much of the work, but she's seen some of the magic that spell put upon us and hasn't tried to run away," Willard began.

"Yet." Leopold's eyes were downcast.

"Yes, sire. Yet. She may yet attempt to take her life back, but if she does it won't be because of the power of this place, or what you look like. She showed no fear when she confronted you just now, and I think if you work hard we can break this spell before it's too late." They were at the foot of the south tower stairs and Willard stood aside. "You know, Master, perhaps now would be a good time to clean up the mess you've made of this tower over the years."

Leopold smiled, his ugly face breaking and a hint of his former good looks showing in the crinkling of his eyes. "I have already begun."

Willard's disbelief was plain as his eyes opened wide and his eyebrows threatened to touch his hairline. "My prince, I'm surprised at you."

"I had a hard time getting back to sleep after you roused me earlier. And with a lady in the house, I felt it would only be right that the old place looks its best. Besides, you know this old place will do half the work if you want it to." He shot out an arm, pointing up the stairs. "Come and see."

Willard did as he was asked, motivated by the first true smile he'd seen from his master in months. He was beginning to think his instincts about Jolie were right. Ever since the night the king and queen had died, he'd felt like a surrogate father to the prince and to see him happy made him feel like he was doing the job well.

As Willard made his way up to the prince's chambers, he couldn't help but notice that there was nothing hindering his ascent. Every time he'd climbed up here he'd sworn it would take him days to pick his way back down through all the broken furniture and other detritus that blocked the staircase. Once he was in the room, he marveled at how clean everything was. Every hint of Leopold's rage was gone, right down to the fine scum of dust that had coated everything in the room.

"I am impressed, sire," Willard said as he looked around the room. Just this morning, the stairwell had been impassable. Now, even the room those stairs led to was pristine.

If the care a man put into his home was a representation of the person he was, this was a good sign for the future. If they all got to have a future, that was. He might just be the valet, but he'd be damned right along with his master if he let the prince suffer for eternity. With a woman in residence who might just be the one to break the curse, it was high time his master did the growing up the witch had hoped for.

The old man clapped his hands together and made for the armoire in the back corner of the room, throwing the doors open wide. "There has to be a less shabby wardrobe in here somewhere. I won't have my master looking like an urchin before the lady."

Leopold could hear the smile in the man's voice and knew the gears were grinding in his mind as fast as they could roll. Apprehensive, overcome with a wary anticipation, he followed his most trusted servant across the room and waited to see what the man would come up with.

Chapter 7

"Walk with me," Leopold asked, his gravelly voice making the words sound like a rough command rather than the sincere request he and Willard were hoping for. Here he was, dressed up in his best in his own room, but Willard wouldn't allow him to ask Jolie himself until the old valet was satisfied that his charge said the words just so.

"Ask it like a question, not like you're ordering her execution," Willard said, his smile turning down at the corners in irritation. "Poor girl will turn you down on principle. You have to mean it, Master."

"I do mean it, Willard," Leopold said, slapping his hands on his thighs like a child tired of his lesson.

"Behavior like that, charming as it is, will not help your cause," Willard growled. Remembering himself, he coughed and straightened, giving his lapels a rough yank. Cocking his head back, putting his nose in the air, he resolved to try again. And again, until the master got this right. "Try once more, Master. Perhaps with a smile?"

"God's teeth," Leopold cursed. He followed Willard's lead, though, and straightened himself up, hoping better posture would bolster his confidence. "Mademoiselle Jolie, it would please me greatly if you would join me for a walk around the grounds this morning."

Willard actually looked impressed, his eyebrows rising. "Much better. Perhaps if you could say something about how lovely she looks?"

"Willard, if I'm going to do that, and give her this death rictus smile, she'll never come," Leopold said, trying to lose the petulant tone in his voice and failing. He turned his mouth into an exaggerated 'o,' stretching his cheeks. Smiling hurt when your face has more surface area to move into the expression than most.

"It will have to do," Willard said.

All of a sudden, Leopold's stomach lurched. He hoped the panic he was feeling didn't show on his face, but he felt it all the way to his toenails. Willard was giving him a look that was supposed to be encouraging, but just made the older man look as terrified as Leopold felt.

Before he lost his nerve, he left the room to find Jolie. The door to the Rose Room was wide open and he could see that no one was in it. The library would be his next guess, and it proved to be correct.

She sat on the settee near the window, a book in her hands and stacks of them piled on the floor next to her. He glanced at the titles she'd chosen for herself. Many of them were journals written by men about their travels to America, India, and Africa. Not places one would expect a lady to be curious about.

"Mademoiselle Jolie," Leopold called from the doorway. She hadn't heard him approaching, and jumped at the sound of his voice and the way he'd addressed her.

"Master, you startled me," she said, a hand going to her chest as if to still her racing heart.

"I must apologize for two things, then," he said, trying to smile without looking as terrifying as he usually did with that expression on his face.

Jolie didn't ask what he meant and he hadn't expected her to. She was not a stupid woman and had probably been waiting for him to return to this room to do this very thing.

"I apologize for startling you, and also please accept my sincerest apologies for my behavior this morning," he said.

Her brows pinched as she thought it over for a moment. She looked suspicious, though, as if she was unsure that he meant the apologies. He thought maybe she was thinking there was an ulterior motive for his presence in the library so quickly after his tantrum earlier. Might as well dispense with it, then.

"I wanted to invite you to walk the grounds with me," Leopold said, his brows lifting in a hopeful look that was both surprising and endearing.

"I would like that," Jolie said with a bright smile. All suspicion disappeared from her face, and she even smiled.

"There is a cloak in the armoire that you can wear. I will get one of my own and meet you at the courtyard door," he said, trying to modulate his voice so that it was not an order.

Jolie agreed to meet him, then dug through the armoire for that coat. It was a chilly afternoon, and she was going to need it. It was a long, green velvet coat with big black buttons down the front and a heavy hood to block the wind. She pulled it on and made her way to the door to meet the prince.

****

The wind through the forest was chillier than Jolie would have liked, but the bite in it kept her awake. Leopold was holding himself back, keeping pace with Jolie. As they reached the wall that would encircle the grounds by summer, he pointed through the gap to a herd of four deer grazing just inside the tree line.

"It looks like the trees are starting to encroach on your grounds, sire," she said as she pulled the hood of the green coat up and over her hair. "You've got a lot of shoots coming up just outside the wall."

"The groundskeeper, Micah LaMontagne, watches for those. He'll nip them in the spring as soon as the frost breaks up," Leopold said. "He lives in the gatehouse. Just there."

The prince aimed a big hand toward the northeast gate, to a small stone building with smoke rolling from its chimney. Jolie nodded, snuggling her hands into a fluffy warmer, before turning her attention back to the herd of deer. The animals wandered as if they hadn't a care in the world, just ten feet from where they stood, watching.

"I'd never seen animals so close before the old witch's curse befell my home," he mused, not realizing he was speaking until her head turned.

What curse? An old witch? Jolie thought to herself, but stopped short before she questioned the master. "That is odd," she said, training her eyes on the animals. The deer behaved as if there were no humans in these woods at all. As if the wall, and the château beyond it, didn't exist at all. "The château hasn't been abandoned. Even if it had been, it hasn't been long enough for them to come close to it like this."

"The château protects itself," Leopold said, watching as the deer walked closer and closer to where he and Jolie stood. Just before they ran into the wall, the herd seemed to hit an invisible barrier. Their noses bumped into something none of them could see, and all four of the deer turned on the spot and started walking away. Unperturbed by whatever barrier they'd run into, they ambled away as lazily as they had approached.

"Goodness," Jolie said, an awestruck note in her voice.

"You and your father had no trouble getting in here, and neither did the people who visited right after I was cursed, but there have been men who have tried to get through the gate or the gap in the wall to the south and failed."

"What sort of men were they?" Jolie asked, afraid she probably already knew the answer.

"Just the sort who thought they would make heroes of themselves by killing the monster they thought would gobble up their precious babes," Leopold said, a smile on his face with no humor in it.

"Well, Papa and I didn't mean you or the castle any harm, did we?" she asked. Hoping to reassure him, she turned and offered him a bright smile.

"I thought you might have it in for me once you found out the facts of your father's deceit," Leopold said. It was a harsh truth but still a truth.

"The thought crossed my mind," she said. "Has anyone ever been able to breach the wall? If they were here with ill intentions, I mean?"

Leopold thought for a moment and they came to a stop just past the opening in the wall. "No one has ever come beyond this wall without an invitation at all until your father."

Jolie looked at the wide gap in the wall every way she could, tilting her head and squinting her eyes, but could see no reason one should not be able to just walk through it. Whatever had turned the deer back was invisible to all of them. The legends she had always heard of the old magic bearers had told of the myriad abilities they'd had to repair and to destroy. She'd never seen one, they'd died out when she was young.

"Was there a reason the old witch would have wanted to protect this place?" she asked.

"None that I can think of," Leopold said. It was an interesting thought, though, and a faraway look came over him. He took a step and they continued on their way. "Perhaps it was a measure to isolate me further, by not allowing people to come here and alleviate my loneliness."

He had said too much, and tried to ignore the way her eyes softened at his admission. They walked on in silence for a while, both of them thinking too much to speak.

The cold was starting to stiffen the muscles of her face. Jolie thought about what he'd said, trying to come up with something to say.

"Perhaps, sire, but I suppose we'll never know." It wasn't comforting, but it was all she could think of.

Jolie was hopeful he would tell her more, but he turned away as they walked. The deer passed out of sight through the trees and the silence around them reminded her of how alone they were. Separated from his people, feared and reviled as a creature of the night, and stuck in an enchanted château that wouldn't allow visitors.

"I am sorry this happened to you," she said, her voice just above a whisper.

Leopold kept his face averted so she couldn't see his reaction, but she heard the surprise in his voice. "Thank you," he said.

More silence, but this time was a bit different, as if he were trying to think of how to bring something up. Finally, he turned to her, his eyes wandering everywhere but to hers.

"Would you join me for luncheon tomorrow?" he asked, all of the words coming out in one big rush. If he didn't say them quickly, he wouldn't ask at all.

Jolie stopped in her tracks, her bottom lip pushing out in surprise. They navigated around the stables and servants' quarters while she considered.

"I would be pleased to accept, but I am afraid I don't understand why you don't invite me to join you at dinner tonight."

Leopold thought for a moment, trying to find an excuse without telling her the truth. "I usually eat alone."

A cryptic response, at best, and he could tell it wasn't going to hold her over for long, so he changed the subject. "You chose several books about travel when you were in the library earlier. Why?"

Considering his comments earlier, she was sure he saw no reason a woman should want to leave her dooryard, but that just meant she had no reason to lie. If he believed a woman's place was home, he would scoff at her reasons. If he didn't believe it, he would be interested in what she had to say.

"Father always told me stories of his travels as a young man. He went to India, the Americas, Africa, all over the world before he met my mother. When my sister Mireille was born, he began trading with merchants in India," she said. "He was very successful—"

Jolie clipped the word off, like she hadn't thought about what she was saying before she could stop herself from letting it out. Leopold looked down at her, catching a glimpse of her disappointment before she got rid of it with a shake of her head.

"—at first," she said finally. "He's lost everything he ever earned in the last year, but failed to tell me or my sister about it until now."

"Your father is a man of great secrets," Leopold mused. They were as far as they would get from the castle, at the northeast gate, and they turned a corner to head back toward the keep.

Leopold's eyes were still on her face, and she didn't try to hide her anger at his judgment of her father. Her green eyes flashed and her brow furrowed, a hand coming up from her waist, her finger pointed at his chest. He held up a hand to stop her tirade before she got started.

"Please, don't misunderstand me, Mademoiselle Babineaux. I meant no offense," he said. "I only meant that we don't know why he would hide his misfortune from those his losses would hurt the worst, and why he would send you here in his stead when he is an old man and you are a young woman who has barely begun to live."

Dropping her hand back down, she huffed a breath as she turned back toward the path.

"You never answered my question," Leopold said, tucking his hands into the pockets on his coat. "Why is it that you wish to travel?"

"I have only gone between Fontainbleu and Port Lucerne when Papa would take me with him to deliver goods to one of his ships. He allowed me to help load the crates when I got older, and to make sure the men didn't break anything, but I never got to go along on the journey," she said. Her eyes grew wistful and she looked at a point far away, at the opposite wall, like she was trying to see the horizon.

"Men think women on a ship are bad luck, and Papa was too attached to me to let me go. I always dreamed I would go on my own, someday," she said, her voice cracking.

Leopold was surprised by the feeling of guilt that rose up in him at that small, heartbroken sound. He squashed the emotion with a grunt, turning away from her so he couldn't see the way her lower lip quivered. He ignored her when her hand raised to her cheek and averted his eyes when she dabbed at her face with a handkerchief. A part of him wanted to offer her words of comfort, a small part deep inside him that was growing larger and more insistent by the minute. But there was still too much of the spoiled prince still within him to allow it.

Jolie was a prisoner now, paying for a crime her father had committed. If Armand had wanted his youngest child to travel the world on the high seas, he would have seen to it she did. He hadn't, and there was no reason for Leopold to feel bad about it. That she might never do it on her own, because she was trapped in his home, was beside the point as far as Leopold was concerned.

When Jolie finally collected herself, she sighed and watched the ground at her feet as they walked. They were almost to the northwest corner of the wall.

"Why were you looking at what books I chose?" she asked, surprised, as if the thought had just occurred to her.

"Your selections surprised me," he admitted. "I did not expect a young lady, particularly one of gentle breeding, to choose Marcus Aurelius."

"Gentle breeding," she scoffed, more to herself than to him.

Leopold laughed, forced to admit to himself that what she'd just told him of her life and education was anything but gentle. "You are nothing I would have expected from the daughter of a merchant, Mademoiselle Babineaux. You have surprised me a great deal."

"How so, Master?" she asked as they turned the corner.

"You are strong enough to accept things as they are, rather than run screaming the first time you see something out of the ordinary," Leopold said. "And you seem to already be willing to try and make the most of your situation."

"I see no sense in trying to deny what has happened here. I'm no fool, obviously there is some magic here, but I don't believe I'm in any danger from it," Jolie mused. *Though whether I'm safe from you remains to be seen.* She didn't voice her thought, but the words hung in the air between them like the steam from their breath.

Jolie stopped and dug her hands into the rabbit fur that lined her warmer. Even though it was not yet evening, and the sun had only begun to dip, the air was growing colder. As she struggled to get herself warm, a weight fell over her shoulders and startled her.

Leopold draped his heavy wool cloak around her shoulders and tied it at her throat. His warmth seeped into her skin through the fabric of his cloak, taking the chill away in an instant.

His heavy brows relaxed and his eyes softened. The corners of his mouth lifted in a small smile. "I can't have you freezing to death on my watch. Shall we return?" he asked, holding out a meaty forearm and turning to make a straight walk to the keep's rear entrance.

When she placed her hand on his arm, she could feel the heat of his skin through the fabric of his tunic. He led her to the giant doors, opening one of them with a big hand. As they stepped through the door into the near-darkness, he swept a few steps away.

"I didn't invite you to dinner tonight because I'm afraid," Leopold said, his voice soft. "I need more time to ready myself."

"Afraid of what, Master?" she asked, surprised by his admission.

Her eyes were adjusting to the lack of light and she took a step toward him. His hand came up to stop her, and she could see he was embarrassed in the way his shoulders slumped and his eyes dropped to the floor. The hand he'd held out went up to massage the back of his neck.

"Myself, Mademoiselle Jolie," he whispered. "Always myself."

With that, Prince Leopold swept down the corridor to her right and, she imagined, to his south tower. That left her standing in the hall, just inside the doors, wondering just what he'd meant by that.

****

Quentin made it all the way home before losing his temper. In the privacy of his room, he tossed his overcoat on a chair, then pinched the bridge of his nose, unsure of what to do next. Everything he planned for himself had fallen apart this morning. He'd been so sure that he would walk out of the Babineaux home with an official engagement and a marriage agreement, maybe even a heavy dowry. Armand Babineaux was one of the most successful merchants in Fontainbleu and had been for decades.

Pierre and Malcolm had lied to him; he was sure of that. Armand wouldn't leave them out of such important news. A daughter's marriage was one of the biggest events in a family's history, and a father wouldn't neglect to tell the other people in the household about it, even for a night.

A thought occurred to Quentin, and he stopped his pacing to consider it. Mireille's son had said Jolie was with the Grey Man. There was a chance that Armand was delirious and his words meant nothing, but what if the boy was right? She was at the castle, and a child said she was with the Grey Man.

His parents were still away, which meant he had time to remedy the situation. His older brother, Alphonse, had just welcomed his first child and they were visiting for a few weeks to help the new parents adjust. It was a long chance, but he'd hoped to have his marriage secured by the time they got back. That would show them once and for all that he could take care of himself and make a responsible match for himself without their help.

Instead, here he stood in his parents' home, empty-handed again. There was nothing worse than waiting to hear their incessant nagging about how he was squandering his life and their fortune. The longer he went without a bride, the worse they got about the path he'd taken in life.

The way his parents would see it, he'd just ruined another attempt at a good marriage. He would wind up marrying a woman his mother chose, he thought with a shudder. Some English cow desperate to get back in the court's good graces. Or worse, she might find some plain bourgeois woman to keep the Revolutionists happy.

Pacing his private quarters, his steps echoing, he tried to formulate a plan, each idea worse than the last. He'd never been able to stop the compulsive thoughts that ran through his mind once they started. More often than he cared to admit, these thoughts went in a dark direction, and now was no exception.

What began as finding another woman to marry became Quentin running off to England to live with his cousins became breaking into Château Villeneuve and kidnapping Jolie became something he couldn't let go of once he'd thought it. If he killed the Grey Man, it would solve all of his problems. He could have Jolie back and his parents could get off his back about his inability to grow up. As a bonus, the village would see him as a hero for ridding them of the monster.

Quentin clutched his head with both hands and paced the room faster and faster as the words repeated again and again, louder and louder until he felt he had no choice. It was the only thing that made any sense in the world.

He had to kill the Grey Man.

****

Jolie ate supper alone in the dining hall. To break the silence, she scraped her fork against the plate, the screeching sound echoing off the walls of the cavernous room. The sound would bother her any other day. When she finished, she placed her napkin in her plate with a sigh and pushed her chair away from the table.

She went to the Rose Room to grab the cloak the master had lent her earlier and found it right where she'd left it after the walk: folded carefully on the bed. The way odd things had been happening in the palace she'd been afraid it would be gone. She didn't want to think of the consequences of losing a piece of the prince's personal property.

It was late, but she thought it would be best if she returned the cloak to Prince Leopold before she retired for the night. She hoisted the heavy thing into her arms and crossed the Great Hall. For once the candles in the sconces along the walls were all lit for her. The room was bathed in a flickering glow. As she crossed the hall toward the south corner of the room, a soft ringing sound followed her.

Jolie slowed her pace as she set off again, trying to find the source of the sound. Halfway across the hall, she turned on her heel, moving so quickly she almost fell over. There was no one behind her, and no reason for the sound.

Ping! Ping! Ping!

This sound was new, and was coming from the floor. Looking down, she felt no surprise in finding the silver ring bouncing up and down as if trying to get her attention. It hopped a few more times, then fell still, standing on its edge.

Stooping to the floor, she held out a hand and the ring hopped into it and was still. She slipped it onto her index finger so she wouldn't drop the poor thing, then continued toward the south tower. When she got to the foot of the stairs, she risked a glance up.

"Mademoiselle Jolie?" Willard called from behind her. He was coming out from the Great Hall when she turned.

"Willard, you surprised me," Jolie said. "The master lent me his cloak this morning on our walk. I wanted to return it, but I haven't seen him since we returned."

Willard nodded, an amused smirk on his face. "I understand. The master is in his chambers. If you would like, I can take it to him."

She handed the cloak over to Willard and backed away.

"He will need it for his walk this evening," Willard said, hoping she would take the bait.

"Where is he going?" she asked, and saw Willard's satisfied smile.

"Sleep does not come easily to our master, and most evenings, he walks to the river in order to tire himself. Once he returns, he might walk the halls or in his chambers until he can no longer stay awake." Willard tucked the cloak under an arm.

"I saw him pacing when I looked into the mirror," Jolie said, remembering. "When Papa told me about the Grey Man being here, I wanted to see what I was getting myself into, and I asked the mirror to show me."

"I am sure that was very frightening to you," Willard said,

impressed that she had come even after seeing the master.

"It was, but my situation at home had become less than ideal. I felt I had two undesirable choices," she said, sadness darkening her green eyes.

Leopold stopped on the stairs when he heard Jolie's voice, keeping himself out of sight around the corner of the stairwell.

"Papa had promised my hand in marriage to a man I only met once," Jolie said, her tone changing as she spoke. "When I spoke to the man I was to marry, there was nothing in his eyes, and it frightened me."

Leopold thought he heard a nervousness in her voice that hadn't been there before she mentioned her betrothed. He sneaked forward another step, putting her in view but keeping his big frame hidden in the shadows.

"I could stay and marry Quentin Garamonde, or I could leave everything I have ever known and take a chance that I might be happy in my new life." She crossed her arms over her chest and looked down at her feet. "Papa didn't say that in so many words, but he left the suggestion there, and I took it."

Leopold hadn't realized how bad the odds were for her outside this keep. At her age, most women were already married and had borne at least one child. Marriage was a commodity— bartered like a sack of flour to the highest bidder. A young lady with a wealthy father would bring in suitors of quality. He knew the name Garamonde, knew that the family had been wealthy and influential for centuries, but had never met a member of the family himself.

There was no reason for him to believe the Garamonde man would make a poor match, but he didn't like that Armand had matched Jolie with someone who frightened her. Then her father had presented her with two bad options, all but forcing her to run away to a fortress that housed a monster. He didn't know what to think of Armand Babineaux, but none of the thoughts he was having right now were nice ones.

"Was there any contract drawn for your marriage?" Willard asked. "Is there any way that you can back out of it with no one the wiser?"

"Papa had to wait until the next morning to call his solicitor to draw up the contract," she said. "With me gone, I see no reason the marriage contract could be written, or that I could be held to any agreement."

Leopold felt an odd sense of relief at the knowledge that she wasn't officially engaged. He couldn't understand why he felt that way.

"Well I suppose that's a good thing. We won't have an angry fiancée knocking down the door trying to get you back," Willard said. Leopold could hear the smile in the old man's voice, reassurance in his tone.

Jolie nodded, but the movement was tight, as if she wasn't fully comforted by Willard's words.

Leopold stepped into the weak candlelight, resolved to show himself now, but feign ignorance of their conversation. They didn't need to know what he was going to do, but he knew where he would go on his walk tonight. Garamonde scared Jolie, and he felt as her master it was his duty to find out if the young man was going to be a threat while she was here.

Jolie caught the prince's movement out of the corner of her eye and turned toward him. She smiled up at him and Willard handed the cloak to her so she could return it herself. "I meant to return this to you, so you would have it on your travels."

The question was in her eyes, in the slight lift in her brow, but she didn't ask and he didn't offer. He took the cloak from her hands, careful to keep his hands from touching hers, and wrapped it around his broad shoulders. "Thank you, Mademoiselle Jolie."

Pursing her lips, she stepped back as he swept by. He headed down the east corridor and out of sight.

Willard bade Jolie goodnight and slipped back into the Great Hall, leaving her alone with her thoughts.

Chapter 8

Candles guttered in the weak moonlight. Guests milled about, their solid black garb unsettling in the darkness. The room was dark enough that Jolie would lose sight of the people in front of her only to have them suddenly reappear, their movements jerky.

The huge room was silent, and Jolie got the feeling she'd had this dream before, memories of it dancing just out of reach. The only sound Jolie could hear was the ticking of a potbellied Comtoise clock across the hall. The clock was ten feet tall and three feet wide, made of ebony and glass. Its ticks and tocks shouted in her head, driving her further from sanity. She could feel the sound in her feet, thudding through the floorboards.

The deep, resonating ticking made her nervous as she tried again to navigate the crowded room, a feeling like the clock was counting down to something important. The dais in the middle of the floor still held the same two thrones, but on the seat of the one on the left rested a single rose, pale ivory and pink petals glowing against the rich blue cushion. It was the same rose that the handsome stranger had offered her.

As she reached for the bloom, petals began to fall from the stem until there were only a few left. The light the rose emitted dimmed and went out. Confused, she took a step away, backing into someone as she tried to escape.

"I'm sorry, excuse me," she said, turning toward whomever she had offended.

A handsome stranger looked down at her with a gentle smile. He didn't speak, but bowed his head to her and offered a hand. She couldn't see his features clearly, but what she could see was beautiful. He was tall, dressed in a beautiful uniform of Delft blue and ivory, with gold braid on the shoulders. Long, dark brown hair was tied back in a queue. His face was strong, with prominent cheekbones and a strong jaw. If she didn't miss the mark, she thought his long nose had been broken at least once, but the feature only added to his attractiveness. Dark eyes bored into hers beneath thick brows. Something about this face was familiar, but she couldn't place it.

Soft music from across the room, slow and romantic, began. Strains of violins and the deep moans of the cello sang to her from meters away.

Jolie settled her hand into the stranger's and he led her toward the dais. Guests moved aside, creating a large open area. He placed one hand at her waist and raised the other high, lifting hers up level with her head. Her free arm rested on his forearm.

"I've never danced like this before," she whispered, a flush of

embarrassment coloring her cheeks.

His chuckle was warm, his voice as soft as hers. "I shall teach you," he said.

With that, he pulled her closer and her heart started pounding. Her father had told both of his daughters about the Waltz. "It is sinful how closely the couples hold each other, right out in front of all the other guests!"

Armand had said this with a light in his eyes that belied how he really felt about the dance; that it was intriguing as nothing else could be, holding a partner so close you could feel the heat from their body on your skin.

Jolie looked up at her partner, saw the flush coloring his cheeks, and knew he was feeling the same way she was. He swept her around in circles for what felt like hours, twirling and stepping with a lightness of foot she didn't know possible from a man his size. It didn't take long before they were both laughing, drinking in the gaiety of the occasion.

Guests clapped as they finished, he with a bow, her with a curtsy. As she stood, he dropped to a knee, producing the red rose from inside his coat.

"Will you marry me?" he asked.

Jolie stood in front of him, unable to control the mad rush of thoughts through her head. "Why have you asked me this?" she asked. "I do not know you."

"But you do, Jolie," he said, his smile unwavering.

The stranger didn't elaborate further though, and Jolie woke, still unsure of just who was asking for her hand. She wrapped herself in her blankets and sat up against the headboard, wondering what the dream meant.

****

Leopold slipped in through the back gate just as the sun broke the horizon. Once he was inside the keep, he untied his cloak and draped it over a meaty forearm. He hadn't seen whoever it was that had followed him, but he'd felt eyes on him from the moment he'd left the village. Twice, he'd caught a glimpse of movement out of the corner of his eye, but hadn't slowed enough to pinpoint his pursuer.

His footfalls were loud, flat-footed thuds on the stone floor and when he mounted the stairs to the south tower, the sound of his huge boot turning sounded like a mill grinding meal. His breathing was heavy, forceful, and his arms swung at his sides.

The steps wound up the tower, past arrow slits that let little light fall on the prince's form as he ascended. With no sign of his past tantrums left after his cleaning yesterday morning, his path was clear. The staircase narrowed at the top until it was just wide enough for him to pass. He walked down a short hallway and shoved his way through the door. His past abuses to the heavy door left it hard to open and close, and he had to throw his weight against it to manage the task. He closed it with a shove, then fell against it, closing his eyes at the exhaustion that was creeping over him.

Leopold tossed his cloak— the one Jolie had returned to him— across the room, not caring where it landed. This walk had frustrated him more than relaxed him. Throughout his journey, Jolie's soft lavender perfume had been in his nostrils, and was a constant distraction. Their walk earlier had told him little, but enough that the little woman was taking over some of his thoughts. It didn't help that last night, when he'd finally fallen asleep, he'd dreamed of her. He couldn't remember much of his dream, only that she had worn a gown worthy of the royal court and that her beautiful hair had been down around her shoulders.

Leopold made his way across the room to stand before the desk. On it was the hand mirror the magic bearer had made. He'd brought it here the night Jolie had arrived; grateful it hadn't broken on the violent journey she'd taken through space.

"Show me the one who follows me from the village," he demanded and the mirror went to work, the metal glowing as images swam into focus on the glass. Leopold saw a man, younger than he and well dressed, in that glass. He took a moment to study the young man's handsome face, so he would remember it.

This young man appeared unarmed, but warmly dressed for a walk through the forest in the early morning. Leopold could hear very well across great distances, and was sure no one had been following him until he had left Tremonde road for the path to Château Hill. He supposed it was possible this man could have lain in wait for him there, but why would he have then only followed him? In the dark woods, there would be no witnesses to any altercation they may have had.

Leopold recognized where the man was standing, and walked to where he could get a better view. From the south tower balcony, Leopold could see the gap in the wall. He threw open the French doors and walked out, turning south. Ten feet beyond the gap, the young man stood, fists on his hips, surveying his surroundings. He kept trying to step forward and stopping short, like his leg wouldn't go past a certain point. He tried it with a hand, but it would only go a foot in front of him before it stopped, too.

Leopold had long known his home protected itself and its occupants from harm. How else could one explain a village full of able-bodied men allowing a monster to survive in the stronghold that once housed their royal family? Especially once the legend began to spread that the monster had developed a taste for children?

The stranger took one last look around him, then turned back toward the village. Leopold went to the door to his chamber and as loudly as he could, called for Willard. The servants were in town often enough; the valet might know who this man was.

It took a while, but eventually the prince heard Willard's slippered feet shuffling up the stairs. When he reached the top, the old man looked at his master, eyes swollen with sleep.

"Who is this?" Leopold asked, thrusting the mirror into his valet's face. Willard's eyes widened, then narrowed as he tried to focus.

"It is very dark, sire, but I believe that is Quentin Garamonde," Willard said. He squinted at the image, then nodded. "Yes, that is the son of Antoine, Earl of Nice, and his wife Odette. Supposed fiancé to our Jolie, as I recall from earlier today."

"I went into the village tonight, Willard," Leopold admitted, skipping over the fact that Willard had figured out he'd listened in before his walk. "I went to the Garamonde house to see what sort of man Jolie was engaged to."

Willard sighed in irritation and Leopold shot him a look.

"I didn't see anything there, and I was sure no one had followed me until I reached the road up Château Hill, and then I just knew someone was there." Leopold set the mirror back on the writing table.

Surveying his chamber, Leopold's eyes lit on the third artifact of his eighteenth birthday. On the wall, near the doors that led to the balcony, was the pink and ivory rose. Since the night of the magic bearer's visit, it had lived there in a glass globe fitted into a sconce. His twenty-seventh birthday was over eleven months ago, and since then the flower had begun to droop in earnest. Most of its petals, puckered and drying, rested on the bottom of the globe. The stem and leaves, once a deep emerald, was now a withered brownish green like the moss that grew on ancient stones in the forest.

"Thank you, Willard. That is all," Leopold said, his eyes fixed on the old flower. He let his mind wander as Willard descended the stairs without a word.

Nearly a decade had passed since Leopold was the handsome boy who could cut an old woman with his words. Now, there was a woman in his keep who was not offended by him. In truth, she seemed intrigued and warm when they spoke, and in the library this morning, he'd felt such a strong connection between them he hadn't been able to shake it, even after this long and tiresome walk. She was afraid, and he knew she had unanswered questions, but there was something between them he could not deny.

Thinking of Jolie and the curse and the man that had followed him from the village was not going to help him get any sleep, so he decided to try lying down to see if it would work. He worked his boots off and left them in the floor by the desk, then flopped on the bed and closed his eyes.

Behind him, on the table, the mirror's glass face flickered as if it sensed some new energy in the air. As if it knew something Leopold didn't.

****

Rosalie came to Jolie's Rose Room early the next morning. A stack of ledgers were piled high in her arms, nearly blocking her line of sight. Jolie darted to the door and helped her bring them in, setting the books on the desks before taking a seat.

"It's relieved I am that you want to take these over," Rosalie said, what remained of an Irish brogue charming Jolie into instantly liking the older woman. "This old woman needs less to do these days."

"I'm happy to help. I need something to do around here, and I did all of my father's once I was old enough. I'm sure this won't be too much more difficult," Jolie said, confidence in her voice.

"Of course not, dear," Rosalie said with a small smile, and they launched into a detailed lesson about finances.

Two hours later, Rosalie was already letting her do all the work on her own. The older woman was impressed with her ability.

"If you have any questions, you know where I am," Rosalie said. "But I think you'll do just fine."

"Our master invited me to luncheon today," Jolie said, more to herself than Rosalie.

94

"That's lovely," Rosalie said, her smile broad this time. There was something in that smile, a mischief of some sort that Jolie couldn't reconcile. "When did he ask you?"

"While we were on our walk yesterday afternoon," Jolie said, feeling color rising in her cheeks at Rosalie's quicksilver expressions. The old woman managed to look proud, hopeful, and conniving all at the same time.

"Well, I must get you dressed for your meeting when the time comes, haven't I?" Rosalie said. "But for now, why don't you take a break from all this and head to the music room or the library until luncheon is ready?"

"That sounds lovely, Rosalie," Jolie said, standing up and stretching the stiffness from her shoulders. "I'll see you soon."

Rosalie smiled and left the Rose Room, looking lighter than she had when she'd walked in. Jolie was happy to help. Easing the older woman's burden was a pleasure, and would help occupy at least some of her time here.

Jolie went to the library and as hard as she tried, couldn't get into the book she'd left there earlier. Her mind hummed along even as she read one of the books she'd plucked from the shelves, trying to figure out what Willard could have meant.

What could he mean when he said that time was running out? Any number of things, she supposed. The prince's infamous birthday was just weeks away, and it was the most obvious answer, though she didn't know why. Any answer she could come up with sounded like superstitious nonsense. She had years to find out the truth, after all. That thought didn't make her feel better, though, and she turned her focus back to the book in her lap.

The sun was nearing its peak, the midday light streaking through the window and warming the room. Despite the constant hum of her nerves, the warmth of the room and the boring book in her hands started to lull Jolie's senses. When she lay down on the settee her eyes were still focused on the book but it wasn't long before they drifted closed. The book slipped from her fingers and dropped to the floor with a dull thump.

If she'd been awake, she'd have seen the way the book landed open. She'd have seen that just a moment after it landed a force like an unseen hand closed the book, then picked it up and replaced it on the stack she'd made. The curtains that let in the bright winter light untied themselves from their moorings on either side of the window and doused the room in darkness, letting their mistress nap.

Jolie's mind flooded with images, flashing like the flickering glass of the hand mirror. The naked trees of the wood, the rough road that had brought her father here, the howls and moans from the keep the night the king and queen died. Her mind went black and she slept.

Standing in the Great Hall, she was dressed in an immaculate white silk gown, broad panniers widening her hips and accentuating her waist. White satin gloves extended from her fingertips to her elbows, embroidered with pale pink roses. Her hair wasn't powdered but hung in loose red ringlets around her shoulders, flowing down her back to her waist. She could have been any other courtier.

The room was filled with people in odd costume, even stranger than last time. The men were all in full royal court regalia, but everything they wore was black. From their wigs to the buckles on their shoes, the only parts of them that weren't obscured by their dark clothes were their faces and hands. The women wore dresses like hers, but black as the night sky. Fashionably cut, elegant gowns, but all black. She felt self-conscious, sticking out like a sore thumb this way, one white dove in a flock of ravens.

Trying to find a familiar face, Jolie walked through the Great Hall, trying to catch sight of the faces of the people milling about. As she passed, each one turned away from her, keeping their faces averted. His height and build gave him away as Willard, but when she looked up to meet his eyes, she saw he had none. Stunned, she looked at his face, but there was nothing there. He looked as if someone had stretched the skin of his forehead over his entire face, leaving it featureless.

Startled, she backed away, putting her hands up as if to ward him off. He bowed and went back the way he'd come. Now, everyone turned to her and she saw that all the guests looked the same. Frightened she'd been cursed with the same affliction, she put a hand to her cheeks, but everything felt normal.

It took her a while to notice that the whole room was silent. No one's shoes clicked on the glossy wood floor, not one voice could be heard, and no clinking of silver or glassware broke the silence. Thousands of yards of fabric swished as she walked and yet she heard not a sound.

A long table of food sat at the north end of the hall, but no one was eating. Casks of wine and ale had been tapped, but no one was drinking. Musicians were at the ready, but none of them were playing. There was a dais in the center of the room, draped in brilliant blue velvet. On it sat two gilt thrones, identical in height and with matching blue velvet cushions on the seat and back, both empty.

Jolie had heard the term 'deafening silence' all her life but had never had occasion to understand what it meant until now. For all its silence, though, there was a heightened sense of apprehension within the walls of the Great Hall. She felt as though something incredible were about to happen, and once she left this room nothing would ever be the same. With no idea what was going to happen or why it would have anything to do with her, all she could do was wait as the tension built.

As one, all the guests turned toward the entrance to the South Tower. The silence was broken at last by booming footsteps descending the stairs. Two men stood in front of Jolie and she had to crane her neck to see. As soon as she could get a glimpse of the tower door, someone else would step in front of her.

In frustration, she started weaving her way through the hall, getting closer and closer to whoever was coming. The heavy footsteps echoed through the halls, louder and louder as they approached the party.

Winding her way between stiff panniers and broad shoulders, it felt like every time she made any headway someone would step in front of her to block her path. No matter how hard she tried, she made no progress. The footsteps stopped after several minutes of struggle, so she gave up, thinking it wasn't that important that she see this person after all.

'If I'm meant to see him, I will see him,' she thought.

No sooner were the words formed in her mind than the guests fell away. Half of them moved right, the other half moved left, leaving an empty swath of the hall open between Jolie and this guest of honor. She peeked down this strange hall and saw him standing in all his splendor. This was the same stranger she'd seen in her last dream only now she could pick out his features better. He wore a knee-length blue coat with gold braid at the shoulders and an ivory vest. A white shirt with ruffles at the wrists peeked out from under the coat, and a white cravat was tied around his throat. Breeches that matched the color and fabric of the vest and deep brown leather knee-length boots covered his legs.

Though she was afraid to find another featureless ghost staring back at her, Jolie forced herself to look up at his face as he approached. His eyes were as dark as walnut skin, rimmed with dark lashes. His nose had been broken once, just as she'd suspected, leaving it just slightly off-kilter. Lips, caught in a smile as he looked at her, were full. As unfashionable as it was, he wore a beard that covered most of his face in dark hair. He wore his hair longer than most men did, as well, and only had the top half of it tied into a tail at the back of his neck, leaving the rest loose around his shoulders.

Something about his face was as familiar as it was beautiful, but her mind couldn't make the connection. She was positive she had never met this man before, but as his eyes roamed over her she was just as sure that she knew him somehow.

As he drew closer, she saw that he held something in his hand. A rose, its petals pale pink at the edges and ivory in the center, was cupped in one big hand. The blossom glowed with a soft light that emanated from its center. The closer he got, the more the rose began to wilt, but he seemed unfazed by the change. By the time he stood in front of Jolie, his body just inches from hers, it was just a shriveled shadow of its former self. Petals, dry and withered, fell at his feet with each step. On the ring finger of his left hand, the stranger wore the silver band Armand had brought home. In his belt, where a man would usually carry a saber, was the hand mirror.

Jolie looked up at him again to see the smile had faded from his face and in its place was a look so stricken she felt her heart constrict in her chest. Holding out the hand with the naked rose in it, he dropped to one knee at her feet, his eyes meeting hers.

In a deep, gravelly voice, the stranger asked, "Will you marry me?"

Jolie woke with a start, her heart slamming against her ribs with such force she thought the bones would break. As she sat up, the curtains behind her opened, letting her adjust to the light. Surprised to find herself still alone in the library instead of the Great Hall as in the dream, she looked around, foggy images of the bizarre party lingering enough to make her feel confused about where she was.

Her dreams had been the same since she had come here, but this one left her rattled. In the others, she had always been alone, other than the black-garbed guests. The handsome stranger hadn't been there at first, but now he'd appeared in two dreams. She'd never had dreams like these. She tried to shake the images but her mind struggled to let them go, clinging to the unanswered questions these visions left her with.

Why were her clothes and the handsome stranger's the only ones that weren't black? And why was his face the only one she could see? Questions raced through her mind, and she spent a few minutes lying on the settee trying to work through what she'd seen and failed to come to any kind of conclusion.

A soft squeaking interrupted her thoughts. The sound drifted through the door and when she looked, a cart was rolling toward her under its own power. She'd seen it already, but she couldn't help but look everywhere she could on the cart. Of course, she could see no mechanism or means by which the thing should be able to move on its own.

There would come a day when a cart serving her a meal would be normal and she wondered if she would ever be able to explain it to anyone outside this place.

Part of her knew how unlikely it was that she would ever see anyone who might demand an explanation of the affairs in Château Villeneuve. The only way she could see herself as a free woman was when she would be old, grey, and long forgotten. Jolie shook her head to rid herself of the thought, then looked at what the cart had brought her.

Atop the cart was an assortment of snacks; a pot of tea along with fresh bread, more of the smoked ham from breakfast, cheese shot through with dark blue mold, and a thick pat of butter. A roasted pear with mottled brown skin swam in spiced juice in a white porcelain bowl.

The food was light and delicious, and she ate her fill. The second she pushed her plate away the cart shuttled out of the room as if on orders. She found the book she'd been reading before she fell asleep and picked it up from the stack.

That's not where I left it, she thought. She gave the stack of books a sidelong look, hoping she could catch some movement, but nothing happened and she stood to leave.

In the hallway, she had to remember which way to turn to get to the corridor. By the time Jolie realized she'd gone the wrong way, she'd walked past the drawing room and had to walk past the doorway again. When she did, she caught a flicker of movement out of the corner of her eye and turned to see what it was.

Standing by the window, looking out over the south courtyard, was Prince Leopold. He had removed his cloak and was wearing a crisp white linen shirt, this one gathered at the neck and wrists with ruffles. His hair hung loose around his shoulders, thick, shiny, and dark. So tall and broad he nearly blocked out the light coming in the lower half of the window, he stood with his hands hanging at his sides, feet shoulder-width apart.

Jolie was struck again by how big he was, his shoulders massive with muscle, his arms thick and long. Something about the way he was staring out the window, looking out at a world he could no longer be a part of, filled her with sadness. Even from the side, the longing in his features was as clear as if she were standing directly in front of him.

Someday, she knew, she would look out these windows in much the same way. She imagined how he must feel after years of being afraid to let the world see his face and for the first time she felt more than a passing sympathy for the man in front of her. Jolie knew the only way he'd seen the outside world was in darkness, hiding in the shadows where no one would see the monstrosity he'd become.

When he turned toward her, for a fraction of a heartbeat she thought she saw a different face, the face of the stranger from her dream, but then she blinked and knew it wasn't true. She didn't know why her mind had put the two men together as if they were one, when they couldn't be any more different.

"Do you always linger in doorways?" Leopold wasn't angry with her for not revealing herself to him, but curious, and hoped she heard the amusement in his words. Jolie smiled, and he was relieved she'd understood.

"Are you well?" she asked, concern furrowing her brow as she crossed the room to him. "You looked sad when I first saw you."

"I will be fine," he said. His voice was gruff, offering no room for argument, and he regretted the way he'd said it as soon as he did.

The prince's tone gave her pause, and Jolie stepped back. She backed far enough away from him she would have a head start out of the room if he got angry. They were going to be stuck with each other for a long time, and if they didn't get to know each other life would be more miserable than it needed to be. To get to know him, she would have to learn to calm him down.

Jolie looked at Leopold and asked, "How long has it been since you had a guest?"

Leopold turned back to the window and surveyed the grounds as he calculated. "Before you arrived it had been seven years, four months, two weeks, and a day."

His count was so precise Jolie's eyes widened.

"Most of my parents' friends and family came for my parents' funeral, but none of them knew what had happened to me. I refused to see them, and they stopped coming. Not long after that, I stopped receiving calls from society mothers trying to get me to marry their daughters as well."

There was a long pause after that, but neither of them felt it was an uncomfortable silence. They listened to the sounds of their breathing, the wind whipping against the walls, and let the conversation continue when Leopold was good and ready.

"The last woman that spent any time in this hold was Princess Ursula VanHeuven-Hurst of Denmark. She and her parents had no idea that my parents were dead, nor had they heard a word about me. So Ursula still thought she had a chance of becoming my bride," Leopold said, a faraway look in his eyes. "At one time, I would have given a great deal to marry her. When she showed up at the door, I couldn't wait to send her away. Willard had the honor of that task, of course."

"Did you refuse to see anyone?" she asked. "They'd come all this way to see you, did you leave them with nowhere to stay?"

"I couldn't let them see me like this. If they needed to, I would allow them to stay, but often they were so insulted when I wouldn't see to them personally that they left straight away," he answered. "When Ursula left, she spread the word of what a brute I'd become and I went from one of the most eligible bachelors in the world to a man no one would accept as their son-in-law."

Jolie sighed and he looked at her, trying to gauge her expression. She wore her emotions on her sleeve, letting everything show on her pretty face. As she worked through her confusion, she nibbled on her lower lip, her arms crossed over the book she had pressed to her chest.

Leopold took the opportunity to look at her while she was focused on her thoughts. She was so short, her head barely coming to his chest, but he could see the strength in her body as well. Jolie was not fat by anyone's standards, but she was softer, rounder than the women he was used to. Her wild shock of hair made him smile. He liked that she wore it down and that he got to see how long it was. It never looked the same twice, its crazy curls everywhere at once. He wanted to touch those curls, to pull one straight with his fingers, then let it bounce back to its natural shape.

"I'm sorry this happened to you," she said, her voice soft and low, jerking him out of his reverie. "The last ten years can't have been easy on you."

His face must have shown his shock because when she turned to him she looked apologetic until he put up a hand to stop her. No one but Willard had ever said anything like that to him. Leopold had been angry at first, of course, but over time had accepted his fate as deserved.

"My punishment is no less than I deserve, Lady Jolie," he said, adding the appellation to her name without thinking.

The stricken look in her eyes surprised him again, her brow drawn up and her lips parted. She set the book down on the floor, then straightened and met eyes with him.

Unsure, she opened her mouth to speak, thought better of it, and tried again. "Master, forgive me if this is an odd request, but would you please kneel?"

"Why?" he asked with a sardonic grin.

A flush stole its way up her throat to her cheeks, reddening them to a shade of crimson that clashed obnoxiously with her hair. "It is only that you are so much taller than I, and I wish to look into your eyes."

Something about the way she explained what she wanted made him feel as abashed as she was. Kneeling would put him at the height he'd stood before the witch's curse had changed him. Putting himself at that level would be akin to chipping away at the distance he'd put between himself and the rest of humanity.

Without his self-imposed ostracism, he would be naked, exposed to Jolie's scrutiny. He wasn't sure he could do this, but if she had been brave enough to ask, he thought he could be brave enough to grant her request.

Patient, she waited for him to either kneel or curse her for a madwoman for making such a ridiculous request. When he nodded, her heart picked up its pace, pounding in her ears. Something so small shouldn't make her nervous, but she'd always believed you could see what a man was made of by looking into his eyes. Whatever Leopold was made of might scare her to death.

"I want you to know, I kneel to no man," Leopold said as he dropped to one knee, a mischievous smile curving his thick lips. He got his other knee under him and clasped his hands at his waist.

"Well, then," Jolie grinned back, "it's lucky we are that I'm not a man."

His smile widened so that it looked as if his cheeks would close off his eyes and he chuckled. It was a pleasant sound, rusty like his voice.

Their levity died as Jolie stepped toward him, her hands behind her back. His head was still above hers by a good measure, but much closer than it had been. Their eyes met and a strange feeling stole over her, sending a shiver down her spine and giving her a sense of disjointed recognition. Like her mind knew something but couldn't piece it together to paint the full picture for her.

His face was fascinating, like the grotesques that guarded Notre Dame Cathedral. Covered in coarse hair, like he'd grown a beard over his whole face, his features were obscured even more. She could almost believe all the old tales about werewolves looking at this face. What was more, she could understand him not wanting anyone to see him like this, especially if he had been as handsome as everyone had said before.

Something touched her shoulder, startling her, and she looked down to see his fingers twining into her hair. He pinched one of the thick ringlets and pulled, drawing it out straight before letting it bounce back. Her eyes flew to his, and even in his distorted face they were soft and warm on hers. His hand lifted to her face and he pressed a palm against her cheek, his fingers threading into the hair at the back of her head. If he just squeezed, he could crush her skull. The fear was real and she had to brace her muscles to stop from running away.

And yet, there was something in his eyes that she'd never seen before. She couldn't put a name to it, but she saw something in the depths of those dark eyes that her soul recognized. This feeling made her breath quicken and her heart ache, like she had found something she'd never realized she was missing.

Leopold felt strange, like his chest had too many organs in it. It was hard to breathe with Jolie this close, with his hand in her hair just like he'd wanted. No woman had ever looked at him the way she was right now, even before he'd been cursed. It filled his chest with a warmth he had never known.

Jolie lifted a hand, stretching her fingers out to his face as if to return his gesture, then thought better of it and dropped it to her side again.

He rubbed a thumb over the skin at her temple, closing his eyes at how soft she felt. Her hand came up again, her fingertips brushing the skin over his right eyebrow. Every hair stood on end, his scalp prickled all at once, and his eyes fluttered shut on a wave of sensation that fanned out over his whole body.

Overwhelmed with emotion, he pulled her toward him, not sure what his intentions were but needing more of what she'd just made him feel.

"Ahem," Willard coughed at the drawing room door.

The two of them flew apart, cheeks flaming and hands shooting behind their backs like children caught with their hands in the sweet jar. Jolie stooped and picked up her book and left the room without a word or a look at either of the men. Leopold stood, clenching the hand he'd had in her hair, still feeling her skin in his palm like they'd not been interrupted.

Willard watched as Jolie stormed down the hall, making a sharp right at the end into the corridor and out of sight.

Turning to Leopold, Willard raised his eyebrows, looking askance at his master. "What were you doing, Prince Leopold?"

The spell was broken now, but Leopold could still feel her in his hand. "I forgot myself, Willard, I'm sorry." He turned to the window again, his eyes still closed on the wave of emotion Jolie had caused in him. "I will make amends to Jolie for my actions later."

He couldn't see it, but Willard was grinning behind him, leaning on the doorjamb like he was standing in his own home and not his employer's. In truth, the older man was thrilled that this young woman had made the prince forget himself, even for a moment. This was a good sign, the best they had seen in years.

"Perhaps, Master, you could invite Jolie to dinner tonight to make up for your mistake?"

"I have already invited her to have luncheon with me today. Please let her know that the invitation still stands," Leopold said, his head hanging in shame.

"Of course, sire," Willard said. He cut a neat bow he knew the prince wouldn't see, then left, grinning like a fool as he went.

Chapter 9

Jolie sat in the Rose Room reading her book without seeing a word. Emotions swirled through her like hot water, not the least of them confusion. The encounter in the library, coupled with these dreams she kept having, was tainting her thoughts, carryover from it muddling whatever had happened between she and Leopold in the drawing room afterward.

Annoyed with herself, she paced the room, her footsteps heavier than usual. She had too much time on her hands. The collection in the library could take her the rest of her life to read, but even she needed more to do than just reading. Even the added task of balancing the ledgers wasn't enough and she already knew it. Even if she quadruple-checked her sums, they wouldn't take her more than a few hours a week. The household didn't exactly need much in the way of goods and services, with how few people lived here and how small a strain it was on its resources.

As if he'd heard her thoughts, Willard came to the doorway with a soft rap of his knuckles on the doorframe.

"The master would like to reaffirm that his invitation to lunch with him today still stands, my lady." He offered her a warm smile, and she returned it.

"You may let the master know that I accept his invitation. I do have a question, though?" she said, stepping closer to Willard.

"Yes, my lady?"

"Why would he invite me to luncheon and not dinner?" she asked, her brow quirked. "After all, it's not as if I have any plans."

Willard laughed, but then his face fell. "I'm afraid the only one who can give you that answer is the master himself."

"I asked him while we were on our walk yesterday and right after we returned he said it was because he is afraid of himself," she said. "Why would he say that?"

"You've seen that the master doesn't have a firm grasp on his own temper." It wasn't a question, but Jolie nodded anyway. "I believe our master has begun to care what you think of him, and he's trying very hard to control himself, despite evidence to the contrary."

Nodding again, Willard's answer both helpful and not, she turned to the window.

"The master takes walks into the village some nights to exhaust himself. He doesn't sleep well at night. I feel that lately, even this has been of little help."

Jolie thought of the Grey Man legend, and where it had gotten its start. "It makes sense now," she said. At Willard's odd look, she continued, "The Grey Man stories the children tell."

Willard smiled, the turn of his mouth a little sad. "Superstition can amuse, can it not?"

"To tell the truth, I didn't think it was superstition when I came face-to-face with Prince Leopold that first night," Jolie said, smiling back at the valet.

It felt like it had been months since she'd arrived, not just days. Through all the confusion and oddity she'd witnessed here, she wasn't uncomfortable. She missed her family and her home, of course, but she had done the bulk of her grieving in the weeks she hadn't left the Rose Room.

"I imagine you didn't."

"I do wish there was more you could tell me," She took a few steps closer. "I get more confused the longer I'm here."

Willard looked uncomfortable, his hands twisting into one another. "As do I, Lady Jolie."

"Perhaps that is the purpose of my punishment, to see the world the way Prince Leopold does, always as an outsider looking in."

Willard stayed at the door, watching her as she resumed her pacing. He didn't know what to say. Though he knew the prince better than anyone else in the world, he had no idea what the younger man had been thinking, coming up with the sentence he had for Armand, let alone suggesting a daughter take his place. The appalling threat of murdering the old man's family if no one came to serve the term was outrageous, but a sign of how long Leopold had been alone.

"I saw something in him this morning that I've never seen in anyone, and it frightens me," Jolie admitted. "There's something in his eyes that I thought only I felt, and it took me a while to realize what it was."

When she didn't elaborate on her thought, Willard stayed silent, letting her come around to it on her own.

"I've felt alone most of my life, unless I was with my father. He took me along on trips, kept me a part of his life even when he was working," she explained. "My sister was always more like our mother, beautiful and feminine, whereas I am unremarkable and more like a boy than a girl."

Willard couldn't see a part of her that a man would mistake for boyish, but he knew she wasn't speaking of her body.

"Mireille drew the attention of every young man in the village. She had her pick when it came time to marry and she married well. Once any of my suitors saw me, or got to know the things I like to do and am good at, they lost interest and left." Jolie was surprised by the emotion that rose up when she thought of the rejections she'd suffered. "I look out at the rest of my life and know there will come a day when I no longer care that there's not a husband or a gaggle of children, or even a friend who I can talk to."

Willard was stunned by her admission. She was too young to feel the way she did, like there was so little hope. "Mademoiselle Jolie, you mustn't—"

"I already do, and so does our master. That's what I saw when I looked into his eyes," Jolie said. "My father once told me that when you look into a man's eyes you see his soul. All the stuff he's made of is right there. I feel like Prince Leopold and I might be made of the same stuff, and that frightens me."

She could be right, Willard thought. If he hadn't believed Jolie was the woman who could break the curse, he did now. He smiled to himself, letting it spread over his face as he thought that the master's time as a monster who haunted children's nightmares could soon be at an end. There was little time to waste, and if he was going to make anything happen, he had to get the two of them in a room together again.

Willard knew what he'd seen between them this morning, and with what Jolie had just said, he knew it was real and mutual. But attraction and commiseration did not a true love make. He had work to do.

"My lady, you have nothing to fear from our master," he said. "I will reiterate your acceptance of the invitation."

"Thank you, Willard." She stopped her pacing and offered him a weak smile.

He bowed and left the room, making his way to the south tower. *No time to lose*, he thought with a grin. Mounting the stairs, he had no idea what he was going to do once he got the master's attention. Once he got to the top of the stairs, he saw the mirror and the ring on the table, and he had an idea.

"Master," he said, knocking on the door. The prince was seated at a desk in a chair that looked like it was seconds away from breaking into pieces under his weight.

Even nearly a decade into his isolation, Leopold was still unsure what he was meant to do with himself from day to day. He knew how Jolie felt better than anyone.

On the desk was a sheaf of paper, a pen, and an inkwell that had probably been bottled around the time his parents had died. Practicing his letters seemed a boring but serviceable way to spend some time. "What is it, Willard?" he asked as he finished a Q with a flourish. He put the pen down in the well and turned to his valet.

"I saw you and Jolie this morning in the drawing room and I am certain she is the one you've been waiting for," Willard said. "There is nothing I would love more than to see you happy and this curse lifted, but if you ignore her it will never happen."

"I am aware of your thoughts on this matter," Leopold said, and Willard saw the loss of hope in his eyes. "But you are wrong. I've run out of time."

"Across the Great Hall, pacing her chamber like a madwoman, is a young lady who is as lonely and lost as you are. She sees in you fragments of her own soul, things she feels that she didn't know anyone else did," Willard said, pointing a finger at Leopold's chest. "I saw you as well, and you can't tell me you feel nothing for her."

"She is lovely, I admit," Leopold said, thinking only of appeasing his servant, but then he remembered what her touch had made him feel. Closing his eyes, the waves of sensation danced over his skin all over again. Tingling head to toe, he let himself feel it again but only for a moment before he shut it down with a shake of his head. "It is an attraction, nothing more."

Leopold heard the doubt in his own voice but refused to acknowledge it. "I will scare her away eventually."

"How will you ever know if you are too fearful to try?"

"I am afraid of nothing," Leopold said, a glimpse of his old boastful self showing through the veneer of civility he wore.

Willard didn't buy it and pursed his lips, one eyebrow quirked. "I think she frightens you more than the whole rest of the village and their childish stories. And do you know why I think she scares you?"

"I'm sure you're about to tell me," Leopold droned, rubbing a big hand over his face.

"Because above all else, you fear what might happen if you take a chance and fail," Willard said and the words hit home, leaving Leopold dumbfounded. "You would rather walk into Fontainbleu naked as the day you were born than walk across the Great Hall and talk to a twenty-year-old girl."

Leopold was blushing and Willard knew he was right.

"We both know that she feels everything you do," Willard said, his voice low and pleading. "But there is more to it than just that, sire. I think, Master, that she needs you just as much as you need her."

Leopold's eyes came up to meet Willard's and the older man saw all the emotion in them. Fear and uncertainty, but also hope.

"Why would she need me?" Leopold asked, and Willard didn't hear the same conviction in his voice that had been there at the beginning of the conversation. "She's never been alone—"

"Just because someone is in the middle of a crowded room doesn't mean they're not lonely, sire," Willard interrupted.

Leopold thought back to the way he'd always felt when his parents held a ball. Hundreds of people milling around, including children his age, and still he'd felt like he was the only person in the world. Back then, it had been because he set himself apart from the rest of them, always thinking he was better than the others. Now, he was separated by more than his own overblown opinion of himself.

Could Jolie feel the way he did? Surely not, with a father willing to steal from the palace garden for her. Even if she'd been close to her father since she was a child, that closeness would have to change as she grew into a woman. Even any bond she had with siblings would change as they went their own way as adults. People grew apart, it was inevitable.

"What shall I do, Willard? I don't even know where to start," he said, hanging his head.

"This from a young man who had his pick of brides ten years ago," Willard said, remembering the boy Leopold had once been.

"I didn't deserve any of them. We both know that. I would have ruined any woman who stayed long enough to marry me, and myself and our children in the process," Leopold said.

"The fact that you can say that right now proves to me that you deserve another chance at happiness," Willard said, his smile so paternal it made Leopold miss his own father.

"I don't deserve her," Leopold said.

"You must stop pitying yourself, sire, and take a chance. You don't know where to start? Try kindness." At Leopold's confused look he continued, "Control your temper, and be kind. It's as good a start as any."

The prince still looked unsure, and Willard said, "The time will pass whether you are doing anything with it or not."

This seemed to work, and Leopold stood from the chair, which creaked loudly as if in relief. He straightened his shoulders and headed for the door. Willard led the way down, then left for the servants' quarters with a whispered, "Good luck."

Leopold walked toward the Rose Room, trying not to lose his nerve. He felt like a child— unsure of himself as he'd ever been. As he approached the door, he realized he hadn't thought about what he wanted to do. He slowed down, trying to allow himself more time to think, but as he came up to the door, all thought left his mind.

Jolie sat at the desk, much as he had just been in his own room, with papers spread out over its surface. Instead of letters, though, she was scribbling numbers down, adding sums. The thick ledgers were spread out over the desk. One pen was lost in her hair, the other twiddling between fingers of her right hand as she thought through the problem she'd given herself. Ink stained her fingers, and a smear painted the back of her right hand.

It was so amusing to see her this way, unguarded, that he didn't want to interrupt her. He did, though, knocking on the doorjamb.

Jolie, focused as she'd been on her mathematics practice, didn't notice him until he spoke. As soon as he did, she got the feeling she had ink all over her face and hands. Self-conscious, she tried to find a handkerchief to clean herself up.

"Here," Leopold said, drawing a square of the linen from the pocket of his shirt and offering it to her.

"Settling the accounts will be a lovely job for me," she said as she tried to get the ink off her hands. "I used to do it for Father."

"What does your father do again?" Damned if he hadn't forgotten as soon as he opened his mouth to ask the question.

"He's a merchant. He buys spices and tea from India, then ships them to the Caribbean Islands to sell them," she said, looking at herself in the mirror on the vanity. "I used to help him in any way that I could."

"Rosalie has been handling the accounts but she is getting on in years and I've been meaning to lessen her responsibilities so she can get more rest."

"Thank you, sire. I shall do the best I can." She looked at the cloth in her hands and, realizing it was beyond salvation, left it on the vanity. "I will get you a clean one."

"No need. I will get one myself if I need it," he said.

"I wanted to thank you again for inviting me to lunch with you. It will be lovely."

"I hope so, thank you for accepting," he said. Talk was growing stale, he could feel it like a curtain between them, and he yearned for the closeness he'd felt with her earlier.

"Is that all you came here for?" she asked. She was still turned toward the desk, ready to get back to her work if he gave the slightest indication that he was leaving.

The prince looked suddenly uncomfortable. He was thinking hard, his brow scrunched up and his mouth opening and closing as if he had more to say but wasn't sure how to go about it.

"I find it very difficult to talk to you at times," he admitted. He dropped his gaze to the floor. "I am forever afraid of saying something that makes you fear me. After what happened in the library this morning—"

The prince cut himself off so quickly, the echo of his words hung in the air. She turned in her chair to face him straight on.

It was all still right there, everything that had passed between them, and yet neither of them could find the courage to say anything about it. Jolie didn't think he would ever finish the thought, so when he spoke she was pleasantly surprised.

"—I was hoping to make a new start between us," Leopold said, meeting her eyes finally.

Her smile was beautiful, lifting her cheeks and showing straight, white teeth. "I would like that."

"Then, I will see you at lunch in about an hour?" Leopold asked, his voice lifted in genuine hope.

"Of course, Master." He loved her smile, so pure and happy. Something made him want to keep it on her face as much as possible.

Leopold gave her a nod and left her to her work. Ten feet from the door, he turned back to see her bent over the desk again, her hand scratching figures in the ledgers as fast as they could move. With a smile, he left to meet Willard in his chambers. He wanted to get the 'dressing' portion of the afternoon done. The valet could be fussy about how he looked for events, and they could be at it the full hour that remained before the meal would be served.

****

Quentin ran a track in the floor of his parents' foyer. The knock he was waiting for came to the door and he leapt to answer it before the butler could get it. The old fool would turn away his guest without allowing him in.

The man on the other side of the door was a shabby old fellow. It had taken him two weeks to arrive from Paris, and Quentin suspected he had done all of his traveling on foot. His clothing was stained with time and too many wearings. The fetid smell coming off of the man was a combination of sweat, hay, and manure. His beard was matted and his hair hung in lank, greasy strings around his face.

"Monsieur Thomas Brilliande, I assume?" Quentin asked, trying not to wrinkle his nose at the odor.

"I am, Monsieur. And you are Quentin?" the old man asked, showing off what was left of his teeth, just a mouthful of yellowed stubs. Despite his moth-eaten appearance, his voice was cultured. The man was educated and had fallen on the hard times that left him the shambles he was only recently.

"Yes, I am. Please, come in, and we'll get straight to business." Quentin held the door open for the man to pass, hoping this would only take a few minutes. If this man stayed very long, the maid would have to clean the entire house with ammonia to get rid of his stench.

"Of course, Monsieur. I have brought a drawing of the château with me, to show you where everything was," Thomas said, producing a document from his inner coat pocket that, thankfully, looked cleaner than the rest of him.

Quentin led him to his father's study, and to the giant mahogany desk that dominated the room. He plucked the map from Thomas's hands, careful not to touch the man's skin, and spread it on the desk.

Drawn in grease pencil was a square within a larger square, with a circle at each corner. A compass rose sat in one corner of the crude map, pointing north. The gate and every door he would need to navigate through were clearly marked, as were the south courtyard and the break in the wall that Quentin would have to cross.

"This will help me very much, Thomas. Thank you," Quentin said, his voice bright. "Where does the Beast sleep?"

Thomas pointed to the South Tower. "This used to be the watchtower, back when it was first built. It's the only tower with a room all the way up at the top of the stairs. All the other tower rooms were bricked off fifty years ago. This is where the monster sleeps."

Quentin nodded. He slid open a drawer and took out a pencil, then drew an 'X' on the south tower's circle. "What else do I need to know, Thomas?" he asked, keeping his voice even despite the pounding of his heart.

Thomas scratched his oily head, then jabbed a finger at the gap in the south wall. "This wall only went up after I left, but even though there's a big hole in it, no one's tried to go after the monster before. From what you told me, the old man Babineaux is the only person to cross into the south courtyard for years. Don't you think that's odd?"

"Tell me what I need to know, old man, and not your theories about what's kept lesser men from killing the Grey Man." Quentin's eyes were wide, his sudden flare of anger pursing his lips and furrowing his brow.

"Of course, sir," Thomas said, bowing his head. "There is a powerful magic in that place," he spat. Quentin tried not to roll his eyes at the man's words, but it took a good deal of effort.

"Ever since the night the king and queen died," Thomas supplied, as if trying to make the younger man understand.

Thomas had a hard time meeting Quentin's eyes, knowing the younger man would never believe what he had to tell him.

"Keep your stories, old man, or our deal is off. I'll keep the map and you'll walk out of here lucky to be leaving with your life." Quentin straightened up and took a step closer to Thomas. He puffed out his chest and met the old man's eyes, taking pride in the way the old man seemed to wither under his glare.

"Yes, sir." Thomas looked back down at the map, pointing his grubby finger at it again. "This path comes off the old Tremonde road. You can hardly see where it turns off, but it's there. I'll mark the path with a black cloth for you tonight, on my way home."

Quentin nodded, watching Thomas's finger wind up the path on his map.

"He goes out most evenings to the Chaud. He doesn't sleep well, and takes long walks up and down the shore looking for the wit—"

114

Quentin shot him a look and Thomas backpedaled.

"—Woman that did this to him. When he starts to tire, he comes back home and collapses, sometimes for whole rest of the day."

"Will he compromise her?" Quentin didn't really care, but he knew if he didn't ask the old man might find his lack of concern odd.

"Only worked there while the boy was a child so I couldn't tell you. It won't matter, anyway. You can rescue her all you want, but no one will ever believe he didn't take her virtue, sir," Thomas said. "You might save her reputation if you tell a tale that she was held there against her will by the monster."

"Her father sent her there to serve his sentence. Her brother-in-law told me she's to stay there the rest of her life," Quentin grumbled. "Where would he keep a prisoner?"

"Don't know that either, sir. I worked there two years and the whole time, there was never a prisoner. There are dungeons below, but my guess would be a lady like your Jolie would be kept in one of the other rooms in the towers." Thomas stabbed a finger at each of the other three towers.

Staring at the map, Quentin felt a rush through his whole body. Anticipation and excitement prickled on the back of his neck and danced over his skin, making his heart pound and his blood rush through his ears. He reached into the pocket on his coat and dug out a hefty bag of coins.

Passing it to Thomas without looking at him, he said, "Don't forget to mark that road for me, old man, or I will find you." He waved a hand and Thomas slipped out the front door, closing it behind him with a click.

Quentin stood at his father's desk looking at the dirty, scribbled map with a smile on his face. Anyone who saw him might have thought he was as excited as a child with a treasure map.

Until they looked in his eyes and saw the great yawning nothing that looked back at them.

****

"Rosalie, what does one wear to luncheon with a prince?" Jolie asked, sidling up next to the maid and looking through all the gowns in the dressing room next to her bedchamber. Her stomach fluttered with nerves, and she wasn't sure what to do with her shaking hands. Why

115

she was so anxious about this lunch was a mystery she'd give a lot to solve.

The gowns were all beautiful, but some were obviously meant to be worn either at court or for a much finer appointment than she was used to. This was just luncheon, after all. The fact that this would be her first meal taken with a member of her country's royal family was making her sweat through the dress she had on. At this rate, she would ruin whatever gown Rosalie chose for her.

"Don't rightly know, Mademoiselle," Rosalie said. "I think that pink one would look lovely." She stopped, lifting her head as if a good idea had come to her. "Though I would choose the printed one." The older woman crossed the room and held a cotton gown up to Jolie.

The two women turned to a full-length mirror propped up against the wall by the bed. The fabric was ivory in color, block printed with red and purple blooms, the stems and leaves a pale green and vines creating a delicate pattern all over the gown. The gathered elbows swept the top of the full skirt, and the neckline was low enough to be provocative without revealing too much, with a little frill of lace for a little bit of extra coverage.

"Yes, child," Rosalie said. "I would choose that one."

Jolie, watching as Rosalie took a square hoop out of the huge armoire to shape the gown's skirt, gave her a smile that looked even less confident than she felt. Rosalie put a hand on each shoulder and turned her around.

"Nothing to be nervous about, child. The master is not to be feared. Surely you know that by now." Rosalie met Jolie's eyes with her own, her eyebrows raised to her smooth mass of white hair. "Terrible you have to see him like this, without benefit of seeing the handsome man he once was. Turn, and I'll help you dress."

"He'd never have given me a second look if he looked the way everyone describes," Jolie muttered as Rosalie went to work on her blue morning gown, working it off with deft fingers.

"What makes you say that?" the older woman asked. The bodice of the dress disappeared and Jolie grabbed her hand for support as she stepped out of the skirt. Thank God the thing didn't have a frame under it or she'd have to be buried in it. As it was, it stood in almost perfect form once it was unlaced and she had to raise her leg above hip level to get out from under the mountain of fabric.

"The way every man that's ever come into my life has reacted when they see me for the first time," Jolie answered. "I have all the qualifications of a good wife, but then they meet me and realize they'd rather run away to the Americas than have their children born looking like me."

Rosalie feigned indignation, but Jolie saw how her eyes wandered over the mass of red curls parading around her shoulders.

"I've had offers of marriage from three men, only to find out later that they were just desperate fools who needed an heir to inherit, or they wanted what my father had," Jolie said. She hung her head and corrected herself. "Or what they thought my father had."

"Anything your father did or didn't do," Rosalie said as she strapped the frame to Jolie's hips, "isn't your fault, though I'm sure you would be the one to pay for it. And your sister, I assume."

"My sister is already married," Jolie said. "And she chose well. Her husband is a master carpenter who makes a handsome living."

"So the burden would likely have fallen on you," Rosalie said, her voice lifting as if in question. She helped Jolie step into the skirt. Jolie helped as much as she could, but this was a job usually handled by three women and it took longer than it should have to get it done.

"I don't know for sure what his plan was, because I came here," Jolie said. "He was planning on marrying me off to a young man from a wealthy family so I might have been able to make it. But I only met the man once and he scares me."

Rosalie started lacing the bodice up beneath the back pleats. Her eyes met Jolie's in the mirror. "Your brother-in-law doesn't have a brother?"

"Five sisters," Jolie answered. "And it's like I said, anytime I would draw the attention of a suitable match, they would see me and run away, or I would talk to them about what I like to do and next thing I knew, they were gone. There was one that I thought would actually marry me. But then, a friend of mine overheard him talking about me to his friends and I knew he was just another one cut from the same bolt."

"Perhaps you could do something different with your hair," Rosalie suggested. "In Paris, you can have any color hair you like. Some makeup to hide your freckles, make you a blonde, you would be quite fashionable."

"And then once I wash my face, and my hair grows?" Jolie asked. "I shouldn't have to change my face or my hair to get married."

Rosalie, having been around royalty and the court her entire adult life, knew how fickle high society were in their tastes. She had seen the cruelty courtiers could mete out to anyone who didn't fit their idea of perfection. If a person looked a certain way, and had enough money and the right attributes, they could get away with murder, literally. If they were different, either due to financial or physical reasons, they could be ostracized.

At court, Rosalie had seen a kind, smart young woman go from a gentle and generous girl to an empty, weeping shell of a person in a single Season. The girl was a peasant from a poor farming family, sponsored one summer by a society matron. The girl had been showered with gifts and dressed in the finest dresses, only to arrive at court to whispers about her parentage. Hoping for a good marriage to get herself out of the wheat fields, instead she was ignored by men and women alike for an entire summer. Rosalie heard that after the girl went home, she wound up in trouble and was forced to marry her father's farmhand.

This standard was the reason their master had become the unbearable child he was, and had created the mess they were in today. Handsome as the sin you never dreamed yourself brave enough to commit, but without a scruple in his pretty head, the boy was a terror with no reckoning.

Rosalie had only worked at the palace a month before the fateful day the magic bearer had cursed Prince Leopold, but in that short time she'd seen enough. Enough to know that there was nothing anyone could do to change him, and that he would never change himself unless something drastic happened. She could never have imagined what the 'something drastic' would be, or that time would ever run out for things to be fixed. She'd had the same hopes as Willard and even the master had since Jolie had arrived, but she wasn't sure there was enough time for these two misfits to even like each other, let alone fall in love.

If it was going to happen, there was much work to be done. Lunch with the prince could be a good start and Rosalie could help by making Jolie look as beautiful as possible. As she started sweeping the girl's long hair off her shoulders, she heard a soft rap on the door. "Who is it?" she called, fishing for hair pins in a drawer.

"It's Willard," he called. His next words were muffled through the door.

"Mademoiselle is nearly ready, you may enter," Rosalie called, pinning a hank of hair high on Jolie's head.

Jolie heard Willard come in the room, his shoes clicking on the floor. "The master has not yet seen her in full dress. Do your best, Rosalie."

Without a word, Rosalie started working on an elaborate coiffure, smoothing and piling hair everywhere she could reach. Short curls framed Jolie's face and trailed down the nape of her neck.

"Why do I get the impression you two are plotting something?" Jolie asked, scrunching her eyes closed as her hair flew in all directions under the older woman's ministrations.

"Not plotting, my dear, not at all." Willard said. His voice sounded choked and when she looked at him, he couldn't meet her eyes. "You should make your way to the dining hall. You look lovely." He turned on his heel and left the room.

When Jolie looked to Rosalie, hoping for some explanation, the woman turned away and left as well.

Odd, she thought. Definitely a plot of some sort, but she was sure she'd be the last to know what it was all about. She'd heard about palace intrigues since she was a child and had to admit it was a little exciting to be a part of one, even if she didn't know yet what it was all about.

Winding her way through the room, she tried not to knock anything over with the voluminous skirt. The frame made her bottom half twice as wide as it usually was and navigation was all the more difficult for it.

The curtains were already open in the Great Hall, candles lit in the breezeway between it and the dining hall. Curtains were open in that room as well, opening windows she'd not seen in the dark yesterday. The table was already laid with the meal she would share with the prince. The master hadn't arrived yet and she was suddenly unsure what she was supposed to do. She stood in the doorway, clasping and unclasping her hands and pacing as she waited.

Leopold kept his head down as he crossed the Great Hall. His shirt's high collar was strangling him, the ruffles at his cuffs pulling the hairs on his wrists. The buckled shoes he'd forced on made him yearn for his broken-in boots. Willard had shoved every piece of clothing he owned at him this morning, determined not to let him out of the south tower room until he approved of the prince's outfit. The valet walked in front of him until he reached the breezeway, where he turned and stood with his back to the wall, hands clasped at his waist, back ramrod straight.

Leopold looked up once he got close to the breezeway leading to the dining hall, catching sight of Jolie standing near the table. She was turned to the side, looking away from him and he was glad she couldn't see his reaction to her. She looked beautiful, wearing a gown that his mother had commissioned just before her death. Queen Adele had never gotten to wear it, and he had a feeling Rosalie had chosen it for that reason.

One of his shoes scraped on the floor and she turned. Without the cloud of hair obscuring her features, he could see her high cheekbones and stubborn jaw, the graceful curve of her neck. He didn't like the way her hair looked and it took him a moment to understand why. With it pulled tight against her head, she looked like any other courtier. He wanted to ask her to take it down.

Instead, as he approached, he stopped and bowed. "Good afternoon, Mademoiselle Babineaux," he said with a smile.

"Good afternoon, Prince Leopold," she said, falling into a deep curtsy. "I must thank you once again for inviting me to share this meal with you."

"I must thank you, as well, for accepting my invitation."

The prince looked so civilized, wearing better clothes than she'd seen him in before. When he held out an arm to guide her to the table, she smiled broadly, surprised at the gesture. She rested her hand on his forearm and followed his lead. He pulled out her chair and pushed it in beneath her when she sat, then went to his seat at the opposite end.

Willard appeared from a door in the back of the dining hall that led to the kitchens. She squashed a flash of disappointment that she wouldn't be able to witness whatever magic she'd missed at her other meals. Whatever secrets the château held about food service would stay secrets at least for now. Willard served her first, then their master, then slipped back into the kitchen.

The table was fifteen feet long, and put so much distance between Jolie and the prince that she didn't think they would be able to have much of a conversation. After their walk yesterday and the encounter in the library this morning, it felt odd to be sitting so far away from him.

The distance stifled any attempt at conversation. Every time one of them opened their mouth to speak, they shut it again rather than shout. After a few minutes of silence, Prince Leopold picked up his plate and wine glass and walked down to her end of the table, putting himself in the seat to her right.

"This is better, isn't it?" he said, smiling. He took a sip of his wine, his thick lips making the task difficult. He managed to handle the task with more decorum than she expected, and she returned his smile, pleased with the effort he was making at their *'new beginning.'*

"Yes, it is," she said.

Still, they ate their food mostly in silence. There was only much two people could talk about when they needed to fill their bellies. It was only once they had started to nibble rather than gobble that either of them felt the need to talk.

"Why won't you tell me what happened to you?" she asked, knowing she was diving into a pool she couldn't hope to swim but not caring.

Leopold's nostrils flared, a simmer building low in his gut, and he didn't answer.

"I've told you everything about my life," she coaxed. "I know it's not as exciting, but we've both been through something I think is, if not the same, at least similar—"

He raised a hand off the table, his face puce. "You think what you've been through is anything like what happened to me?"

His tone scared Jolie more than the words themselves. Deceptively soft, with a flinty edge meant to cut to the bone, she knew if she didn't choose her next words wisely, he would snap.

"Of course not, Your Grace," she said. Her heart was pounding in her ears, limbs ready to run at any moment with the adrenaline coursing through her system. It took everything in her not to jump out of her chair and run from the dining hall.

"Whatever pain you think you're in right now, you at least know your family is alive and well! You can look in the mirror without being ashamed at what you've become!" Leopold was even more terrifying in that he hadn't gotten up from the chair. He slouched back in it, punctuating his words with his hand, stabbing it at her and slashing the air.

"I misspoke, sire, and I apologize," Jolie said, trying to blink away the tears that were blinding her. Her heart was pounding so hard she could feel her pulse in her eyeballs. "I beg you, let me rephrase—"

"No!" he yelled. "You said what you meant. You think there's some similarity between your story and mine? You think that you have any idea what loneliness is, when you can still go about in the daylight without inciting terror?"

"Please, calm down, Master, you're scaring me," Jolie said, her voice choked by the massive lump in her throat. She had just remembered Prince Leopold's threat to get Papa to come back. She was afraid to ask it with him in such a state, especially since he had refused to answer for his threats the night she'd arrived. But suddenly, she needed to know the answer like she needed air.

"Would you have killed my family if Papa or I hadn't come back that night?"

Leopold's face didn't just fall, it crumpled. His mouth hung open, his pique shattered by her question. This was not the reaction she had been expecting. "Why would I have ever said that?" he said, breathless.

"Papa said that was what you would do if neither of us returned. That you would find his home and kill his daughters and he would live the rest of his life knowing it was his fault they were dead."

"Is that what people in the village think of me?" Leopold dropped back down into his chair, the wood groaning under his weight.

"They call you a monster," she said. She was more afraid now that he had calmed than when he had raged at her.

"I was nothing more than a handsome boy when I was younger, now I am doomed to be a monster," he said, an ironic smile on his lips. "All because that's what others think of me."

"You've never come forward to tell anyone what really happened. One night, we have a royal family who govern us, the next we have a senate to elect and the king and queen are dead, their only son presumably so." Her voice grew stronger, "And then we see a beast stalking our village and are left to our own conclusions. My father said you threatened to kill his entire family if he didn't return on time. Did you or did you not say that?"

"I am not the monster your villagers speak of," Leopold said, his voice going soft again. His eyes flashed and she saw the danger in them. One more word from her and he might lose control altogether.

"I don't believe you," she said, unable to stop herself now. She was starting to think that her father had outright lied to her, if Prince Leopold's reaction was any indication, but she needed to be sure.

"Of course you don't," he stood again, walking away from her, one hand rubbing his forehead in disbelief. "Believe the father who betrayed you and sent you to serve a prison sentence in his stead. The father who, if I may remind you, squandered whatever chance you had at a good life. Or have you forgotten?"

That horrible feeling was building again, and he was afraid of what he might do or say. He kept himself across the room, sure he wouldn't hurt her but not willing to take the chance.

Jolie looked at him like he had slapped her. The stunned silence started to draw on, but his temper made sure he filled it.

"Your father lied to you, Jolie, about everything you thought you knew about him. If you weren't here right now, you would be in the street by now, wouldn't you?" he asked, the spoiled brat in him reveling when she flinched. "At least, you would know which day you were going to be. Am I right?"

Jolie knew he was but she'd be damned if she would admit it. Her father had his reasons for lying to her and Mireille. Pain bloomed afresh in her chest at the thought of never seeing him again, and she choked back a sob that was equal parts anger and sorrow. Two weeks and a couple of days wasn't enough time to come to terms with anything in life, and here Prince Leopold was rubbing salt in the wound.

"I was right before, when I said that all that witch had managed to do was give you a body to match your black heart and the soul of a devil," she hissed, leaning over the table toward him. He was four times as big as she was and could snap her back like a chicken bone, but she would not back down from anyone who called her family's honor into question.

Just as they had the first time, the words hit him like a club. The slow simmer that had been building within him boiled over, becoming a tidal wave of untenable rage. He grabbed the edge of the table with both hands, and with a roar, tossed it onto its side as if it were made of paper rather than oak. Candelabra went flying, hot wax forming pale white runners on the floor and the walls, food splattered in all directions.

Jolie backed away, unable to take her eyes off the prince as he loomed over the table, his breaths coming in great gusts. She wondered where the odd whistling sound was coming from until she realized it was the breath wheezing in and out of her own chest. Without another thought, she took off at a dead run for the Rose Room, not daring to look back.

Chapter 10

Mireille and Malcolm drank their tea in the kitchen, neither of them able to look at each other. In less than three weeks, Armand had deteriorated so much they were sure he wouldn't survive. They weren't even sure how they themselves were still alive after everything that had happened. Malcolm was arranging the sale of Armand's things, finding buyers for the house and land, and had already sold all but two of the horses. Last week, the Babineauxs had owned thirty fine riding horses, now they had just enough to pull a carriage.

Down the hall, three of the rooms were empty. All the furniture and artwork it had taken a lifetime to purchase, gone. Armand's study was emptied first, due to the simple fact it held the most valuable possessions in the house. The library had been next, then the drawing room. The bedrooms and nursery were still intact, but it wouldn't be long before they would be empty shells.

Malcolm had insisted they leave Jolie's room for now, in case she came home for her things. Mireille was unhappy that he had so easily come to her sister's defense, but was just too tired to complain about it right now.

Doctor Hervé Monscion had diagnosed Armand with pneumonia and pleurisy, and had said it was only a matter of time before the old man died. All that could be done was to make sure he was in no pain, so he was fed laudanum all day and night. The doctor said they would go in one morning and he would be gone.

"At his age, it's a miracle he's held on this long," Monscion said with a shake of his withered grey head before he left two days ago.

Everyone knew why he was hanging on like he did. Every time the laudanum wore off long enough for Armand to come out of his torpor, the only word on his lips was "Jolie."

****

Jolie stood on the Rose Room balcony, thinking of her family and wishing someone would come rescue her. Someone always climbed out of a window in the adventure novels she read. Jolie had climbed out the windows of her father's house dozens of times, just to see if she could. She was confident she could make it to the ground. With no rope in the room, and no time to put together a makeshift one out of the linens, she decided to see if the wall could be scaled. It sounded ludicrous, even to her, but she couldn't stay in this godforsaken keep another night.

The Rose Room was not a tower room like the prince's chamber, but the balcony was still a good fifty feet above ground. She hoisted herself onto the balcony rail and over, swinging her feet until she felt the edges of the stone blocks that made up the whole of the keep. They were as she had hoped, sturdy and rough, with enough uneven edges to give her good hand and toe holds.

Her only other option would be to wait until the middle of the night, but Prince Leopold didn't sleep well and could catch her even then. She screwed up her courage and took a fortifying breath.

The moment she went over the rail, the skies opened up and dowsed her in a frigid rain. Her lovely gown was soaked through in minutes and she could feel a rivulet of cold water running down her spine. Water ran off her skirt in torrents, splattering on the bricks. She looked between the balusters at the Rose Room, considering postponing her escape. But what if fear stopped her trying again later?

If she could just get down this wall, she could be out through the gap in the south wall and gone with no one knowing. She could be home with her family for supper.

Jolie couldn't bear to think about the consequences, because she didn't want to know what Prince Leopold would do once he discovered she had escaped. He would know right where to look for her, at her father's home or at Mireille's, so her freedom might be short-lived. It wasn't worth thinking about right now, though, when she had more pressing matters at hand. She could plan her way out of reimprisonment later.

The stones grew slippery under her hands, and more than once her slippers lost their grip. Not quite halfway down, she realized she'd been wrong about her own strength. The muscles in her arms and legs were burning, hot and angry over the exertion she was putting them through. The weight of the waterlogged gown threatened to pull her down. There was no way she could climb back up. She looked down and saw there was still fifteen feet to go before she could hope to survive a fall.

If she fell from here, she would die as soon as she hit the ground. Papa would never believe it wasn't Leopold's doing. While she didn't want to stay, she didn't want Armand coming after Leopold for her untimely death.

"Now what, smart girl?" she asked herself, resting her forehead on the cool stone. Water ran through her hair to her scalp, sending a chill over her skin. Her grip on the stone was tenuous at best, and she knew if she didn't come up with a plan soon she would fall.

****

Leopold paced the great hall. Willard stood a few feet away, his eyes following his master's movements through the huge room. If he tried to keep up with the big man, he would wear himself out before Leopold burned through half the energy this pique had built up.

"Master, take deep breaths," Willard implored his employer, the same way he had every time the young man lost his temper.

"I'm trying, Willard," Leopold said. Most times, he would say anything to appease Willard. This time, though, Willard could hear in Leopold's voice that the young man was trying to calm himself. His chest heaved with big gulps of air and he closed his eyes.

"Try to focus on something that makes you happy," Willard said. This was usually the portion of the argument where Leopold lost his head entirely, stomping off to the south tower and smashing a few of his possessions.

"I don't have anything to focus on, Willard. I'm trying but—"

"—Miss Jolie looked lovely at lunch, did she not?" Willard said. He'd seen how his prince's eyes widened at the dress she had worn. "With her hair up like that, one could hardly tell how wild it is when she leaves it down."

"I like it better down," Leopold said and even through the heavy facial hair Willard could see the blush that painted his face crimson. "Her hair suits her better that way, is all I meant."

Willard smiled and didn't comment when Leopold changed directions, turning his back on his valet and heading toward the kitchens. He walked fifteen steps, then turned on his heel and came back, changing the route but not the manic pace.

"Of course, Master," Willard said. "She did look lovely, though, didn't she?"

Leopold groaned, knowing the old man's persistence meant he'd already been caught out. "She looked pretty. What does that matter?"

"Has it not crossed your mind, Prince Leopold, that she might feel the same way you do?"

"I've long regretted the amount of freedom I've allowed you these last ten years. Maybe today is the day I drop you out the South Tower window and end my agony."

"Then who would go into the village and have a new pair of boots made every time you wear through one on your many walks through the forest, sire?" Willard's voice was even and calm, belying the sarcasm in his words. Leopold would no sooner throw him from the tower than he would walk, stark naked, through the Fontainbleu town square.

To that, Leopold had nothing to say. In his mind, even as he spoke threats to Willard, he was still picturing the way a single long curl had escaped from Jolie's coiffure and trailed down the back of her dress. "I don't dare hope she feels anything for me, Willard."

"You will only know her heart if you learn to control yourself. It will be of no benefit to us at all if the poor girl is too frightened of you to speak when you're near."

"I believe we don't have to worry about that. She had no compunction speaking to me this morning, even when I was angry."

That was true, Jolie had spoken her mind with aplomb at lunch. Willard took a cue from her and launched into his master. The soft approach he'd always taken wasn't working, so obviously he needed to change tactics.

"I'm getting very tired of having this conversation with you," Willard said, with enough force the prince took a step back. "Time is running out, master. Don't you understand that?"

It took a moment for Leopold to recover from his shock at having Willard speak at him in such a way. But when he did, Willard saw there was no change in the anger Leopold had allowed to take control again.

"How could I not, with everyone other than Jolie reminding me every five minutes?" Leopold asked.

"You are wasting what little time you have left by yelling at your only remaining chance at happiness," Willard hissed right back. "You will drive her from here, and then what?"

Leopold didn't have to work hard to imagine what would happen if he squandered this chance. He had thought of the consequences more than Willard knew, but now he would also have to imagine a life without Jolie in it, because he was certain she would not stay if they didn't break the spell. At some point, she would leave and he would have no reason to blame her.

"At this rate, we'll be lucky if she doesn't—" Willard paused and cocked his head to the side, sure he'd heard something in the distance. "Did you hear that?"

Leopold turned his head. At first he heard nothing. Then, off in the distance, toward the East Tower, came the sound of a voice. Through the sound of the driving rain, the words were hard to make out and the two men started for the north tower.

"HELP!" the voice called, and Leopold recognized it as Jolie's. His heart throbbed in his chest and he took off at a dead run for the tower.

Leopold leapt over the bed and to the balcony door, which stood open, the wind driving the frigid rain into the room in stinging sheets.

"Jolie!" he called, his voice booming through the forest.

"Master?" Jolie called, surprised. The last person she'd expected to come for her after this afternoon's debacle was the prince himself. His head popped out over the balcony rail.

"What are you doing?" he called, shocked at how far she'd gotten. "Damned fool, you'll be killed if you fall."

"I know that now!" she said through her teeth. "I can't make it all the way down, and I'm not strong enough to get back up, either."

Leopold looked around the room, searching for anything he could use to help her. The only things he could find were the drapes, but if she couldn't climb back she might not be able to hold onto them long enough for him to pull her up.

Willard came through the door, out of breath. "What's happened?"

Leopold was frantic, his whole body tense. His eyes were wide and bright, his voice tight when he spoke. "You were right. She tried to escape."

"What can I do?" Willard asked, at full attention now.

Leopold dropped to the floor and started taking off his boots. After that, he stripped off the hose that covered him from knee to foot. "I'm going after her," he said. "Get Rosalie in here to clean up the water. Fetch her dry clothes. Light a fire."

Willard nodded and started stacking wood for the fire, leaving Leopold to his task. He leaned out over the railing again and rolled up his sleeves to his elbows. "Jolie, I'm going to need you to move over to your right so I can come down to you."

Leopold tried to keep his voice calm, even though he felt like screaming. Taking a deep breath to quell the shaking in his limbs, he watched as she moved, so careful.

"You're coming down here? Are you mad?" she screeched even as she did as she was told.

"I could build a scaffold, if you'd rather," he said and as he looked down on her, saw her cheeks rise in a smile. "But it's wet and cold and I'm sure this will be quicker."

"Do you think now is the appropriate time to be funny?" she said, trying to keep the laugh out of her voice. Looking up, she saw him swing one hairy leg over the railing, then the other. She worried that his feet wouldn't grip the stones. Hers certainly hadn't, but he came down the wall like he'd been made to do it.

His eyes met hers before he answered her question. "I was just hoping to see your smile one more time today."

He got himself into position alongside her and braced himself. She saw not even the barest trace of his temper in his eyes, only concern in the way his brows quirked up. Concern for her, she realized as his hand crept toward hers on the stones.

"You have a beautiful smile, Jolie." he said. His eyes held on hers for a moment and she felt like that moment stretched on for hours.

As she looked into his brown eyes, she thought again of what her father had taught her about a person's eyes. If Armand's words were true, and she could truly see what Leopold's soul was made of, his was deeper than any she'd ever seen. His words echoed in her head, telling her over and over that she had a beautiful smile. Everything she had felt in the library at his touch and at the look in his eyes came back to her in a mad rush.

Leopold hadn't meant to say that out loud, but now that he had, he didn't regret it. He would give up his fortune to keep that smile right where it was. She was looking at him like she could see into him, past the exterior, and in that moment he felt like he was just a man.

Jolie's lips were turning blue in the cold and he was afraid she would shake herself right off this wall if he didn't get her inside, and fast.

Flattening himself against the wall, he took her left hand in his right and drew it up onto his shoulder.

"Climb onto my back, then I'll carry you up," he ordered, his voice calm.

Her eyes widened, but as a fresh torrent of rain hit the walls, she started to move. There was little space for her toes to fit as she slid along the stones. The slippers didn't help, and she had to reposition her feet more than once with each step.

"Let the slippers fall," Leopold said, his voice a low growl.

"I don't want to lose them." Even she heard how silly that was.

"I can buy you more slippers, Jolie." His hand tightened on hers in case she fell as she wriggled her feet out of the slippers.

Progress got a bit faster without the waterlogged footwear. She didn't realize she was resting her head on his arm, turning it against him with each step, until she came nose-to-nose with him at his bicep.

"Keep going, little one," he whispered with a smile. Papa had always called her that and at a flood of memories, her heart throbbed and she nodded. "Stretch over me and put your hand on my other shoulder."

She did and his hand closed over it, pulling her further across his broad back. Her right hand flew across his shoulder and she grabbed a handful of whatever was there. At his grunt, she started to let go, not wanting to hurt him.

"Hold on!" he bellowed, and she did. The handful she'd grabbed had been of the thick hair that covered his neck and shoulder beneath his shirt. It hurt but if she let go he wasn't certain he could stop her from falling. "Hold on to me."

"I'm so scared," she said, pulling herself up to grip him around the neck. Her feet dangled free and all of a sudden the twenty foot distance to the ground looked more like miles.

"I've got you, I promise," he said, looking at her over his shoulder as he started moving.

This close to him, Jolie was surprised at his sheer strength. A man's size only told half the story. She knew fisherman shorter than her who could lift crates that carried a hundred pounds of cargo. Papa had hired men who stood six-and-a-half feet tall who had to strain to carry a baby. Leopold was solid throughout his big frame, and as his muscles worked under her, she felt a thrill at the power in his body.

It was indecent to be so close to him, but rather than shame she felt a powerful sense of gratitude. A weaker man would drop her, or still be at the balcony planning her rescue as she fell when her own strength gave out.

As they climbed, she kept her grip on his neck tight. He scaled the wall faster than she could have, and it seemed to her that he didn't feel her weight on his back. His brow was furrowed in concentration, his lips pursed against his teeth. His hands fluttered over the bricks, searching for the best place to grip as he pulled them both up.

When they reached the balcony, Leopold slid his body against it. "Go on, I'm right behind you," he said, out of breath. Willard hadn't returned yet and she had to pull herself over the railing.

Leopold watched as she went over with a hand ready to help if she needed it. Once she was safe, he hauled himself inside, then closed the balcony doors behind them. Jolie flopped down on the padded bench at the end of the bed. Shaking, she stared into the grate at the flames.

Once she was situated, he held himself away, standing near the door. Twice, he started to speak but stopped himself with a whoosh of breath.

"Would you rather die than stay here with me?" he said when he'd built up the courage. In his voice was a childish disbelief, like he couldn't conceive of what her reasons could be.

"You have no idea how frightening you are, especially when I have spent years hearing stories about you," Jolie said, her shivering making her hard to understand.

"Ignorant superstition," he said, waving one hand and planting the other on his hip as he turned toward the door.

"That may be, but even the most ridiculous story becomes truth if you hear it often enough," she countered. The warmth of the fire was seeping into her body and she scooted closer. "Why do you do nothing to refute these stories?"

"What would you have me do, Jolie? Go into the village at midday to buy a ham?" he asked, satisfied when her eyes flew to his. "We both know what everyone would do. I'd be the next one in the pillory."

"What happened to you? The point I made at lunch still stands. Everyone in the village knew Prince Leopold was the most handsome young man in the country," Jolie said, turning toward him. "Society mothers were desperate for an audience for their daughters, just in case you sparked with one of them. What happened to make you like this?"

Someone was coming up the stairs, and Leopold wasn't about to start that tale now. He took a few deep breaths, preparing himself for the rush of anger he was sure her words would trigger once again. It didn't come.

Rosalie bustled into the room, her pouf of brownish grey hair bobbing and bouncing as she moved her girth to Jolie's side. "You poor dear!" she cried.

Jolie looked from her to where Leopold had been standing, but he had already gone. She stood to let Rosalie help her change. The old woman wanted her to recount the story of her attempted escape, but all Jolie could think about was Leopold, his quiet strength and the sadness in his eyes when she asked again about the night his parents died.

****

Darkness settled over the château and Leopold felt the familiar edgy anxiety creeping in. Willard and the other servants had retired to their rooms, and supper was laid on the table. He didn't expect Jolie to join him but he was hoping she would. She had questions and wasn't the kind of woman who would just let them go. He had plenty of his own to ask her, which was why he'd sent everyone away.

Sitting at the head of the table, with the other setting placed at the foot, he wondered to himself why there was always so much distance between people when they dined. There was no reason to be so far apart, and he stood, picking his plate up and carrying it down the table as he had at luncheon. Once that was done he brought all the serving dishes down as well.

Jolie stepped up to the door in time to see Leopold pick up the tall candelabra and carry it from one end of the table to the other. The place settings were across from each other at the foot of the table. An intimate setting, she thought, and one made for conversation. The thought made her nervous after what happened after their last talk, but she was also hopeful that this was a sign that he was ready to tell her his story. Her slipper scraped on the floor, making a soft sound, and his eyes met hers.

If one could ignore his immense size and the hair that obscured his features, he looked like any other aristocrat Jolie had ever met. In a black dinner jacket and breeches, his long hair knotted at the back of his head, he looked every bit the gentleman. Rosalie had brought her a cobalt gown to wear, and for once in her life she felt like a lady, as if some transformation was happening that this dress made possible.

Leopold couldn't take his eyes off her. If she'd been pretty in the printed dress this afternoon, she was breathtaking in this blue one. Her hair was down, flowing around her shoulders in tight little ringlets. Not a pin or comb in sight. *Much better*, he thought. He pressed a hand to his stomach, trying to calm the nerves that had erupted there at her appearance.

As she crossed the room toward the table, he circled the end and pulled her chair out for her. His father had done it for his mother many times. As a boy the gesture had always seemed antiquated and silly, but when her eyes met his and he saw the warmth there, he understood why Alaric had done it. He smiled too, pleased with himself, as he went back around to his seat.

She stood to pour the wine and he held up a hand, filling her glass first. Then he filled her plate, giving her the best bites of the dishes on the table before serving himself. Only when both their plates were filled did either of them speak, and then they both tried to talk at the same time.

"I meant to—"

"I'm sorry—"

They laughed together, and Leopold held out a hand, letting her speak first as he tucked into the meal.

"I meant to thank you, for rescuing me," she said.

"And I'm sorry for getting so angry at lunch. I was supposed to make a clean start with you, and I mucked it up in the worst way possible. I'm hoping to make it up to you." He said the words slowly, as if he had chosen them with great care. She took her first bite of the quail and he saw how pleased she was with it before she spoke again.

"When I noticed you were upset I should have walked away, but I pushed," she said. "So, I'm sorry, too."

"Might we start over?" he asked, the boyish hope in his eyes endearing. "Again?"

It wasn't easy for her, but she nodded.

"With one addendum, if I may."

"What is it?" she asked, her eyes meeting his again.

"I refuse to apologize for my honesty about your father. I know you love him, and you should, but you need to see what he did for what it is and stop romanticizing about what might have been and what used to be," he said. His eyes were locked on hers, soft and kind.

This was a hard truth to swallow, but she had to try. "Just because the truth is hard, that doesn't make it any less true," she agreed.

Leopold wanted to offer her the chance to talk to her father, to clear the air between them about everything that had been said and done, and knew that someday he might have to.

Not today, he thought. *Not just yet.* Instead, he could offer her something he'd never given anyone else. The only people who knew what he was about to tell her were either dead or had been in the Great Hall the night of his eighteenth birthday.

"I've struggled my whole life with my temper," he began, seeing how she came to attention, straightening in her chair, her plate forgotten. "I don't think my parents had any idea what a monster—"

He broke off mid-sentence when he realized the word he'd chosen. His jaw worked as he fought to continue and Jolie waited.

"—what a monster they were raising."

"I doubt you were all that bad," Jolie said, shaking her head. She was thinking of her own nieces and nephews, of course, and how they could have bad days and good. "Children can be difficult, but I don't think you were a monster."

Jolie's reaction was unexpected. She'd passed over his choice of words as if his appearance were of no consequence. *Remarkable,* he thought.

"You asked me a question earlier that I never got to answer," he said, and her pulse picked up. He took a long drink of wine, set the glass down, and twirled the stem in his fingers.

"You asked me one first," she said, hoping that if she told him something about herself he wouldn't be so reticent about his own story.

"Would you rather die than stay here with me?" He couldn't meet her eyes when he asked this time. Her answer was important, and she would have to frame her reply with caution.

"I wasn't thinking about that at the time. I was thinking only of the way you acted, and that I've never seen a grown man behave so abominably as you have the last couple of days," she said. Now was not the time to answer without thinking, and she allowed herself time to think before each word. "I was afraid of you."

Though they weren't unexpected, the words had a deep effect on Leopold, and his face fell. She was right, he had behaved like a man with no self-control. Again. He'd never had his own inflated sense of entitlement thrown in his face that way before. Including the frustration he'd caused his parents, he'd never paid any attention to what his behavior did to others. If he was ever to prove to anyone that he was more than the Beast-boy the witch had branded him as, he had to start now.

"I'm sorry I frightened you," he said.

"I appreciate your apology," she said, picking at a roll.

"When I heard you call for help, I've never felt such fear," Leopold admitted, his eyes dropping to his plate. "All of my anger just went away. I don't know why, but making sure you were safe was more important than being angry at you for confronting me."

There was a tenderness in his eyes that made her blush.

"I feel like I've spent half of our time together apologizing for being an ass," he said, biting his tongue so he wouldn't apologize for the curse.

There was that smile again, the one he'd told her he liked. She lit from within with that smile. He couldn't help but return it, but knew it wouldn't last long once he started to answer her question. He sat up in his chair and jerked the front of his jacket to straighten it.

Here it comes, she thought, unsure of whether she should lean forward or tell him to stop. Suddenly, she didn't know if she wanted to hear the story after all.

"On my eighth birthday, I was playing on the River Chaud with my parents when I saw a very old woman making her way down the bank," he began. "Instead of helping her on her way or offering her a smile, I threw stones at her and called her horrible names."

As he spoke, everything seemed to fall away and she saw the story unfolding before her as if she'd been there through the whole affair.

Prince Leopold came upon the old woman on the banks of the River Chaud. Upon seeing her shabby dress and ancient face he threw stones and made cruel remarks, his words and actions callous and unthinking of her struggle. That day, beside a babbling river and in the presence of the country's royal family she promised to return. He remembered her words as if she'd just spoken them.

"*Thou shall pass ten years growth from boy to man 'ere I return. A thousand prayers I shall say for thee, Beast-child. Thou shall suffer great if thou refuse to cast aside such childish prejudice. I will cast you to a hellish place, show you the ways of the Beasts and thou shalt recoil at thy own image.*"

The boy Leopold laughed and turned back to his playthings. The King and Queen knew better than to scoff at the old woman's words. Her reputation as a powerful magic bearer was without question.

"*As for thee and thy wife, who hast begotten the Beast-child, thou will not escape mine punishment for his cruelty. Should I return in ten years' time to find the same beast-boy in the skin of a man, 'twill signal the end of thy* chances to change him and thou both shall fall dead 'ere the hour strikes twelve."

The King and Queen's faces paled, their skin ashen, and they nodded.

"Thou wilt never betray to the Beast-prince of what I speak, or I shall strike him dead whence he stands as he harks to thy tale." She turned away, her old hips letting her complete the task only in the most peripheral sense. Pivot by slow pivot she moved, as if her hip bones were each hooked to chains attached to two different faraway points.

"Witch!" the Queen called. She took an involuntary step forward, reaching for the old woman. "Is there to be some reward for our son, should we be able to turn him into a fine man?"

With an effort, the old woman managed to turn herself around and face the royals again. Her eyes radiated a bright white glow like the flash of a flint spark in shadow. She tipped her head back and raised her twisted arms up over her head. A ball of light formed in her upturned palms, glowing so bright the King and Queen had to look away lest their eyes burn from its intensity.

The ball grew to fill the old woman's hands, then the light overflowed their scant limits and poured down over her body. As the edges of this dripping pool of light spilled down her shabby clothing and bent body, she transformed. Her skin smoothed, her eyes brightened, her bones straightened, her hair darkened and grew into a thick sheaf that ran halfway down her back in a heavy black fall.

In a moment's time, before Adele and Alaric stood a woman of such beauty as they'd never seen.

"I shall become a wife that will make him the envy of every royal family in the land. I will bestow to him wealth beyond his ability to measure, and bear him many strong sons. I will also vouchsafe a peace that will continue in this land for five hundred years. I will lay-to the last of mine own charm to create this reward for him."

Once again the dazzling light returned in her hands, this time moving upward as it stole away her beauty and youth. The hag brought her hands to her waist, heaving great exhausted breaths that showed the King and Queen just how much this sorcery cost her.

"If we should fail?" King Alaric's voice quavered as he spoke and the crone gave him a crooked, toothless smile. This man knew his son and how difficult their task would be.

"'Twill be as I said. Thou both shall die before the stroke of twelve on his eighteenth birthday, and he will know what it means to be the Beast of his playact." She turned, levering her body away from them, and they watched her

136

walk away.

Leopold stopped there, his eyes locked on the table.

"I never thought I'd see her again, but ten years later, on my eighteenth birthday, she came to the door, hoping to be let in. Willard took over when a footman got flustered. He tried to turn her away, but then she revealed her purpose." He swallowed the last of his wine, his eyes black as the night sky. "My parents never told me that she'd promised to return. I'd forgotten about her, to be honest. I didn't know how powerful she was, but everyone else did." He stopped, closing his eyes as the memory of her power washed over him.

"I came to the door, and proved myself to be everything she had accused me of being so long ago," Leopold said. Jolie thought he was purposely avoiding her eyes. He retold the tale for the first time since the night it had happened, and Jolie saw the old woman as if she already knew her.

The food had become like ash in Jolie's mouth, dry and tasteless, and her stomach turned.

"Mother and Father were terrified, but I didn't see it."

Jolie pushed her plate away, knowing what was coming next would explain the ungodly howls that had echoed through the valley that night. She'd only been thirteen herself at the time and she could still feel the hairs stand up on the back of her neck at the memory.

"I tried to turn her away as well, but then she told *me* her purpose. When I turned to look at Mother and Father I knew the old woman spoke the truth. She turned into a beautiful woman, more beautiful than I'd ever seen, and told me that if I had worked hard and improved my character, she would have been my reward." His whole body shuddered and he reached for the wine. "Prosperity for centuries, healthy sons, a beautiful wife, greater fortune than I could measure. If I had just grown up."

Jolie gulped down her wine, knowing that the worst was coming.

"She forged the ring and the mirror, then dropped dead on the steps. When I turned around, my parents were both dead on the floor," he said, his throat tightening. "I cried, I screamed, but that's when I started changing into—" he held his hands up. "—this."

Confusion was painted on all of his features, telling Jolie that he himself didn't understand everything that had happened to him. That he hadn't even had time to accept his mother and father's deaths was despicable, and she found herself angrier at the old magic bearer than anyone.

"All of a sudden I realized that my whole life, they had tried to warn me," he said, admitting this for the first time. "They'd tried to raise me into a better man, but along with everything else I was, I was stubborn. And every time one of them tried to correct me, the other would reward me for my horrible behavior. I was a beautiful child, grew into a handsome man, as you heard, and I was untouchable. I was a prince, I could do whatever I wanted with no consequence. I thought nothing could ever happen to me, and I thought I would always have the world at my fingertips." Fat tears rolled down his cheeks, running a zigzag pattern through his beard. "Why change when I already had everything?"

"Is there any way you can reverse the spell she cast that night?" Jolie asked.

The eyes that had been averted so far locked on hers, and an odd expression came over Leopold's face, at once hopeful and lost. "Some things were possible, but I'm afraid their time has passed. It is only a few days until my twenty-eighth birthday, and at midnight on that night, the curse will be permanent."

"Permanent? You mean, you'll stay like this—"

"—forever," he cut her off and for a moment she saw that flare of anger like she had at lunch. It faded after just a moment, though, and she was relieved.

Such a fantastic story, one she wasn't sure she could believe, and he must have seen something in her eyes. "Will you come with me? I want to show you something."

"Of course," she said, nervous at his sudden energy. He rounded the table and offered her a hand. She tucked her fingers into his huge fist and he led her toward the south tower.

At the foot of the stairs, he hesitated. "These stairs lead to my bedchamber. If you would rather not join me without a chaperon, I will wake Willard or Rosalie."

When he looked at her, his eyes were still pinkish from his tears and she thought she would do just about anything to take them away. The thought made no sense, but neither did anything else that had happened in the last three weeks. Still, it took a lot of courage for her to say what she said next. "I trust you."

Leopold stood up a little straighter, his chest puffed out and a smile spread across his face. He let her lead the way, glad that he'd thought to clean the room out when she'd arrived.

"When I was six years old, I started coming up here to hide. After a while, Mother and Father turned this into my room. I hated climbing all these stairs but I liked being separated from everyone." He stopped in his tracks, a foot hovering. "I suppose that even then, I felt I was better than anyone else."

"No one should be condemned for their actions as a child," Jolie said, tossing the words off almost as an afterthought and Leopold knew she believed them. The only words that come that easily are the truest ones.

They'd come to the top of the staircase and he had to reach over her shoulder to help her shove the door open. The globe on the wall caught her eye and she went to it, hand outstretched. "Is this the rose?" Her voice was breathless with wonder as her fingertips brushed over the glass.

"Yes," he said, leaning against the door frame. Willard would read him the riot act if he did so much as touch her hand in this room, so he kept his distance. It was odd having her in here, but an oddity of a pleasant sort. Butterflies fluttered in his stomach, his heart tapped out a rapid rhythm in his chest, and the palms of his hands felt clammy. There was an apprehension building within him, a jumpy anticipation, like his heart knew something his head didn't.

On the table just inside the French doors that led to his balcony, the silver ring rested. As she approached, the little metal band jumped up to stand on its edge. With a smile, she looked up at Leopold. "Why does it do that?"

"If I knew the answer to that, I would tell you," he said, smiling.

"The old witch must have been very powerful," Jolie mused. She walked around and around, taking her time as she looked at everything in the room on her way back to him.

Jolie stopped just inches away, her eyes on his. "I'm sorry this happened to you," she said. She lifted her hand and touched his cheek. At her touch, his eyes closed and he took a breath that was more than a little unsteady. "Goodnight, Master."

"Goodnight, Mademoiselle Babineaux," he said. She took a few steps down before she heard him say, "Call me Leo."

She'd stopped when he'd said it, so he knew she'd heard. Her footsteps resumed and he heard her whisper, though he knew she was sure he couldn't hear her.

"Leo."

Chapter 11

Quentin watched through his spyglass as the huge creature came
down the old Tremonde Road again. He was hidden in a tree forty
yards down the road, concealed by heavy branches. Thomas had been
good on his word, and had tied a black handkerchief to a tree at the
entrance of the trail. Quentin had followed the Grey Man up the road
the led to the front gate, but he needed to know every route the animal
took.

Knowing your quarry is the surest way to a successful hunt, he'd
learned from his father. He could hear the words in the old bastard's
droning voice now, if he thought hard enough.

Quentin waited while the creature lumbered toward him, headed
for the River Chaud. Contrary to all the talk, the thing rarely came into
the village, if ever.

Damned aggravating, it was. If he could catch it in the village and
either snare it or kill it there, it wouldn't be nearly as much work to
show everyone what he had done. He could simply tell the constable of
his triumph and lead him to the thing. By the time his parents got
home, their youngest son would be an embarrassment no longer. He
would be a hero in this sleepy little town, able to marry Jolie as planned
and take over not only his own fortune but hers as well.

The latest rumors running through Fontainbleu were about the
sudden sale of property and chattels that Malcolm McHenry and his
wife Mireille had been conducting. Good prices, too, from what
Quentin had heard. Why they were selling off old man Babineaux's
things was a mystery to most of the people Quentin had talked to, but
what difference did it make?

The old man was sick, possibly dying, and they had no need for
his house or possessions if Jolie was trapped here for the rest of her life.
The other possibility that occurred to him was that they were selling it
all off to move him in with them. That pompous solicitor, Pierre, hadn't
said what was wrong with Armand, just that the old man was sick.
Maybe it was bad enough to warrant special in-home care. Malcolm
couldn't stay away from his work forever.

There is a rational explanation for everything, Quentin told himself,
even as a little voice niggled him that he was missing the real reason.
He refused to think that shrewd old man Babineaux had driven himself
to penury. His other reasons made more sense.

The Grey Man started to walk out of sight around a bend in the road and Quentin shinnied down the tree as fast as he could without breaking something. Once on the ground, he ducked into the trees and started tracking, his footsteps silent even in the crunchy fallen leaves. The rain last night helped, softening the ground cover so his feet made no noise as he walked.

The hulking beast kept up its slow, ambling pace until it reached the shore of the river, then it plunked down on the ground. If he'd thought to bring his bow, the monster's broad back gave Quentin a perfect shot. One arrow between the big thing's shoulder blades would at least leave it grievously injured, if not kill it outright.

Quentin held up an imaginary bow in his hands, aiming down his arm, imagined nocking the arrow, drawing the string against his cheek, taking perfect aim, and loosing the arrow into the monster's back. He even made a soft little *pew* sound with his tongue against his teeth, then had to duck as the Grey Man turned toward the sound.

Quentin dropped to the forest floor, clamping his hand over his mouth to stifle a laugh that would surely get him found and ruin this whole plan before he'd even gotten started. There was still too much work to be done, too many things he had to get right before his parents came home and ruined everything.

When the monster turned to face the river again, Quentin stood and pointed a finger at its back.

"Soon," he whispered, then left the way he'd come.

****

Leo heard the soft sound and the word his pursuer had said as clear as if the stupid boy had been standing in front of him. He'd known, once again, that the blonde boy was behind him this whole time. Many better men had tried to best him at this game. All had failed, and this pup was no exception. Thanks to the magic bearer's hand mirror, he knew who the boy was without the boy having even an inkling that Leo had seen him.

Quentin Garamonde, the boy who wished to marry Jolie, and reminded Leo so much of the young man he used to be. He didn't know why the boy followed him, or what he wanted to accomplish in doing so. But if he hadn't been sure he was going to find out eventually, that whispered, "Soon," had confirmed it.

Not tired enough by half, he stood and paced the river bank, working through whatever thoughts needed hammering. Of course, the only thing he could think about was Jolie. Throwing the table at lunch was a terrible thing to do, especially when he could have hurt her, but it had made him see how out of control he was. If he didn't work on himself, he could hurt or kill someone. The thought of his actions harming Jolie made an unpleasant warmth bubble in the pit of his stomach.

The moment she'd run out of the dining hall, he'd known he had no more time to learn how to control his anger. He either had to do it or let her go and with her, the chances of ever breaking the curse. He would never be able to bear it if she was injured by his own actions, or worse yet, if he lost control and did something that – it didn't bear thinking about.

There was a light in Jolie he wanted for himself, but what was more, he wanted to see it *in* himself. The moment they'd shared in the library, with such an innocent touch, had lit a flame within Leo that he'd never felt before. If he didn't work very hard to make himself a better man, right now, it could blow out. It was a fragile thing, and it needed everything he had left in him to keep it lit. Jolie would help, but only if she was able to stay, and she wouldn't if he didn't take himself to task and take this curse seriously.

How many times had Willard told him there was very little time left? He knew it, but had believed for so long that there was no hope for him to change, there was no point in keeping track of the days. Until now. Until Jolie. She'd come to him not only a woman of beauty but one of substance. One who refused to be cowed by a man whose, as she had so eloquently put it, 'outsides matched his insides.' Jolie didn't let him push her around, didn't just accept him for who he was but wanted him to improve. She had given him more chances than he deserved from her already. And the time for chances was running out.

His birthday was in just a few days, and if he was going to break the spell, he had a lot of work to do.

Leopold dropped to his knees in the wet, cold loam of the riverbed, bringing his hands up in prayer for the first time in so long he couldn't remember the last.

"Lord, I pray for strength," he whispered. He felt foolish, praying with his knees in the mud like this, but he figured he needed all the help he could get, and whose help was stronger and better than the

Almighty's?

"I pray for strength, and for the chance to prove that I am a better man than I once was," he said, still in a whisper. "Keep Jolie safe, and keep her family in your right hand, for their loss would cause her immeasurable grief. And hers is a suffering I cannot bear.

"If I fail to prove to her, and to the rest of the world, that I am not the selfish child I used to be, I will gladly let her go and provide her with a good living for the rest of her days. Do what you will with me should that come to pass, just keep her safe," he said, then took a moment to try to remember how his mother had always ended her prayers. "In the Lord's name I pray. Amen."

Leo crossed himself and stood. He didn't feel as if he were a changed man, but he felt lighter, as if voicing his concerns and hopes, and making promises, had eased his burden. Promising to the Lord that he would fix himself made him accountable to see that it would be done. And he aimed to see that it would be.

Still not tired enough to sleep, he headed back anyway. He was hopeful, truly hopeful, for the first time in almost ten years. He didn't know if it was the prayer or knowing that in a few days, his fate would be decided no matter what, but it was like he could see a light after a long walk through a dark wood.

A noisy part of him kicked up a fuss that the real reason was the way Jolie had looked at him tonight, and the way she'd made him feel when she'd whispered his given name, but he wasn't hopeful enough to believe that. Yet.

****

Music played, soft and slow at first, in the background. Trilling notes from the flutes and high, plaintive strains from the violin prickled against her skin like sentient things. Her skin broke out in goosebumps and her spine straightened with anticipation.

The guests danced and swayed, their arms akimbo with their hands on their hips and their heads cocked awkwardly to the side as if they were listening to something above them. Their movements were jerky, and Jolie realized they were moving not to the music, but to the ticking of the gigantic black Comtoise clock.

The music suddenly grew louder and louder, blaring in her ears as the band played their instruments to a discordant rhythm. The clock's ticks and

144

tocks grew louder, too, until she thought her head would explode. She opened her mouth but couldn't hear the sound of her own screams.

Booming footsteps added to the din, and Jolie landed on her knees on the wood floor, arms over her head and her nose buried in her skirt. The footsteps stopped directly in front of her and at the same moment, the music stopped. The ticking of the clock quieted back to normal, and all the guests froze in place.

Jolie knew without looking that it would be the handsome stranger again, with his beautiful face and soft brown eyes. When she met his eyes, it was definitely him, but when he tried to speak to her, nothing came out but the dull roar of waves hitting the shore, like he was the voice of the sea.

Confused, he cleared his throat and tried again, but the sound didn't change. His face grew concerned, but every time he tried to speak to her, that same roaring sound was all she could hear. Panicking, he reached a hand to her, that same rapidly wilting rose in it as last time, only now when it finished its quick death, just three petals remained on the bloom.

'Three days, Jolie!' he mouthed to her, and it took her a moment to understand. He held up three fingers and mouthed the words again.

"Three days until what?" she asked, reaching for his outstretched hand. He took her hand in his, the rose between them, and she pricked herself on a thorn.

Pulling her injured hand away, she saw bright red blood on the palm. Without permission from her own mind, her hand went to her right ribs, smearing her blood on her immaculate white gown.

Hoping the stranger had an answer, she looked at him again, but in his place stood a leering woman who looked too old to still be living. Stooped over, holding onto a gnarled walking stick as though her life depended on it, the old woman took one look at Jolie and cackled, opening a wet, overlarge mouth missing all of its teeth, the laughter silent.

"Three days," the old woman said in a musical, sing-song voice, then vanished.

The handsome stranger was nowhere to be found. Jolie looked down to where she'd smeared blood on her dress again and saw blood pouring out of it in buckets, as if from a large wound.

Looking up again, she saw that the stranger had returned, the front of his usually impeccable shirt splattered with crimson. She checked herself once more, and all the blood was gone, her dress as perfect as if nothing had ever happened. The cut on her hand was gone as well. Instead, the stranger had a gaping gash low on the right side of his chest, and she could hear a wet, *sucking sound coming from the wound.*

The man tried to speak, but all that came out of his mouth was blood. Trying again, he mouthed words to her.

'Marry me,' was all he said before he, too, vanished.

The music started back up again—

—jarring Jolie from her sleep. The dreams kept getting stranger and stranger every night. She'd never had dreams that continued a story like this, or repeated themselves so much. Same guests, same costumes, same place, but what was changing was the urgency of the dreams.

In the first dream, the atmosphere had been weird, but fun. She had had that dream every night for the first two weeks of her imprisonment. It was only when she had left the Rose Room and started to participate in her own prison sentence that they began to change.

Now they were starting to scare her. Blood, ticking clocks, warnings about how many days were left until...who knows what?

Brain fog wasn't letting her think just yet, but she knew the prince's birthday was in three days, so maybe the dream was just trying to make sure she didn't forget it. She already knew what it meant, that if he didn't break this curse on that day, he was stuck the way he was forever.

"Just another fact of your life, now, Jolie," she said to herself. It was still dark outside and she wondered if Leo was still out and about or if he had returned yet. It wasn't proper to go looking for him, with all the servants asleep in their quarters, but she'd already reconciled with the fact that just being here with the prince had left her reputation in tatters the minute the door closed.

She wrapped herself in a robe and left the Rose Room, slipping on a pair of silk slippers as she went. The corridor was dark and as soon as the door closed behind her, she realized she hadn't thought this through. Holding her hands out before her, she tried to feel around for any landmarks. To get to the dining hall, all she had to was turn right and walk about twenty feet to find the breezeway.

Why did she not bring a candle with her from the room? Why did she only think of it now, when she couldn't even find her way back to the room? She could be stuck in the corridor until sunrise. *More importantly,* she wondered, *why was tonight the night the candles on the wall decided not to light when I walked into a dark room?*

The curtains didn't open either. For weeks now, she'd heard them whip open at night to allow moonlight in, and she'd never seen the candles on the wall without a flame even in the day. When she looked toward the east doorway into the Great Hall, there was no glow from the ever-present fire in the great fireplace at the northeast end of the room. Was the château's magic fading as it counted down the days until Leo's birthday? Was what power the magic bearer had used on this curse starting to weaken?

That thought made her heart do a funny thump in her chest, and she kept moving, sure the recalcitrant organ might stop altogether. She felt along the wall to keep her bearings, going slowly so she didn't trip over anything. As she got about halfway to the breezeway, she heard footsteps. Not heavy ones, like Leo's, but ones that were much lighter, like someone trying to move silently.

They moved too quickly to be Willard's, and Rosalie's were lighter still. Jolie supposed they could be Micah's, but even if they were she'd never heard his to compare and confirm. She froze, praying that whoever it was hadn't heard her making her way through the halls.

Jolie waited through eight breaths without hearing another footstep—her heart wouldn't let her wait through the full ten—then started on her way again. She lifted her feet off the floor so she didn't make noise, and moved as slowly as her muscles would allow.

Holding her hands out in front of her again, she walked a half dozen steps before she heard them again. Soft, skittering footsteps, like a pair of leather soles on the stone floor of the corridor. She felt a breeze go by her, jostling the curls that brushed her forehead. The hairs on her arms and the back of her neck stood on end, and a full-body prickle stole over her skin.

Freezing again, she sucked in a breath through her nose, forced herself to hold it for a beat, then let it out slowly through her mouth. Her body was tense, waiting, and somehow she knew she was going to touch something the moment before her palms flattened on the fabric of a person's clothing.

Knowing it was going to happen didn't stop the blood-curdling scream that tore from her lungs.

Jolie sucked in a deep breath to let another one fly when she heard chuckling. Soft, so she almost didn't believe she'd heard it, but it was accompanied by those same footfalls she'd been hearing through the corridor. They ran away behind her, down the way she'd come.

Collapsing against the wall, she tucked herself into a ball and wrapped her arms around her knees. Heavy footfalls were coming toward her from the south, and even though she knew whose they were, she still steeled herself as Leo approached.

"Jolie!" he called, his voice as frantic as it had been when he'd rescued her from her ill-fated escape attempt. He came around the corner and saw her on the floor.

"What happened?" He knelt in front of her, his big hands gentle on her face as he turned her head to look for injuries.

"Someone is here, a man," she said, her voice coming out in sobs.

"Where did he go?" Leo asked, chucking her under the chin to lift her eyes to his.

Unable to speak, she pointed and Leo scooped her up off the floor. He took her to the Rose Room and set her down on the bed. Moving so quickly she wasn't sure how he didn't stumble over the furniture, he searched the room. Once he was sure it was safe, he locked her inside, leaving without a word. She lit a lamp for herself and tried not to cry, or obsess over looking around the room a thousand times in Leo's absence.

When he returned, after what seemed like an eternity, the look in his eyes told her he had found nothing. He closed the door and leaned his back against it, his barrel chest rising and falling with his heavy breaths.

"Did you see this man?" he asked once he'd caught his breath.

"No," Jolie said. "I only heard footsteps and I touched him, which is why I screamed. Then, I heard a chuckle."

"A chuckle?" Leo's brow pinched and one corner of his mouth lifted. He was remembering his near encounter with Quentin on the riverbank. That whispered '*Soon*' rang in his ears. Not wanting to scare Jolie any more than she already was, he pulled the corner of his mouth up in a smirk.

"You don't believe me, do you?" she asked, pulling herself up straight in her indignation.

"Why would this person chuckle? It seems an odd thing to do for a person skulking around at night. And how do you know it was a man?" His expression didn't change, and she was sure he was only amused by what had happened.

"The château protects itself, doesn't it? It wasn't Rosalie or Willard, that I'm sure of," Jolie snapped, crossing her arms over her

148

chest. "Unless your groundskeeper likes to play jokes on women alone in the dark—"

"—the halls are never unlit overnight," Leo said defensively, his back straightening. This was news to him. When he'd heard her scream, he'd run so fast he hadn't had time to notice.

"Isn't it? Look out in the hall and see for yourself," she said, aiming a hand at the door he was leaning against. "I went into the hall looking for you, and it is as dark as a tomb out there. How did you not notice?"

"I see well at night, so I guess I've never paid any attention. I don't need the light, so I don't look for them," he mused. "And I was rather in a hurry when I came here." He worked the doorknob and leaned out of the doorway, looking down the hall.

"It makes me wonder if the magic is starting to fade now," Jolie said as he leaned back in and closed the door.

"That still wouldn't explain a stranger in my home," he said, but as soon as the words were out of his mouth, he knew he was wrong. "If the magic is weakening, whatever wards have been keeping people out all this time must be doing the same." When he looked at her this time, his eyes were softer, apologetic, and there was no amusement left in them.

Jolie didn't know what to say to that, but didn't feel the satisfaction she normally would have at the quick turnaround his thoughts had taken. This was just another reminder that there was a great chance he would spend the rest of his life as the Grey Man. And now, on top of that threat, there was a brand new one: the threat that a person could easily get into the château.

"I never should have told Willard to allow the workers to leave for winter with the wall unfinished," Leo mused to himself. "You're not safe here."

"Neither are you," Jolie pointed out.

Leo almost laughed, but instead he opened his arms, reminding her of his immense size. Even if a militia were to breach the wall, they would be hard pressed to defeat this man. "I will not go outside the walls anymore. It is my duty to protect you while you are here."

"Protect a prisoner?" Jolie said, smiling to herself. Leo winced, as if what she said physically hurt him.

"I never said part of your punishment here was to suffer poor treatment or be in danger," Leo said. "I would like to think that while you've been here, I've shown you kindness and care."

She couldn't argue with that, but she could remind him of a few things. "You have thrown a table in my presence, and yelled at me more than once, but overall, yes, you have been a kinder warden than I expected."

"I will say that I'm sorry every day of my life if you would just ask me to," Leo said, his eyes so sad in his hairy face that she knew how sorry he really was.

Jolie smiled, wrapping her arms around her body a little tighter. "Thank you, for coming to my aid tonight."

"You are welcome, as always," Leo said without hesitation.

There was something different about him tonight, Jolie thought. He stood up straighter, keeping his shoulders wide rather than sunken, like he was no longer ashamed of his size. When he looked at her, he didn't look away when she met his eyes, holding her gaze. He looked to her like a man who had made a decision that pleased him.

"Did you go on one of your walks tonight?" she asked, wondering if that was why he looked so much better.

"Yes I did, to the river," Leo said.

"Willard said that you go every night because you want to wear yourself out so you can sleep," Jolie said, hoping to lead him to reveal more about himself. It was hard to figure the man out when he guarded himself so tightly, but she thought tonight he might be more willing to open up to her.

"That is part of the reason, yes," he said, his eyes flickering away for a short moment that made her think that was all she was going to get out of him. "I have nightmares, Jolie. I walk so I can be too tired to dream when I return."

At first, she didn't think much of the revelation, but his eyes jumped to hers again and held, like he was waiting for her to catch onto something. When she did, when she realized what this man might have nightmares about, she closed her eyes, wishing she'd never asked.

"I'm so sorry, Leo," she said, calling him by his given name for the first time since the day he'd asked her to. She wanted his torment erased, and on instinct, she stood and crossed the room to him. She couldn't give him a proper hug, her arms would never wrap all the way around him, but she pressed as close to him as she could, her hands gripping the front of his great cloak.

Leo tried to remember the last time someone had hugged him and couldn't. It must have been when he was a child, before his behavior made him the unlovable creature he'd become. He knelt and buried his face against her shoulder, closing his eyes as her arms wrapped around his thick neck.

Leo left his arms at his sides, afraid he would crush her, but he wanted more than anything to hold her. If this curse never lifted, he thought his worst regret would be that he never got the chance to wrap Jolie in his arms like she was doing to him now.

"How long have you been having these dreams?" Jolie asked. "Since the first night?" She couldn't tell if he was crying, but his voice sounded choked when he answered, like he was trying not to.

"Until you came, I had them every night," he said. "But since I met you, my dreams have been different."

So have mine, she almost said, but decided to keep the thought to herself. She stepped back, letting him go, and looked into his big brown eyes. There was moisture in them, and his jaw was clenched so tightly that she wondered how his teeth didn't crack under the strain.

"I don't like seeing you hurt," she admitted, patting his hairy cheek. "I wish I knew how to help you."

Fall in love with me, he didn't say, and wasn't sure whether he wanted to laugh or cry. It sounded so simple but, at the same time, so impossible. Looking into her beautiful eyes, filled with concern for him, he would have given up every ounce of wealth he possessed if he could find a way to make her love him. He had a feeling she felt something for him, as he did for her, but didn't know what those feelings between them were and what difference they would make. He had a real fear of only getting part of the way there and having to let her go, as he'd promised.

Now that she was here, he didn't know how he would handle watching her leave, but he knew if he was never going to be able to live as just a man again, he couldn't keep her here, either. The thought came to him that he should tell her what would break the curse, but if he was wrong and she felt nothing, she could just as easily avoid him until the time came. That possibility sounded even worse. Better to leave things as they were, then decide once they had a result of some kind.

Leo said nothing, but offered her a smile that still seemed a little sad. Jolie stood on tiptoe and pressed a kiss to his forehead, the hairs there tickling her nose. "I bid you goodnight, Prince Leopold."

Leo lifted his hand and cupped her face, as he had in the library, and felt the same thrill shooting through his body as it had that morning. Judging by the way she tilted her hand into his palm, she felt it as well, and he smiled.

"Goodnight, Jolie. Sleep well," he said, then turned and left the room. She heard the lock click behind him and for the first time didn't feel threatened by being locked in her room, but protected. This huge man was doing what he felt was his duty, keeping her safe, and despite all the goings-on that night, as soon as her head hit the pillow, she fell into a deep, dreamless sleep.

****

If only Quentin could have seen Jolie's face when he'd finally found her! He would have given up a significant portion of his inheritance to see that.

After days of testing the invisible barrier that kept him out of the grounds, he'd finally been able to get past the stone fence tonight. He should have waited until daylight, when he could have gotten around the keep without a torch, but dousing the flame had been worth it to meet his wayward fiancée fumbling her way through the halls.

As he walked back to the village, taking the main road that wound down Château Hill to Fontainbleu, he couldn't pry the smile from his face. Before too long, he would be able to walk right in, bold as you please, and kill the Grey Man as he slept.

The monster had nearly caught him making his exit, but he'd managed to duck out the front door before it caught up with him. Once he was outside the château, he found his way by moonlight.

He'd heard the beast speaking to Jolie as he'd run through the corridor, the concern the thing had for her as he'd asked what was wrong. He wondered to himself if she had some sort of feelings for her jailer.

That would be just like a woman, he thought. *Serving a prison sentence and she goes and falls in love with the creature that's keeping her prisoner.*

Fickle woman probably wouldn't even be grateful when Quentin freed her. But Jolie would marry him, of that he was sure. She would be his bride after he went to all this trouble to free her. Women clamored over heroes. Everyone knew that.

After he went to all this trouble, she would have to marry him. And he would ensure that the world knew how much work he'd put into this endeavor. The night the Grey Man was killed would go down in history as a night of legendary heroism, and Quentin's name would be written in books as the man who triumphed over a child-killing, woman-stealing monster.

Jolie could never refuse him after that.

There was much to do before he would be ready to go to the castle to complete his task, and the next few days would be critical. He would go under cover of night and hide weapons on the grounds, so that he could get to them easily even if he were being pursued.

If the beast believed Jolie that there had been an intruder in Château Villeneuve tonight, he would be on his guard, and getting in again might not be possible. Quentin would have to try, though, because if there were weapons within those walls, he could vouchsafe himself an almost sure victory.

This would take some planning, and he picked up his pace for home to do just that.

Chapter 12

Armand's condition stabilized over the following day. A second physician, Guillaume LaFitte, had taken up temporary residence in the Babineaux home to tend to Armand at night after Malcolm and Mireille fell into bed, exhausted after their own shifts as nursemaids.

"Do you think we should try to reason with someone at the château?" Malcolm asked, voicing a concern he'd had for several days now. He had a suspicion that Armand was only hanging on in hopes of seeing his youngest daughter again, but the old man's suffering had gone on long enough. As much as it would hurt to lose his father-in-law, he couldn't stand to watch the old man's agony any longer.

"I've wondered that myself, but was afraid to mention it," Mireille admitted. Her blue eyes were rimmed with red from lack of sleep. Henrietta was a godsend with the children, but between the children and Armand, no one was getting enough rest. "I know he wants her here, but I'm afraid that if he sees her, he'll let go, and I'm not ready yet." Her throat closed off and Malcolm reached for her hand.

"I understand, lass, but I think he'll let go one way or another," he said, giving her hand a hard squeeze. She stepped into his arms and he wrapped her in a hug.

"I don't understand how she could run off like that," Mireille said and Malcolm rolled his eyes. "At the worst possible time, with Papa so ill."

"You heard what your father said, she had no say in the matter," Malcolm said. "We have no reason to believe otherwise, and I'll not hear another word about it."

He pulled her into the empty study and away from prying ears of children and servants. "Let's wait another day or two, then one of us will go and request an audience. If we tell them about Armand, they should let her see him. We can promise she will be brought back as soon as possible and we will be held to that promise, but they must let her go. Even the Grey Man can't be so cruel as to keep her from her ill father."

Mireille nodded, but in her eyes Malcolm still saw his wife's jealousy and scorn. As she left the room, he looked skyward as if searching for guidance. No matter what happened, these next few days were going to be some of the most difficult of his life. His wife would make sure of it.

****

"I feel ridiculous," Leo said as he tied the cravat for the thousandth time. "Why must we insist on dressing, and redressing, and redressing, every time we change the pace of our walk?"

"It is convention, sire," Willard said on a sigh. "And you might as well learn how to do it well. After all, you will rejoin society in just a few days' time. You must relearn all the things you took for granted before."

"How are you so sure that the curse will be broken?" Leo asked, untying the cloth and starting over.

"I know what I've seen so far, and a little push is all you two need to do all the work on your own," Willard said. He became· very interested in his cuticles and Leo smiled, knowing the older man was going to be the one doing the pushing.

"What can I do to help?" Leo asked, finishing the tie and standing back to admire his work in the mirror.

"You need to be interested in her, not just in her looks but in her mind. Jolie is very smart, and she desires things beyond the village and her home. Perhaps you could encourage her interests," Willard said, standing up from the settee to pace the floor.

"She enjoys reading," Leo said and heard Willard scoff behind him.

"Yes she does, but you've given her an enormous library to read from," the valet said. "It must be something bigger, something she dreams of. Maybe something her father couldn't provide for her, or that she knows may not be possible anymore, now that she's here."

Leo thought, trying to remember every word she'd ever said. When it came to him, his smile was one of pure bliss. "She has always wanted to travel, ever since she was a little girl." His face fell. "But how can I give her that as a gift?"

Willard held up a hand as he paced, one finger pointed toward the ceiling. "What has stopped her? Her father being a merchant, he could have sent her on one of his ships, with a proper chaperon of course."

"Her father would never allow her to go and many seamen think women are bad luck on ships," Leo explained, remembering what Jolie had said. "And she said once she marries, she will lose all ability to go, which I don't understand entirely."

"A woman must give in to her father's demands as a girl and once

155

she marries she must give in to her husband's. Once he dies, which men almost always do before their wives, she must then hope her son will care for her until she dies," Willard explained. "It is the way of the world. Imagine how she feels, almost on the shelf and already she feels she's accomplished nothing, and if she gets married none of her dreams will ever come to pass. Her best hope will be that her children will achieve them in her stead."

Leo wanted to toss off what Willard had said as so much manure, but he knew it was all true. He had never thought about a woman's life this way, but now that he was, he understood how Jolie felt a little better. The two men paced the floor together in silence as they both tried to think of something to do for Jolie.

"It must be personal," Willard mused.

"Of course, but what can I give her? A ship?"

"It's not a terrible idea, considering you could commission it, and a crew," Willard said. "But for now, I think we need to think smaller. Perhaps something else that would mean a great deal to Jolie."

Leo thought over their conversations again, combing through every word trying to find one thing that he could do that would mean the most. Willard did the same, and when he got the idea he tried everything he could to dismiss it, but knew how important it would be to Jolie.

"Her father just lost everything he's ever earned," Willard said and heard Leo's big boots crunching as he turned on the spot to face him. He turned himself around and met the master's eyes, which positively sparkled with excitement.

"Let's get to work, Willard," Leo said, running to the desk, already making plans.

****

Jolie was in the library again, with *The Meditations of the Emperor Marcus Aurelius Antoninus* open in her hand. The curtains were drawn behind her, but she'd had to do that herself today. It appeared that the château was losing every bit of its magic, and fast.

The book was fascinating— a look into the mind of a brilliant leader— but she just couldn't stay interested. There was such a change in Leo last night, and she couldn't quite put her finger on it. It made her angry, because she got the feeling the difference should be obvious, but

156

it wasn't. Confidence was part of it. She saw it in the way he stood and the fact that he seemed to have stopped trying to make himself look smaller. He seemed resolved, Jolie could see it in the way he seemed so sure of himself. But neither of those things were the whole answer.

The surprise in his eyes when she'd kissed his forehead was charming, as was the way he'd dropped to his knees for a hug. She wondered how long it had been since he'd been held in someone's arms, even in the mediocre way she'd been able to do the job. Intimacy was something she knew he must have sorely lacked these last years and she was glad she could give him that.

Acceptance of his situation, if he had come to that on his walk, could have instigated all those changes. If that was what had happened, she was glad for it. She just wished she knew what part she could play in ending this curse. There had to be something, but Leo held too many secrets close to the vest.

In the beginning of this sentence, she had been determined to just survive, believing that all she had to do was outlive her warden and she would be free. Unable to stand the interminable boredom that her life would have been filled with, especially considering the age of the man responsible for keeping her here, she'd looked to do more to help pass the time. Personal involvement with anyone else who lived here was not part of that goal.

Then everything had changed as she'd gotten to know Leo. He scared her at first, but after last night she could see now that there was more to him than the brutish creature he looked like. She regretted many of the things she'd said since she came here, and now wanted the fresh start Leo asked for as much as he did. If he was willing to change, she could be too.

At the thought of change, though, her mind wandered back to the white house in the village, currently filled with her sister's children. She wondered what her father was doing right now. He had sent her here, had manipulated the situation to make her think it was her choice, when there were no other options. Marrying Quentin would have been more of a prison sentence than the one she was serving, and something about the man made her think the one she was serving here was much easier.

Mireille had probably not stopped smiling since the day Jolie had been missed. Her sister would have been thrilled to learn that she was chained in a dungeon with no hope of escape, rotting away in some dank cellar like a common criminal. Despite Papa's mistakes with his fortune, she would still live a good life and Jolie would be stuck in this prison. If Father had told his eldest daughter who was master of this castle, Jolie had no trouble imagining how excited her sister was.

If only she could see them, just one more time, and know that they were all healthy and happy. Mireille would take care of Papa as he grew older, and Malcolm would make sure they always had a good life. If they thought of her less and less as time wore on, perhaps that was for the better, but Jolie wanted to know that her family was going to be alright. Not knowing was what hurt the most.

Willard walked by the library door and Jolie realized she'd heard him pass by more than once. She went to the door and leaned into the hall. The valet was walking toward the door that led to the rear courtyard, his greatcoat on and a hat on his head. He pounded his way down the hall, then out the door.

Well, that was curious, she thought. She'd never seen Willard leave the grounds before, though she knew Rosalie and Micah did for the shopping and other household needs. A personal errand for the prince, perhaps? Who knew, with all the odd things that went on around here.

From the other end of the hall, she heard Leo's heavy footfalls. When she turned, she saw him making his way toward her, his long legs carrying him down the hall rather quickly. His eyes were turned down at first, but he lifted his head and, a smile broke out across his face as he caught sight of her. The expression was so warm she thought no one would think him a threat if he'd ever deigned to use it in polite company.

"Jolie, I was hoping to see you," he said. "I need to borrow the ledgers from you for some time today. There is something I need to do."

Loathe to give them up, she stepped out of the library and headed with Leo toward the Rose Room. He was wearing the most conventional clothes she'd seen him in yet, all stiff with starch and clean as a whistle. Right down to the shine on his buckled shoes, she was willing to bet every piece was new and chosen by Willard. A cravat as stiff as a fireplace poker was tied around Leo's throat. She'd never seen him dressed so well.

"What do you need the ledgers for?"

"There are a few things I need to look over." Leo, if he were to keep his surprise for Jolie a secret, needed to be vague. He also needed to keep the ledgers from her, and any other accounting of what he was about to do, until the time was right. If everything he was planning could be handled quickly, he could tell her tomorrow, or the next day at the latest, but he had to keep this secret until then.

A chuckle escaped her and her head tilted back, he thought in amusement. "Of course, you need to check my figures, to make sure I'm doing everything correctly."

He jumped on that with both feet. "Yes!"

Surprised by the vehemence in his reaction, she shot a sidelong look at him. "I understand. I'm sure you did the same with Rosalie."

Not once, he thought, but didn't dare speak it aloud, too happy to have a plausible reason to take the books from her. "Of course. Must keep everyone honest," he said, hoping she didn't hear how tight his throat was on the lie.

If she thought he sounded odd, she didn't comment on it, but led him to her room, where he waited in the doorway while she plucked the most recent book off the neat stack on her writing desk. "Will you be needing any more of them?" she asked, handing him the volume.

"No, the most recent one will suffice," he said. He flipped the cover open, glanced at the first page, then snapped it shut.

There was a twinkle in his eye this morning. He stood in the doorway a beat too long, holding the book under his arm, a mysterious grin on his face. It took her a moment, but she'd been around her nieces and nephews enough to know the look of a boy with a secret when she saw it.

"What are you up to?" she asked, putting on her best Mean Aunt Jolie face.

"Nothing," he said, backing out the door. He held the ledger in front of him, then tucked it back under his arm. "I came for the book, and now that I've got it, I'll be on my way."

"You are planning something, aren't you?" she asked, keeping in step with him. She crossed her arms over her chest and cocked her head to one side, her eyes wide and serious.

Leo fought the urge to squirm under that gaze. "N-No," he stammered, "Thank you, Jolie." He turned on his heel and made for the south tower a little faster than necessary.

Well her tried-and-true interrogation technique hadn't worked, but there was something going on she wasn't privy to just yet. When Leo poked his head back around the corner at the end of the hall a moment after he'd passed by it, she thought maybe she'd guilted him into confessing his plot.

"Join me for dinner, Jolie?" he called, his deep voice booming.

The hope in his eyes was too much and she smiled. "Of course, Leo," she answered.

Leo smiled as he made his way to his rooms, fighting the urge to run or laugh out loud. It was a lot to hope that he would be able to give her the surprise tonight, but if anyone could make it happen that quickly, it was Willard.

If he'd learned anything since Jolie arrived, it was that hope was a living thing. If you kept it alive, it would return the favor to you, making your heart beat like the wings of a wild bird. Once he'd started believing it, hope had bloomed within him like every rose in his courtyard garden, brightening his entire life and making anything seem possible.

****

"Do you remember your lessons?" Willard asked, sounding as nervous as Leo felt.

"Of course, Willard," Leo groaned, tugging on the gold braid on his jacket. The jacket's shade of blue was his family's signature color, cobalt, and as bright as it was rich. "Mother insisted on my having dance lessons from the time I could walk, I have not forgotten how to waltz."

A thought occurred to the prince, but he was too nervous to voice it. Willard must have seen something in his face, though.

"What is it, sire?"

"I don't know if I can dance anymore," Leo said, his eyes shooting to his shoes. Everything was as perfect as could be expected. "If I misstep now, I could break Jolie's leg. Before I would only have bruised a toe."

"Perhaps, sire, she will not know how to dance. Then she'll never know the difference." Willard said with a smile.

Leo laughed, the joke disarming him when he needed it most. Willard was always good at that. "I feel ridiculous," he admitted.

"You look resplendent, Master," Willard said with a comforting pat on the prince's arm. "I will go down and check on the preparations. I'll return to call for you when everything is ready."

Just as Willard passed through the door, Leo called, "Are you sure everything is arranged? It will all happen just as I asked?"

"Everything I could manage has been done," Willard answered, leaning back through the doorway. "You have all the paperwork there as proof, and all will come to light in the morning."

"And you did everything in your name, yes?" Leo looked more nervous than Willard had ever seen him, and the older man took it as a sign. If Leo cared enough to be nervous, he cared enough to do everything right.

"Yes, sire," he said, his smile indulgent. "No one will know that their prince has done a thing for them, just an unknown benefactor."

Leo breathed a sigh of relief, his shoulders relaxing. He released his grip on his jacket and turned once more to the mirror. He heard Willard's steps going down the stairs and away from the room. On the desk was an envelope full of papers, drawn up and signed in secret, spoken of only today and even then, in hushed tones, between Pierre LeBoeuf and Willard. Beneath the envelope was the ledger book Leo had borrowed from Jolie, with every franc needed for this venture accounted for carefully in its pages.

Some of what had been done today would take time, but enough had been accomplished that Leo could give Jolie her gift at dinner. If it had taken longer, he would have waited until everything was for certain, but all was nearly done.

Leo didn't think he could wait much longer to tell her, anyway. From the moment he and Willard had come up with their plan, he had been giddy with excitement. He tucked the envelope in a pocket on the inside of his jacket, grabbed the ledger, and tried not to pace while he waited for Willard to return.

****

Quentin rounded the last corner in the path off the old Tremonde Road, then looked around to make sure no one had followed him. Reaching over his head, he plucked the black cloth from the tree where Thomas had tied it days ago, cursing himself for not removing it sooner. If he wasn't more careful, the Grey Man would find him and this whole plan would be shot. He knew which tree marked the start of the path now, anyway.

Stuffing the cloth into his pocket, he looked around and didn't see the monster, or anyone else for that matter. Quentin had waited for hours for the beast to take his walk to the river. When the creature hadn't showed up and temperatures started to dip as low as the sun, he had a choice to make.

In a large leather bag strapped to his back, Quentin had packed several weapons. Half a dozen freshly sharpened knives, a pair of flintlock pistols, and a military saber were loaded in the bag. In addition to those, he had a dagger stuck down the shaft of his left boot and another in a scabbard at his hip. The blades in the bag were all wrapped in thick flannel so they didn't make any noise as he made his trek through the wood.

Quentin had dressed in black, from the hooded cloak that covered him from head to calf to the soft boots on his feet. He stayed off the path itself, and stepped on rocks instead of the soft ground. If the monster had even rudimentary tracking skills, he would see Quentin's footprints. He made his way several paces up the hill from the path, picking his path by the bright moonlight above.

Once night fell in earnest, and he was sure the fortress's occupants were abed, he would sneak inside and plant the weapons as he'd planned. He would soon be able to fulfill his true purpose.

****

Rosalie plucked and tugged, trying to get Jolie's mass of curls to at least pretend to behave. "Oh, forget it!" she said, letting it all fall in its usual disarray around the young woman's shoulders. She flicked the ends of her fingers through the hair one last time as if in dismissal.

"I think you're more anxious about meals with the prince than I am," Jolie said, although she felt no anxiety about this meal.

She was still convinced the prince was hiding something, and his energy earlier led her to believe it was something exciting. She should have been nervous, and couldn't figure out why she wasn't.

Rosalie knew everything, of course. Willard was a gossip of a high order, a terrible side effect of working with those who spent all their time in idle chatter. He had told her of the master's good deeds, the whole time minimizing his own role in the skullduggery. Considering the news, she felt that things were moving along quite nicely, and Jolie had every reason to feel good about tonight. If she wasn't half in love with the master by midnight, he would have to screw things up badly.

Pulling a deep plum gown from the depths of the armoire, she held it up to test the gown's color against Jolie's. The gown was like the one she'd worn the day she'd tried to climb out the window, but dark green velvet instead of patterned cotton. With a nod of approval, the woman started getting Jolie changed.

"I think the master likes your hair better this way, anyway," Rosalie said, heaving a sigh. "I'll try to pin up some of it around your face. Don't want these locks falling into your supper."

Jolie smiled as she wiggled into the bodice.

"From what Willard said, our young Leopold stopped breathing when he saw you in that blue gown at dinner," Rosalie said, then stuck her tongue in her cheek.

Jolie thought back, remembering how his eyes had widened at the sight of her, and the way his hand had settled over his stomach like a man who'd had the breath knocked out of him. The idea of him being so stunned by her appearance warmed her, sending flutters through her stomach.

"I think the master is quite taken with you," Rosalie said, hoping that once she put the idea in Jolie's head, the girl would run with it. And hoping, of course, to see how Jolie herself might feel about him, as well.

Jolie nibbled on the inside of her cheek, unsure of how she felt about it. Rosalie was staring at her in the mirror, obviously hoping for some visible reaction, but she couldn't muster one. Not yet.

"I don't know how I feel about the master," was as close as she could get to an admission. "I see much potential in him, and a stronger man I've never met, but his anger frightens me."

"I've never seen him make such an effort before," Rosalie said, her eyes flicking back and forth from the stays in the gown to Jolie's eyes the mirror. "He's working hard for you. Letting you wear his mother's gowns, stay in her room, dining with you instead of leaving you to eat alone."

"Those things don't excuse his outbursts," Jolie said, her tone harsh.

"Of course not, dear," Rosalie agreed brusquely. "Wouldn't dream of making excuses for the boy." She brushed the back of the gown to flatten the pleats.

Jolie nodded, as if her approval had been needed. "Something seems different about him since yesterday, though," she mused, turning in the mirror to see how the dress looked.

"I know what you mean," Rosalie admitted, looking away, her eyes thoughtful. "Not a change, really—"

"Something small, for sure," Jolie agreed.

"But it feels like more than that, doesn't it?" Rosalie asked, returning her gaze.

"Yes, it does, like he's decided about something, or he's happier. He's not slouching around everywhere he goes anymore, he walks like a man who's been given back his pride."

Jolie held sections of hair as Rosalie went around with the pins. They were silent for a moment while the older woman worked.

"I don't know, but if you ask me, I'd say our prince is smitten," Rosalie said and smiled when Jolie blushed. "You'd be surprised at how much the love of a good woman can change a man. Love is powerful, Jolie. And what you feel for your family is nothing compared to the love you feel for a man, or he for you."

"Papa and Maman were betrothed from birth, but they were lucky that they learned to love one another," Jolie said. "I never knew my Maman, but Papa never remarried, and always spoke of her like she was the only one for him."

"They did get lucky, then," Rosalie said. She wanted to say more, but just then, there was a knock on the door. When she opened the door, she was surprised to find Leo on the other side. With a broad smile, she stepped back and let him in the door, keeping a close eye on how he reacted to Jolie.

His jaw went slack as a whisper of breath escaped, his eyes practically glowed, and his cheeks flushed. His big hand opened and closed at his side. When he crossed the room to Jolie, his fingers plucked at one of her curls.

Rosalie wanted to thrust her hands in the air in triumph, to whoop her gratitude and happiness to the heavens. As it was, she could hardly see through the pools of tears in her eyes.

"You look lovely tonight," Leo said, his eyes on Jolie, reverent.

"Thank you," she said, hearing the breathlessness of her voice but powerless to do anything about it. He looked incredible in near-full regalia. All that was missing was his crown and scepter and he would look like a proper prince. She reached out to touch the sleeve of the jacket, then pulled her hand back.

Leo saw her hesitate, and lifted his arm to her hand, eager to close the distance between them. He wanted her to take his arm on their way to dinner. That was why he was here instead of Willard, after all. He'd given the old man the night off, and planned to give Rosalie the same. His intentions would be questioned, no doubt, but if those two didn't trust that she would come to no harm with him, no one would. For his part, Willard had been all too happy to take the night off for himself. Hopefully, Rosalie would do the same.

Jolie slid her hand onto Leo's arm and noticed he was carrying the ledger book under the other arm. "Finished with that already?"

Leo slid the book out from under his arm and handed it to her, careful not to drop the envelope. She saw it, but didn't comment, just set the ledger down and returned to him, replacing her hand on his arm and letting him lead her toward the dining hall.

When they stepped through the door, Leo had a private word with Rosalie, ducking his head down to the old woman's ear and speaking so quietly all Jolie could hear was a low rumble. Rosalie spoke as well, and when the two separated, the maid pressed a hand to Leo's hairy cheek, her eyes wet with happy tears, her cheeks pulled up in a smile. She gave Jolie a wave, then headed off toward the servants' entrance.

Leo stood tall as he walked her to the dining hall, his chest out and his shoulders back, head held high, and his hand covering hers on his arm. He smiled as they walked, as if he were showing her off to a room full of guests. No one else was there, but she could see his excitement and was reminded again of a child with a secret. Maybe it had to do with the envelope he was carrying. She wondered what was inside. He set it on the table next to his place setting, but she didn't comment on it.

Leo seated her first, at the end of the table with his place across from her again. He poured wine and filled her plate, then they tucked in without speaking. She could feel his leg bouncing under the table, and his hands weren't steady, but she didn't want to rush him into revealing whatever had him so excited. Patiently, she waited.

Waiting for the right time was maddening! Every moment seemed like the right one, and at the same time, none of them did. What was worse, he didn't have anything to talk about without bringing up the contents of that envelope. Finally, he couldn't take it any longer and slid the envelope across the table.

Jolie lifted her eyes to his, hoping for an explanation. She smiled, hoping she looked encouraging.

"I have a surprise for you, but now that I'm about to hand it over, I hope you won't be angry with me," he said. He rubbed at his chest with the heel of his hand, trying to soothe the hopeful ache that had started there. With a thick swallow, he leaned forward the pushed the envelope the rest of the way across the table.

Jolie swept the envelope into her lap and opened it, revealing several sheets of expensive paper. There were no seals or other insignia on them to indicate who they were drawn up by, but there was a name near the top of the pages that she recognized at once. "Pierre LeBeouf?" she asked.

"Willard went into town yesterday and sought out which solicitor your father used. Apparently, the man was all too happy to help," Leo said. "Keep reading."

Her brow furrowed in confusion as she turned back to the pages. As her eyes darted over the words and comprehension set in, her shoulders slumped and one hand went to her mouth. All the color drained from her face, and he heard her sniff once.

When she finished, her fingers fluttered over the pages on her lap. Leo let her be for the moment, waiting for her to come to grips with whatever she was feeling.

"This is everything Papa owned, paid for?" she asked, her voice almost completely cut off.

"The home, all of his things, everything," Leo said, leaning over the table. "Everything Willard could find, anyway. Your brother-in-law had started selling some of your father's possessions. Rest assured, Willard hired a man who will recover as many of your father's things as he can."

"All this must have cost you... I have no way of ever repaying you," Jolie said, her voice plaintive. She finally met his eyes, and the sight of hers glistening with tears almost broke him. "I don't know how to thank you for this."

"I'm not looking for repayment or thanksgiving, Jolie," he said. "On my walk the other night, I made some promises. To myself, to you, to the Almighty, and I plan to keep them. One of those promises was that I would care for you, whether you stay with me here or not."

Jolie thought back to what Rosalie had said earlier. If this wasn't a sure sign that a man was smitten, nothing was. The man who Jolie had met the night she came here wouldn't have done this, and when she thought about it, no man would unless there was something in it for him. Even if that something was personal satisfaction, the knowledge that the woman he cared so much about was safe and protected was enough.

"Your father will never have to leave his home, and I—" his throat closed. The look in her eyes, shocked and stricken, was so pure and real he was sure it was taking years off his life. "—I made another promise at the river. I promised that if the curse does not break in a few days, that I will let you go."

Leo looked away, his shoulders slumping and his back curving. He couldn't look at her anymore. He knew that everything he felt at the idea of losing her would show too plainly.

"Look at me, Leo," she said. "Please."

It took him a moment, and she could tell he didn't want to, but he did. She searched his eyes, looking for any sign of deception, and instead saw only hope and something akin to desperation.

"You would really let me go?" she asked, surprised.

"If the curse does not lift, I will release you from your sentence and allow you to return to your family," he said, his eyes on hers. "And I will make sure you are never left wanting for anything for the rest of your life."

Oh, but what if the thing I need most is you, and you let me go right when I'm about to realize it? She closed her eyes on that thought, still too unsure about him, herself, and them both that she couldn't give voice to it.

Instead, she stood and walked around the end of the table, throwing her arms around Leo's neck and burying her face in his jacket. He smelled like soap and fresh laundry, his skin so warm she could feel his heat through the fabric.

Leo kept his arms at his sides, still afraid of hurting her. He tucked his face into her neck, breathing her in, telling himself over and over to just be satisfied with that.

"Hold me, Leo," she said, her breath tickling hairs on his throat.

"I don't want to hurt you," he said, pulling away to meet her eyes.

"I'm not such a simpleton I would let you," she said, a small smile on her lips.

With another thick swallow, he wrapped his arms around her waist, barely allowing himself to touch her at first, but she felt so good in his arms he relaxed and pulled her to him. She felt like she belonged

167

there, and a feeling that had only begun to bud inside him bloomed violently. One moment, he wasn't sure, the next he knew. For the first time in his life, the Beast Prince was in love. It crashed over him like a hammer blow, burning in his chest and making him dizzy. His heartbeat thundered in his ears and the world around him grew silent.

Determined not to let her see what he had just discovered in himself, he pressed a kiss to the top of her head and stood, pulling her up with him. Holding her hand in his, he led her to the Great Hall. Spinning her around, he watched her beautiful hair swirl around her, then pulled her back toward him, keeping a proper amount of space between their bodies. He raised one big hand, holding hers as delicately as he could in his. She placed her other hand on his forearm, and with a fortifying breath, he draped his free hand on her waist.

"There's no music," Jolie said. She lifted her eyes to Leo's, and the delighted glitter in them made her smile. He pulled himself up straight, drawing his shoulders back and planting his feet.

"We won't need it," he said with a wink.

With a smile, he began the steps to a waltz. He wasn't the only one who had suffered through dance lessons, and she proved to be as skilled a dancer as he.

"You never told me you'd had lessons," he said as they slowed down. She was squeezing his hand in hers, as much she could with her hands less than half the size of his.

"My sister insisted," Jolie said, a sour look overtaking her face. "Otherwise, Papa would have made no concessions to my femininity whatsoever."

Leo chuckled, imagining a little girl with red curls flouncing around a dance floor with a grumpy expression. "What about your mother?" he asked, realizing he'd never heard her speak of her family, besides her father.

"She died a few days after I was born," Jolie said. "Birthing fever. Growing up, it was just me, Papa, and Mireille."

"Your father never remarried?" he asked, surprised. Their dance slowed, and he realized he was rubbing a thumb on the bodice of her dress. He made himself stop, trying to concentrate on the conversation.

"No, but there were frequent trips to Port Lucerne when I was younger. I'm not sure he was ever interested in anyone in that way," she said, her forehead wrinkling as she thought back. "I think he was more concerned about marrying off his daughters first."

"That makes sense, considering what happened recently," Leo said, trying to keep the bite of sarcasm out of his voice.

Jolie shot him a look from beneath her brows, her mouth tightening. She couldn't argue with him, though, not when he was right. "I can only imagine how difficult raising two girls was for him."

"One shudders at the thought of raising two like you," Leo joked, turning his head away so she wouldn't see his grin.

"My sister is nothing like me," Jolie said, her voice wistful. She had a faraway look in her eyes, like she was remembering something that happened long ago.

"What is she like?" Leo asked, sobering.

"Mireille is—" she cut herself off, not wanting to be unkind. Her sister had never given her that sort of courtesy, though, and she decided that even if it was only this once, she would say what she meant. "—she's a termagant. Everything must be her way or not at all, and she's never been kind to me. I'm never good enough, pretty enough, or feminine enough. I always knew things she didn't, but they weren't about dresses or dance steps or which man was worth marrying, so they didn't matter. I refused a coming-out ball and I thought she would tear the roof off our home."

Leo nodded, focusing on her bleak expression, on the naked hurt in her eyes when she spoke of her sister. Obviously, there was no love lost between them, but there was something else in her eyes he couldn't figure out for a moment. When he did, he wasn't surprised, just ashamed.

"You miss her," he said. It wasn't a question, and when she closed her eyes against the tears that gathered there, he knew he was right. He dropped to his knees and gathered her in his arms. Her shoulders shook with her sobs and a feeling built in his chest that threatened to strangle him. His heart pounded and his throat tightened, and with every one of her sobs, his own emotions threatened to spill forth.

Jolie pulled away, brushing at the wet spot she'd left on his velvet jacket. "Oh, dear. I'm sorry, I've ruined your clothes."

Leo shook his head, waving off her concerns. He knew he was the one who needed to apologize, but wasn't sure where he should start. There were too many things to be sorry for, he was starting to feel like he would need a week to get the job done properly.

What was she thinking? Leaning on this man, apologizing to him, waiting for him to apologize to her? She'd forgotten the real reason she was here, and along with that had forgotten herself. She brushed the tears off her cheeks and stepped back, her face flaming in embarrassment.

"I'm sorry, Master," she said, still walking backward. "I really must get to bed. I have much work to do tomorrow."

She started to walk away and Leo slumped, sitting on his feet. His arms hung at his sides, his face slack with surprise. She knew she was hurting him, but she couldn't stay in this room another minute. As kind as he'd been to her tonight, and as wonderful an evening as they'd had, she was overstepping her station as prisoner. Getting to know Leo was not going to help her serve her sentence, and could make life here even harder for her.

There was something in his eyes that she'd never seen before, and if she gave into it she might never be able to walk away in a few days. He'd promised her freedom if the curse didn't break on his birthday, and if she stayed here she might not want to leave when the time come. He was so dear to her already that she didn't want to think about how hard walking out of Château Villeneuve would be.

Leo watched as she turned and walked toward the Rose Room. Even with all he'd done for her by securing her father's future, how could she still only think of him as her master? How could he have fallen in love with her when she didn't see him as any more than she had on her first night here? He kept his eyes on her back until her door closed, then looked toward the floor.

Resting on his thighs were the monstrous hands that, tonight, had felt so much smaller, like a normal man's. Jolie had made him feel like a man tonight, and the sight of those huge paws startled him at first. He had looked down expecting to see himself transformed back into the man he once was. When he realized he was still a grotesque form of himself, he put his head in his hands and wept.

Leo wept for the man he wanted to be, for the love he didn't deserve, for the boy he'd been when this all began. The prince cried for so long he was sure there wasn't another drop of water left in his body, and when he looked up at the sky through the Great Hall's enormous windows, the moon hung high and full overhead. He pulled himself to his feet and brushed off his clothes. Pulling his ring of keys out of his jacket pocket, he went to the door of the Rose Room.

No matter what had just happened to change the evening so drastically, Jolie still needed his protection, and he would lock her door as promised. He could hear her crying through the door from ten feet away, and he closed his eyes as he approached. If it killed him, he would keep the promises he'd made to her. If he spent the rest of his life a lonely despot in this prison of his own making, the time would pass easier if he knew she was taken care of.

The thought of living the rest of his potentially long life alone here tightened his chest again, and he rested his forehead against the door, taking deep breaths. When he turned the key in the lock, he heard Jolie stop crying for a moment and knew she knew he was there.

Unable to stay cooped up another minute, he stalked toward the door. He tossed his jacket on the floor and slammed the door when he left. He didn't even think of the most important promise he'd made Jolie, to stay for her protection, as he stalked into the forest once more.

Chapter 13

The monster left, slamming the heavy door with a resonant booming that echoed through the forest. Quentin watched from just outside the front gate as the creature took the main road down the hill toward Fontainbleu, waiting until it was out of sight before approaching the keep. What had happened to make the beast leave the keep unprotected?

With the threat of someone breaking in, Quentin was surprised that the creature hadn't hired dozens of guards. Then again, where would this thing be able to find men who would stick around long enough to make a difference in the keep's security?

Quentin kept just outside the wall and moved quickly in case the Grey Man decided to double back. The pack on his back was heavy, his shoulders were burning, and his feet were tired. He didn't have much farther to go, thank God. He'd be able to dump off the bag soon enough. Once he got around the wall to the unfinished portion, he could slip inside and give himself the advantage he needed.

****

Jolie heard the door lock, then the front door slammed and she knew she was alone. With no one in the keep to protect her if the intruder returned tonight, her mind raced with all the possibilities. An axe was all it would take for whoever it was to get through the door, and without Leo here...

She had to stop thinking this way or she'd never get to sleep. She would be just fine here. There was no reason to think whoever it was would return, or if they did that they would have an ax to get through her door. There was no sign that she was what they were after, or if there was a target at all. The man could have been here to rob the place or he could have been there to find a warm place to sleep for the night. There wasn't a harmless reason for a person to break into a palace belonging to his country's royal family, but she was desperate. The magic was waning, broken enough to allow someone to get in, and there was no one here to protect her now.

Shaking her head to clear it, Jolie started wriggling out of the gown she'd worn to dinner. In just her shift, she grabbed a book off her writing desk without looking at the cover. She flopped on the bed and opened the book to a random page, reading without focusing on or absorbing a word.

The stress of the day caught up with her before long, and her eyes started to drift closed. The building was so quiet; she could almost believe there was nothing to be afraid of. The moonlight coming in the window lit up the room as the candles guttered.

The Great Hall was silent except for the sound of her own pounding footsteps on the wood floor. She was alone in the room, and as she crossed from the northeast corridor to the grand fireplace, a door slammed behind her. She turned and saw a man standing just inside the door, arms at his sides, a dagger in his left hand, and the ornate hand mirror in his right. He was dressed all in black, and a smooth black mask covered his whole face, even his eyes. A short cape draped around his shoulders, and the hood was pulled up over his head, casting his masked face into shadow.

He wasn't a large man, standing only a little taller than Jolie herself, and slightly built, so she knew it wasn't her handsome stranger. He stood with his feet shoulder-width apart, holding the knife handle in a death grip.

In one fluid motion, he bent at the knee and lunged toward her, his legs eating up the floor in long strides. The sound of his feet on the floor was deafening, and Jolie threw her arms up over her head, preparing for the blow. From somewhere off to her left came an ear-splitting roar, and as she ducked toward the floor, the handsome stranger came out of nowhere and threw himself in front of her, his big body covering hers like a shield. He spread his arms wide, presenting an unmissable target.

From between her forearms as she looked past the stranger, she saw the intruder launch himself into the air, both hands on the dagger handle, ready to plunge it into his victim. Just as he was reaching the apex of his leap, everything froze. Her stranger, the intruder, even the dust motes that danced through the air, froze in place as if time itself had stopped. A crow the size of an eagle flew in through a transom high above and lit on the piano seat, its beak opening and closing soundlessly a few times before it let out a rancorous squawk.

The bird made the same sound half a dozen times and Jolie realized it was saying something. She shook her head and, with one last look at the men frozen before her, walked toward the bird.

"Walk uhmph!"

Straining to hear it properly, she kept moving closer until its words were clear.

"WAKE UP!"

Her heart slammed against her ribs with all the subtlety of a sledgehammer. A great pounding came from outside the room, someone trying to get in the Rose Room door. She sat up bolt-straight, sweat running down her face and chest. Her shift stuck to her back, and she couldn't stop the tremor in her hands.

"Jolie!" a man called from outside the room.

Not Leo, she told herself. The voice was whiny, too high-pitched, and familiar in a way that prickled just outside her awareness.

"I know you're in there!" he cried, and then that pounding sound. He was throwing himself against the door, trying to break it. For once, she was glad she was not at her father's home. He'd have come right through the door of her bedroom there. This heavy oak door was solid and thick. He wouldn't get through it without an axe and half a day's work.

"Talk to me, woman!" he screeched, and she recognized his voice.

What was Quentin Garamonde doing here? Was he the man she'd run into the other night? Something about him being so near made her more afraid than she'd been in her life. Being alone here scared her even more. What if Quentin had done something to Leo? It didn't seem likely, but her mind wasn't working logically and anything was possible.

Should she answer him? She might be able to make him go away, but the more likely scenario was, he would lie in wait until he could get at her at his leisure. There were plenty of places for him to hide here, and if Leo didn't find him everyone here would be in as much danger as she was. Keeping silent might keep him right there, outside her door, until Leo returned. Unless Quentin had a gun at the ready, there was no way he would be able to stop Leo if the prince got to him. Jolie had heard firsthand how quietly Leo could move around the keep, and if Leo heard the racket Quentin was making, there was no doubt her master could sneak up on the smaller man and make quick work of getting rid of him.

Jolie pulled her legs under the shift, tucking them up to her chest, and waited for whatever would happen next. With nowhere to go if he did break through, she could do little more than watch the door, hoping that none of the seams gave under Quentin's weight.

It seemed like he would slam into the door until Armageddon when he stopped so suddenly, the silence was deafening. He cursed loudly, then she heard his footsteps retreating, heading south toward the rear entrance. The front door boomed shut behind whoever he had heard coming, and she heard second set of footsteps, ones she knew belonged to Leo.

The prince caught sight of Quentin through the many doorways between the corridor and the Great Hall, and came through the Hall at a dead run. Without a sound other than his frighteningly light footfalls, he rounded the corners and took the straights with the speed and stealth of a wild cat seeking prey until he reached the door that led to the rear courtyard.

Leo wanted to keep after Quentin, but it was far more important that he see for himself that Jolie was unharmed. He watched from the doorway until he was as sure as he could be that Quentin was going to continue to the village. Then, the prince turned back toward home. He'd been stupid to leave her unguarded, he wouldn't be so stupid as to leave her that way any longer than he had to.

****

Quentin kept running until he reached the edge of the village. He knew he didn't dare slow his pace a moment sooner. The monster had approached with no sound, and Quentin had only known it was home by the opening of the keep's enormous doors. How had the thing been so damned quiet?

For the first time, Quentin felt doubt gnawing deep in the pit of his stomach. The plan he'd made, which sounded so sound at its conception, didn't anymore. The creature wasn't just huge; it was silent and deadly fast. If he hadn't had a head start, Quentin would be lying dead on the side of the road up Château Hill, and he had no doubt the animal would have pursued him right to his doorstep if he had even paused in his escape.

Stopping at the Golden Arms public house, he leaned against a corner to catch his breath and relieve the stitch that was digging into the ribs on his right side. He dropped his pack to the ground beside him and thought over his plan once more.

He couldn't go back up there again, not without the intention of killing the castle's master. The next time he mounted Château Hill had to be the last. He also couldn't get distracted by the woman living there. He hadn't planted a single weapon in the keep once he'd focused his attentions on the door Jolie lived behind.

175

From his hiding place outside one of the Great Hall windows, he'd seen the whole tableau. From the moment the creature had spun Jolie onto the dance floor, he'd seen the sick adoration on its face. Almost as soon as he'd realized the monster was in love with his fiancée, he'd seen the same feeling reflected from Jolie, and his stomach had turned. He'd been unable to focus on anything else the whole time he was there.

When she'd started crying into the creature's jacket, it had taken everything Quentin was made of for him not to shatter the window and loose an arrow at the thing's chest. His stomach turned again at the thought, and he picked up his pack and started for home. The journey to the house beyond the village wasn't long, and he'd barely had time to figure out what he was going to do when a familiar, if unwelcome, face greeted him at his parents' doorstep.

"Thomas?" he called, forgetting how shabby the man had looked the last time he'd seen him.

The man turned and tipped his grubby hat to Quentin. "Whatever you've got planned for the master of Château Villeneuve, you'd best hurry. There's been some... developments."

Quentin looked about him, then ushered the former footman into his parlor before anyone saw what kinds of guests he was having. "Get inside man, before someone sees you here."

Once they were safely inside the stately manor, Quentin whirled on Thomas, his grey eyes flashing in anger. "I never asked you to come here. What are you thinking, coming here?"

"I have information I thought would be relevant to whatever plan you have. If you're asking me to draw up a map, there's no doubt you are after the man who owns it," Thomas said, his eyebrows lifting in question. At Quentin's nod of assent, he continued. "Just recently, thousands of francs' worth of Armand Babineaux's property was sold off by his son-in-law, Malcolm, and his daughter Mireille."

Quentin lifted a hand, turning it around and around, trying to get Thomas to get to his point. The older man continued, knowing he could skip the details.

"As it turns out, one Willard LeChance bought back almost all this property, and returned every piece to the Babineaux household. He also paid off the mortgage Armand was forced to take when his business began to fail a year back."

Quentin screwed up his face in bewilderment. "Who in God's name is Willard LeChance? As you well know, our prince's name was

Leopold," he looked at the other man like his brain had fallen out through his nose.

Thomas held his hands up, palms out in surrender. "I'm getting to that. Armand was insolvent a week ago, but this week he finds himself in good standing once again, all from this same benefactor, whom everyone says the old man has never even met. But Willard worked with Pierre LeBeouf." He waited a beat for the name to register.

"That son of a whore lawyer?" Quentin asked, his voice jumping an octave.

"One and the same, sir," Thomas said, giving the boy a moment to process everything he'd said.

"Is there more? I sense this is not all you came to tell me," Quentin said, sounding as if he'd had the wind knocked out of him.

"Yes, there is, but I don't know if I should tell you or not. You seem out of sorts and it might be too much—"

Quentin shot across the room, grabbed Thomas by his filthy lapels, and propelled the older man into the wall behind him. Thomas's teeth clacked together and he saw stars.

"Accept my apology, sir. How silly of me to doubt your constitution," Thomas said, backpedaling quickly.

"Speak now, Thomas, and do so carefully," Quentin hissed through his teeth. "Or I shall throw you into the Marchand's hog pen, just to see what they would do with you."

The coldness in the boy's eyes, the complete lack of any feeling whatsoever, frightened Thomas more than anything he'd ever seen, and he wanted to go back in time. Coming to this house again was the biggest mistake he'd ever made, and looking into those horrible eyes, he knew no good would come of this meeting. He knew what a herd of hogs would do to a man like him, though, and didn't want to die that way, either. Self-preservation is one of the strongest human instincts, and it won out over any of Thomas's moral protests.

"That won't be necessary, young sir," he said, hating the wobble in his voice that betrayed his inner turmoil. "Armand's family never met LeChance, but when their things were returned to them, along with the bills of sale for their things was a letter."

Quentin released Thomas's shirt and took a single step back, allowing the man just enough room to breathe.

"The letter was from LeChance, but it was on stationery from the royal family, and was signed with the royal seal, which hasn't been seen on a piece of correspondence for nigh on ten years now," Thomas had to resist the urge to pause dramatically, and kept plowing on. "The letter didn't say it but it all but proves that the Grey Man is the missing Prince Leopold. On top of that, LeChance or whoever wrote the letter promised to take care of Jolie for the rest of her days, whether she stays there or not."

So, that was what her tears had been for: gratitude. Quentin turned away from Thomas, scrubbing his hands over the pathetic whiskers on his cheeks. "Do you mean to tell me, Thomas, that my fiancée is living in a royal palace with a promise secured in writing through a solicitor that she should worry for nothing? She has not only gotten out of marrying me rather neatly, but now she will be taken care of by a monster I have no hope of defeating?"

Thomas shrunk back, trying to edge his way toward the door. He was nearly to the knob when Quentin turned to him again, and instead of the wild outburst Thomas expected, the young man offered a placid smile. That there was still no emotion in his eyes only served to frighten Thomas more. He felt a trickle of sweat run between his bony shoulder blades.

"Who is this monster, Thomas? You worked there long enough. Who are these people?" Quentin asked, his voice soft and saccharin sweet.

"Willard LeChance was the valet for the king when I was fired," Thomas said, keeping his voice even as he could. His scalp prickled and his hands shook against his thighs. "I don't know who the Grey Man is, but if he's using the royal seal, he's either a thief or he's Prince Leopold himself."

Quentin threw up a hand and Thomas stopped. Perspiration ran into one of his eyes but he'd be damned to perdition before he'd raise a hand to wipe it away, though it stung like mad.

"That creature is our crown prince as much as I am a prize stallion," Quentin said, his voice as hard as flint. "It is a monster and that is all I need to know. He had nothing to do with this plan to care for my fiancée."

"Well, sir, if you want to be accurate, she never was your fiancée, was she?" Thomas realized his grave error a split second before Quentin's open hand slammed into his right cheek like a boat oar. The slap snapped his head to the side and blackened his vision for the second time that night.

"I will marry Jolie. I have come too far not to win her!" Quentin bellowed, the sound echoing through the cavernous parlor, rattling glassware on the decorative shelves that lined the walls.

"Of course, sir, my apologies again," Thomas said, his voice cracking. A tooth in the back of his mouth was throbbing now, sending white-hot stingers of pain through his whole head.

"If my intentions do not make her my fiancée, my actions will," Quentin calmed so quickly, said these words so evenly, that Thomas was alarmed. If he'd suspected it before, now he knew that his partner in this clandestine endeavor was a madman. He knew, as well, that if he didn't get out of this house soon he never would.

What Quentin had just said registered and Thomas felt a sinking sensation in his stomach at the implications. "What actions? What are you going to do?"

"I must make a plan, Thomas, because I cannot go back until I am prepared to make my stand. I plan on killing the Grey Man, but I must make myself ready to do so. I must be sure that I will not fail. Even the slightest doubt will end my mission before it begins," Quentin said, his eyes faraway and his hands up as if in prayer. The young man wandered across the parlor, turning his back on Thomas.

Thomas took the opportunity before it was lost, opening the door and bolting out into the night. He'd come tonight hoping the information he had discovered would earn him a few more francs from the Garamondes' deep pockets, but instead had had his life threatened. He wouldn't stick around to make sure the whelp would make good on his threat.

Thomas ran through the village until he came to the stable where he'd slept last night. No one was about, and he wiggled through the gap in the broken door without anyone noticing. As soon as he was sure Quentin hadn't followed him, he let his emotions overcome him, sobbing to the horses and the hay. He had to fix what he'd done tonight.

He'd known that talking to the Garamonde boy again was a mistake but the money he'd gotten from him before was already gone. On that account, the boy was right. He had been hoping for more but not like this.

The Grey Man was a monster, but if he was the prince, as Thomas suspected, had done nothing wrong that anyone had ever proven. And that wasn't even the worst part. If Quentin did what he was planning, and Thomas knew he would, Mademoiselle Babineaux could get hurt as well as the monster. So could the other servants.

Too many innocent lives could be lost in Quentin's madness. And madness was exactly what Thomas had seen tonight. There was no other word for the soul-sucking emptiness in the boy's eyes.

Thomas would have to find a way to repair the damage he'd done tonight. He didn't know how, but he would have to figure it out, and fast. Quentin wouldn't wait forever, and the risks Thomas took by staying silent were too great.

****

Leo returned and opened Jolie's door to find her on the other side of the room, huddled on the bed, shaking but unhurt. So great was his relief that he sagged against the door frame, his knees threatening to buckle.

"It was Quentin," she said, her voice tight through her chattering teeth. Leo crossed the room to the fireplace and got a fire going.

"I know," he said, his back still turned to her. "I've seen him here before."

"Why didn't you tell me?" she asked.

"I didn't want to frighten you. The first time I saw him, he was outside the walls, unable to get through the protective wards. He's been trying to cross it ever since," Leo said. He stood and brushed his hands on his breeches, then returned to the door. "Obviously, he succeeded last night, but I never thought he would come back so soon."

Jolie watched as he fidgeted, his huge fists opening and closing. There was no doubt in her mind that Leo would win any fight Quentin brought to his doorstep. But any man in a fight ran the risk of being injured, and that thought turned her stomach. She thought of the dreams she'd had of her handsome stranger, the blood that poured from the wound he'd taken. Leo would win the fight, but at what cost? He could defend her at the cost of his own life. All it took was one well-placed wound.

"He will return, won't he?" she asked, her throat constricting.

"I never should have left you tonight," he said, trying to avoid the topic of Quentin's return, inevitable though it was.

Leo's eyes were so bleak, as dark and dull as burnt wood. He feared for her, and his guilt was obvious in his stooped shoulders. He'd carried himself so proudly these last few days that to see him shrink into himself was difficult for her. Tears filled her eyes.

"I put you in this position," he said, taking a single step into the room. "I am ashamed of myself for keeping you here, where you are in the most danger."

Jolie stood and saw him drop his gaze from her body, but didn't miss the flash of hunger she saw there, or the blush that colored his cheeks. She knew he wouldn't hurt her, and she needed the comfort he could offer her. If she'd learned anything in the time she'd spent here, she had learned that this man before her was well and truly a man in every sense of the word.

The hair that covered his enormous body only hid the truth, a truth that most were too blind to see, even though it was right in front of them. Leopold was a man like any other and yet so much more a man for the torture he had endured. Hardly older than Jolie herself, he had suffered more than any one person should in an entire lifetime. All it took was one person to see him for what he was on the inside and she was that person.

In what little time she'd been here, she cared for Leo a great deal, and knew that no matter what she did right now, she would come to no harm at his hands. She crossed the room and took his hands into hers, tucking herself between them and forcing him to look at her.

"Don't be ashamed," she whispered as his eyes met hers. Little flutters in her chest made her feel jittery, but in the most beautiful way. "You'll just have to make it up to me when this is all over."

The hope in her own voice made her blush, because it was the hope of a little girl who thought there was no way anything bad could ever happen to her or the people she loved.

"I promise I will," Leo said, his voice deep and gravelly. He closed his eyes and turned away, a thick lock of his hair falling over one shoulder. He wanted to let her go right now, to send her away where she would be safe. But her father couldn't protect her anymore and her brother-in-law couldn't be expected to when he had his own family to protect. If she went home, Armand's house could become Quentin's target. Without knowing the man's endgame, Leo couldn't be sure of what to expect from him.

Leo stepped back his eyes still trained on the floor. "Try and get some sleep. I won't leave you," he said, releasing her hands.

Sure she wouldn't be able to fall asleep now, she nodded anyway and offered what she hoped was an encouraging smile as he closed her door. Once she'd heard the lock turn, she leaned on the thick door, glad it had held long enough for Leo to return. She heard a scraping sound on the other side and realized it was Leo, sitting against it for the night. "Good night, Leo," she whispered, then slipped back into bed.

Leo heard her and whispered a goodnight in return, then braced himself against the door, preparing to rest there until Jolie woke.

****

Willard came in to work early the next morning and nearly fell over his master's legs as he walked past the Rose Room. The sun hadn't yet broken the horizon, and the halls were so dark he couldn't see five feet in front of him. The prince grunted, then stood, pulling himself to his full height.

"My Lord, what are you doing on the floor?" Willard asked. Amusement and concern colored his tone, still rough from sleep.

"I slept here last night," Leo said, leading Willard away from the door so as not to wake Jolie.

"Is it the Garamonde boy?" the valet said as the prince led him into the dining hall. The prince pulled open the drapes, letting in the weak early light.

"Of course," Leo said.

"Hence your bizarre choice of beds," Willard said with a nod. "I see."

"It seemed prudent. I went outside for a short walk last night and though I wasn't gone long, he managed to get into the keep again," Leo said, mystified. "I mustn't leave her again. This will all be over soon, anyway."

Prince Leopold looked sad, his expression sagging and his face blank. Willard thought he looked resigned and wondered what had happened last night to prove to the young prince that there was no hope.

"Sire, how did your dinner with Mademoiselle Babineaux go?" he asked.

Leo thought for a moment, remembering how beautiful she had looked, and thinking about the way she'd looked at him. He thought about what he'd realized about himself as well, and his heart squeezed in his chest. Closing his eyes against the flood of emotions, he turned toward Willard and smiled.

"It was the best night I've had in many years." Even though he'd spent a few scant hours on a hard floor and made one of the most painful realizations of his adult life, those words were some of the truest he'd ever spoken.

"I am thrilled to hear it, my prince," Willard said with a genuine smile of his own. "Now that I am here, you should try to get yourself some sleep. Why don't you go on to the South Tower? I will watch over Mademoiselle Babineaux."

Leo thought it over for a moment and even though he knew he would never get the sleep he needed, decided it was still a good idea to separate himself from the woman in the Rose Room for a while. She needed her rest, as well, and if he stayed near her room he would wind up pacing outside the door. He didn't want to wake her before she was ready, so he nodded and headed toward his bedchambers.

Willard bowed as he passed by and hauled a dining chair along with him, setting it up at the mouth of the breezeway. From there, he could see through the Great Hall and all entrances to the keep, including the servants' entrance beyond the dining hall. If anyone were to get in, he would be the first to know and would be able to raise the alarm. He settled into the chair, ready to stand watch over the keep and her lady.

****

Mireille paced the kitchen, her long legs making quick work of the room. Even from here, she could hear her father's broken wheezing. The sound ached in her head and her heart, engulfing her in a pain known only to those who have lost someone they loved. "I can't take this anymore," she said to Malcolm, who sat, bleary-eyed and lost, at the table.

"I know, love, but I don't know what else we can do," he said, his voice flat.

"I'm going to go to Château Villeneuve. I must try to bring Jolie back here," she said. In her words was a tone of questioning, even though Malcolm knew they were beyond asking for permission for what she was planning. "Papa is miserable, and if she comes, he can see her one last time. Maybe then—" her voice cracked and she flopped down into a dining chair, the wood creaking under her weight.

183

"Perhaps I should be the one to go," Malcolm offered, standing and going to his wife. He held her hands in his, trying to look encouraging.

"No, she will expect you to handle this for me," Mireille said, shaking her head. "If I go, she will know father's condition is serious. She knows I would never come for her unless he was dying."

Seeing both the sense in what his wife was saying and her own immovable will behind her decision, Malcolm helped her to her feet. "Take Garnet, the staff there will recognize him, and give them your full name."

"I'll give them my life story if that will get her home for Papa. He needs her now, more than the Grey Man does," she said. Sniffing, she dabbed at her nose with a handkerchief. "I hope he hasn't done anything horrible to her. If Papa sees she's been hurt, he might convince God himself to move Heaven and Earth to right the wrong."

Malcolm smiled, imagining his father-in-law at Heaven's gate, ordering the angels and saints to do his bidding. "I imagine he would."

A great gust of agonized breath came from Armand's room as if to punctuate the urgency of their situation. The husband and wife's eyes met and Malcolm kissed her forehead. "Dress warmly, and hold on tight. Garnet likes to have his head and will run until he drops."

Mireille said nothing in response, just nodded, then jogged to their shared room a door down from Armand's. If she went into her father's room she would never get out the door. There was too much to say and no time to say it in. If he died while she was gone, Jolie wouldn't live long enough to hear the end of it, but if she didn't try to bring her sister home, their father would never find peace. She kissed her children, wrapped herself in a riding habit lined with rabbit fur, then headed to the stables.

****

Willard came into the South Tower room, out of breath from his jog up the stairs. Each step was punctuated by the high wails of Micah's horn from the grand entrance gate.

"A rider approaches the gate." Willard's surprise was clear. "I'd forgotten what that horn was for."

"As did I," Leo said. He knew he wouldn't be able to see the gate from his room. "See what they want, it's probably a hunter who got

184

lost. Then send them on their way."

Willard hurried to the gatehouse, where Micah was waiting for him outside his door. A beautiful blonde woman was on the other side of the gate. When Willard saw the horse she was mounted on, he was sure he knew who the young woman was. Micah walked with him to the gate, the ring for his set of keys around one wrist.

"I am Mireille Grace Babineaux-McHenry, sister of Jolie Lisette Babineaux, who I know to be inside this keep. I must see her immediately," The blonde woman called through the gate, her tone desperate. The horse champed at its bit, its front feet stomping, ready to take off again at the slightest provocation.

Willard thought for a moment. The last person he had expected to see was Jolie's sister. "Madame McHenry, what matter do you wish to discuss with Jolie? She is a prisoner here and therefore allowed no visitors." He paused for a moment before saying, "I can, however, take a message to her."

Mireille's face fell and her shoulders slumped. She was out of breath, her chest heaving as hard as her steed's after the long ride from the village. "It is our father. He has never recovered from the sickness that he caught on the way here. Doctor LaFitte says he will not survive. I wish to beg your Master's mercy so that he may see Jolie one last time."

Willard closed his eyes at the emotion that welled up in his chest at this news. Jolie would be heartbroken, and he hated to be the one to bear the news. "I am sorry for your impending loss. I will relay the message and make a plea to my master to release Jolie for an audience with your father. Please wait here. I shall return shortly."

Mireille smiled and nodded, blinking against her tears.

"I must warn you, Madame, that our master may not allow her to leave the keep, but I will do my level best to change his mind."

With that, he went to the castle, his uniform straining against his body with every long stride. When he plowed back into the south tower room, Leo leapt to his feet.

"What is it, Willard?" he asked, his body tense from scalp to foot.

"It is Mademoiselle Jolie's father."

****

Jolie rechecked row after row in the ledger. She didn't have any new work to add to the book, but was trying to pass time in any way she could.

Realizing she hadn't dated the page, she wrote down the month, day, and year. Only after she was done writing did she realize the significance of the date. The day after tomorrow was Leo's birthday and at midnight the next morning this magic was set to come to an end. Her heart thumped in her chest, a deep, heavy panic bubbling low in her spine as if it was trying to encourage her into action. But what action, she didn't know, and the feeling only made her restless.

Though she was sure Leo wouldn't want any kind of celebration of a day so full of bad memories, she knew this day was even more significant than most birthdays. Whether the curse was broken at midnight or it made itself permanent, she wouldn't know until the time was at hand.

After such a long, odd night, she'd slept shamefully late this morning and taken her breakfast in her room. The afternoon sun was already streaming in the windows, warming the winter chill from the air with help from the fireplace. Her thoughts were still as jumbled this morning as they had been when she went to sleep, and sleeping late left her brain foggy.

Jolie couldn't focus, and the ledger books seemed to swim in her vision. The second she tried to renew her efforts to sort out the figures, she would remember something that she and Leo had done or said last night and her brain would refuse to work.

Leo had given her the greatest gift she could have hoped for last night, her father's freedom from ruin. He had also promised her own, once this curse came to its end. He had said no matter what happened in two days, she would be free to live her life as she saw fit. Looking forward to that put her at odds with another feeling she was struggling with. She didn't want to leave Leo here, alone. He had suffered so much, and when she left here she didn't want to leave him to more of the anguish he'd already endured for too long.

Leo had never been clear on what it would take to break the curse, speaking only in cryptic terms. No one else had told her how to break it, either. Then again, she'd never asked. Willard and Rosalie seemed like they were plotting something. It felt like the two of them were trying to push her and the prince together, so maybe that had something to do with it. Of course, they could just want to assuage their master's loneliness.

For the first time, she thought about why the magic bearer had cursed Leo in the first place.

The curse had begun in punishment for Leo's cruelty and arrogance. His anger when he'd answered the doors, his callous casting aside of a woman in need had earned him ten years of ugliness and isolation. Even when Jolie first arrived, she'd seen that side of him. He'd thrown a table over in his rage, behaving like a wild animal unable to control his emotions.

But since that night, he'd changed. After his last long walk into the forest, he'd become more confident, kinder, gentler. He hadn't gotten angry even once. He had saved her life, told her he liked her smile. The way he'd looked at her while they danced last night....

None of this helped her come to any conclusion as to how to break the curse, and she was surprised at how at odds that uncertainty made her feel. Leo needed this magic to break, needed to return to his normal self, but she didn't know how she fit into the equation.

The door to the room glided open and she looked up. Willard stepped in and she smiled as she set the ledger aside. When she met his eyes, she caught his expression and her heart missed a beat. All thought of the curse flew out of her mind like leaves on the wind.

"The master would like you to join him in the South Tower at once."

"What is it, Willard?"

"The master must see you right away," he evaded, and she noticed he couldn't quite meet her gaze.

She was on her feet and following Willard before he finished speaking. Something must be wrong for the master to summon her to his tower. She hadn't been in his chamber since the night he'd had dinner with her, when he'd told her of his curse. When they reached the tower room, Leo sat at his desk, and it took Jolie a moment to realize that the object he held in his hand was the hand mirror. She hadn't seen it since her first night here.

"I didn't think that had made the trip," she said with a smile. Behind her, Willard's footsteps trailed down the stairs.

The look on Leo's face was serious, sad, and as he looked at her she thought he looked as at odds as she felt. He looked like a man who had a difficult decision to make and wasn't sure he could live with the outcome. She'd seen this look one other time, on her father's face the night she'd used the ring to take his place here. A sinking feeling settled

187

in her stomach and she thought she might be sick.

Leo looked like he wanted to say something but didn't. Instead, he handed the mirror over the desk to her. "Look in on your father."

Panic sent her heart to slamming into her ribs with terrifying speed. The handle of the mirror glowed and its glass flickered. "Show me Papa."

The old man was in bed, his skin pale and damp with sweat. Great coughs racked his body and he looked weaker than Jolie had ever seen him. It took so much effort for him to breathe his back arched off the bed, his stomach pulling him into a c-shape on the exhale.

"Is he dying?" she asked, her voice cracking.

Leo stood and wandered to the double doors, his eyes bleak. "Your sister, Mireille, came here to tell me you were needed. She thinks he won't last the night."

Pain knifed through her stomach and she covered her mouth with her hand, tears flooding her eyes and a moan echoing through the Spartan chamber.

"I am releasing you from your sentence." Leo said before he could lose his nerve. "Your family needs you, and you are free to go to them."

Jolie went to him, her eyes wide with shock. Her mouth opened, but she couldn't form the words through the lump in her throat.

Knowing he'd never see her again, he wanted to look at her for hours. But her father might not have hours to live and he deserved to see his child one last time. His throat was so tight he almost didn't get the words out. "Take the mirror. I know you won't return, but perhaps you'll look in on me here. Your sister waits outside the gate. Go to her."

If only she had more time, there were so many things she would say to her fallen prince. Thoughts, and her own feelings, boiled in her head and heart until she wasn't sure what to think anymore. Leo held out a hand and she took it, planting a kiss on the rough knuckles, his hairs tickling her nose. Tears filled her eyes as she looked up at him and saw the tender look in his.

"Goodbye, Leo," she said. "And thank you."

With that, she was gone. As she reached the bottom of the stairs, Leo sat on the floor, his eyes closed against the aching in his heart. In his life one moment, gone the next, and in the millions of moments in between he had found what he was looking for. Found her and lost her all in the space between one heartbeat and the next.

As if to punctuate the situation, one of the few petals still clinging to the magical rose fell to the bottom of the globe. Better than the clock in the great hall, it counted down what little time he had left, and he'd just let the woman he loved walk out of his life forever.

Chapter 14

Jolie didn't greet her sister as she passed through the gate but jumped onto Garnet's back and held on tight as Mireille guided them toward Fontainbleu. They rode as fast as the rough road would allow and were back at Papa's house before an hour had passed.

Mireille tied the horse to a post in the barn, then both girls ran into the house, their skirts flying behind them like bright blue and pink banners. Malcolm was just inside the door, his eyes raw and his skin tight with emotion. Jolie's heart sank and her vision blurred, but he held up his hands.

"He's not gone yet," Malcolm said. His teeth were clenched, making his handsome face look much older than his years. "How did you get away?" he asked. Fear was hiding in his eyes, beneath his grief, and Jolie knew what the fear was of, even if she no longer understood it.

"When we have time, I will explain everything," she said and hugged her brother-in-law. Shrugging out of her cloak, she swept through the halls to her father's chamber.

The acrid smell of illness nearly knocked her off her feet. Apprehension rose in her, straightening her spine. She tamped it down by force of will alone, and forced her feet forward.

Armand turned toward the door and through his foggy, fever-glazed eyes made out a cloud of strawberry blonde curls. A smile spread across his face even as he was racked with a harsh, crackling cough.

"Jolie, my baby," he said once he could get breath in his lungs. His eyes closed and he felt her hand take his. "Now I am a happy man."

Jolie's throat tightened and she sank down on the bed next to her Papa. "I am happy, too," she said, even though she felt far from it. Mireille, her husband, and all the grandchildren crowded into the room around them, sitting wherever there was room.

Armand drew as deep a breath as he could and locked his eyes on Jolie's. "How did you get away?"

"He let me go, Papa," she said. "Don't worry about that now."

"That monster didn't let you go without a plan on how to get you back." Armand's eyes were crazed, wheeling about in their sockets. "He steals children, just like we all thought!"

"Papa, don't get yourself into a fit over him," Jolie said. "He's not what we all thought he was—"

"—the Papamontes boy, three summers ago!" Armand yelled, going on as if she hadn't spoken. His head came up from his pillow. "No one ever saw him again."

"They followed his trail and found him in the river, Papa. The poor boy had drowned."

"The Shilling girl!" he said, determined. "Last year, just before the big snow."

"They found her after spring thaw," Jolie said, her voice soothing. "Constable Lockwood said she'd wandered too far and froze to death."

She brushed the old man's hair away from his face, trying to hold her emotions at bay while he raved. "You know as well as I do that the Grey Man is just a story, nothing more. That man is Prince Leopold."

She wanted to tell him the whole story, from the beginning, but she wasn't sure how. Armand's last hours shouldn't be filled with such a fantastic story, anyway. "What happened and who he is no longer matters, Papa. I'm here."

Armand's eyes fluttered closed and he took a shaky breath. A sleepy smile lifted his cheeks and he settled into the pillow. She let go of his hand and climbed off the bed, watching his chest rise and fall. The children started filing out of the room, ushered toward the nursery by their father, and Jolie and Mireille went into the kitchen.

As soon as they were seated, Jolie accosted her sister with questions. "What happened? He wasn't this ill when I left. Why was I not summoned earlier?"

"He got worse that night, probably caught his death trying to make it back home. You know Papa, he thinks he can handle anything." Mireille said, pouring tea for the two of them. Her hands shook as she passed Jolie a cup. "He finally managed to catch something that he can't get rid of on his own. Are you home for good?"

Jolie watched as her sister's glittering eyes locked on her face, shrewd, trying to determine how much Jolie's presence in the house was going to reduce her share of the inheritance.

"Yes," Jolie said. She didn't miss the small rolling of Mireille's eyes.

Mireille composed herself before she continued. "Papa explained everything. I have a hard time understanding someone punishing an old man so severely over a rose. Is it true?"

"It is, Mireille. I know you want to judge him harshly, but the prince, as regent, has the right to punish theft of his property as treason. He could have had Papa hanged."

"He wouldn't have been in that position at all if you hadn't asked him for the stupid flower in the first place," Mireille said, her tone cold.

"He wouldn't have had to take the trip at all if the harbormaster hadn't mistaken another ship for the *Lisette*. Don't waste time blaming me," Jolie said. "This is not any of our faults. Old men get sick."

Even if Mireille didn't accept the logic, she understood that her sister's tone left no room for continued argument on the subject.

"Papa has lost everything we ever had, and now we are to lose him," Mireille said, a faraway look in her eyes as she drank her tea. Jolie could hear her sister changing subjects like a switch had been thrown. "Here is what I don't understand: the only one he thought to protect was you. He sent you to live—"

"—as a prisoner to the Grey Man, or so he believed!" Jolie shouted. "What he did was not of benefit to anyone, except perhaps himself. And of course, you, since it gets me out of your hair."

Mireille looked shocked, but Jolie knew she was right.

"You have a husband to be there for you when Papa—" Jolie's voice broke. She almost couldn't say the words. "—Papa passes. I will be alone. I have no one."

"You could live with Malcolm and me," Mireille offered, the words coming from her throat like they were coated in burning coals.

"I would rather live in a sheep barn the rest of my life than live in the same household as you again," Jolie said, surprised at her own strength.

"We all read that letter," Mireille said, jabbing a finger at a piece of paper on the end of the table. The thick vellum was emblazoned with the royal seal. Jolie stared at it, understanding the bitterness in her sister's tone.

"Your prince is taking care of you now, so lonely or not you will still live a very comfortable life," Mireille said, shoving away her teacup with more force than necessary.

"That was his decision. There has been a curse on him for almost ten years now. Prince Leopold is convinced that the curse will break at midnight after his birthday," Jolie said, talking fast while she had a second's window to speak. "After tomorrow, the only people I will have for company will be the vultures looking for a piece of my good fortune."

"Oh, please," Mireille scoffed, missing Jolie's subtle jab. "What difference does it make if you're alone? You will be rich beyond anyone's imagining, and have the protection of the prince. I swear I don't understand what he could be thinking, letting you live your own life with his fortune at your disposal."

Jolie didn't have a response for that.

"Unless of course, while you were there, this prince fell in love with you?" Her sneer turned her beautiful face ugly.

Two days ago, she'd have been able to sneer right back at her sister, but today Jolie wasn't so sure about the feelings she had for Leopold, or his for her.

"I wouldn't go that far, Mireille. I have no reason to think that," Jolie said. The words left the taste of a lie on her tongue, like sucking on an old coin.

"It seems as if you are at least a little wrong," Mireille said, a wicked laugh lighting up her eyes. "He lavishes you with gifts. Your gown is worth more than Malcolm will ever hope to make in a month. What sort of punishment has he made you suffer when you wear such finery?"

"I was mistress of the keep, regardless of the reasons for my being there. It was my home," Jolie admitted. Seeing the jealous gleam in Mireille's eyes, she grew defensive. "Leo is not a monster to be feared, but a man to be respected."

Mireille was confused. "The name on that letter was '*Willard LeChance.*' Who is Leo?"

"Prince Leopold," Jolie said, a blush stealing over her from her chest to her scalp, prickling the skin. She'd used the prince's given name in front of her sister, and knew the assumption her sister would make.

"Do you love him?" Mireille asked. Her blue eyes were wide; her mouth open in a drooping '*O*' of shock.

"No, I do not, Mireille," Jolie said, that metallic taste blooming on the back of her tongue again. "But I will not have you speaking of him as if he is worth less than anyone else. He feels everything just as we do, and has suffered more than any one person should ever have to."

"The Grey Man is a monster borne of Hell itself," Mireille countered, standing. The sisters were nose-to-nose over the narrow table, faces red and eyes wide. "Prince or otherwise, he haunts the nightmares of children throughout this country—"

"How modern of you, Mireille, to believe in such archaic tripe,"

Jolie hissed. "Magic bearers, witches, and sorcerers once roamed this land but we all know they are long dead. There is no more magic to be seen. The only reason anyone believes anything people say about the Grey Man is they're too afraid to find out who he really is."

"Afraid of what he'll do to them, Jolie! I swear, you act like you've never seen the creature. It's hideous, and huge to boot. It's no wonder everyone in the village is terrified of it," Mireille said, incredulous. She took a step back, goggling at her sister as if the younger woman had suddenly grown an extra limb from her forehead.

"Perhaps it is that I can see beyond the face you think is so hideous," Jolie replied. "No one else has taken the chance because you're all too stupid to see that there is more to a person than expensive clothes and good grooming. He looks different, especially compared to the prince he was long ago, but he's ten times the person these superstitious idiots will ever be, yourself included."

Mireille looked like she would like nothing more than to come across the table, her body shaking and her eyes wild. The older woman's hands opened and closed as if she were fighting the urge to strangle her sister.

Jolie just wanted to shut her up. "That *monster* is the one who arranged for all of Papa's debts to be paid and his property returned to him. Willard LeChance is his valet, and the prince used his name."

With that, Jolie plunked back down into her chair. She'd only been awake a few hours, but as darkness crept in, so early in the winter, she realized nothing would be better than to crawl into the bed she'd slept in as a child and sleep away the rest of the day as well. She sipped at her tea as Mireille stared at her for a moment, her face a portrait of surprise, then left the kitchen. The nursery door slammed and one of the children cried out in alarm, then started crying in earnest. The kitchen grew dark as Jolie finished her tea.

The sun had set completely when the physician arrived. Guillaume LaFitte was only in Armand's room for a moment when he came back out. He sat down at the table and turned to Jolie. By the look in his eyes, she knew what the old man was about to say.

"I'm afraid your father doesn't have much time," he said. "You and your sister should be with him when the time comes, but move quickly. He is nearly there."

A sharp stab of agony shot through Jolie's heart and for a moment, she couldn't breathe. Clutching at her chest, she sucked in a breath that burned in her lungs. She gave the doctor a weak nod, then rose on shaky legs and went to collect Mireille from the room she shared with Malcolm. The women went into Armand's room and perched on the bed on either side of their father.

Each of the sisters took a hand and lay with their father as his body shook and his breaths grew weaker and shallower. LaFitte gave Armand one more dose of laudanum, moving in and out of the room silently, and the old man looked at each of his daughters in turn. As the drug took hold for the last time, there was a small smile on his face.

The smile was still there as he closed his eyes and fell asleep. He squeezed his daughters' hands in his as he took his last breath, and in that moment, they both knew he was happy.

****

Leo hunkered down by the kitchen window, listening to Jolie and her sister as they grieved. His heart broke for them, and the memories of losing his own parents were as solid and tangible as if they were standing right next to him.

He couldn't watch them through the window and risk being seen, but he had heard every word they'd said since their argument in the kitchen. It felt odd, being defended, but a wonderful sort of odd. Like a confirmation that what he felt for Jolie was not in vain. Even if she didn't return his love, she deserved it, and he was proud of her.

A man spoke to the two women and one of Mireille's older children started crying. A door closed deeper within the house as the sounds of Mireille and a man who had to be her husband spoke in hushed tones. Leo stood and walked around the house, trying to find Jolie. When he found her, she was sitting on to a bed piled high with pillows and quilts. On that bed was her father. Armand looked thinner than when Leo had last seen him, his skin already beginning to turn grey with death. A maid of some sort walked into the room and covered the mirror on Armand's bureau with a sheet. An older manservant helped her to drape the windows as well, a custom preventing Armand's spirit from getting trapped in the reflections. The manservant stilled the pendulum on a great clock, as well, stopping time for the family to grieve.

Leo knew he had done the right thing letting Jolie go home. He'd never gotten the chance to say goodbye to either of his parents, even though he was in the same room with them when they died. He was glad he could give her the opportunity to do so with her father.

Mireille walked into the bedroom and spoke briefly to Jolie, who nodded and left without a word. He followed her as best he could through the windows, still careful not to be seen. She was closing a door behind herself when he found her again. The room she'd wound up in was a bedroom, and he could only assume it had been hers. Her face was red, tear-streaks running down both cheeks. Her hair was even wilder than usual from raking her hands through it as she'd wept. There was nothing he could do to comfort her without frightening everyone else in the house, but his arms ached to hold her and try to take away some of her pain.

Jolie walked through the room with her head down, then sat in the cushioned window seat. Leo ducked out of sight, flattening his back against the wall.

Perhaps she was looking out the window, up the hill toward the château, but now he would have to wait until he was sure she was away from the window before he could look in again. For the first time in his life he felt like a criminal, but even though he couldn't do anything but watch over her, he couldn't leave her. Not now.

****

Quentin looked through his father's spyglass toward the Babineaux house. He'd only come to this knoll tonight because he'd seen Mireille and Jolie ride by his house and wanted to see his wayward fiancée. Now, his interest was well and truly piqued. The Grey Man was hiding outside Jolie's bedroom window. Quentin could not believe his luck. Here he was, with a mission to kill the monster, be the hero, and save the wayward damsel in distress, when who should show up at the damsel's own house? It felt like fate.

Quentin couldn't hear exactly what was happening in the house, but he saw the physician's coach outside. His best guess was that Armand had just died. He knew that Mireille and Malcolm had arrived for a month-long visit that had stretched to nearly two months, and that the physician had been in and out of the house for the last three weeks.

Judging by the way Malcolm had behaved with Armand's solicitor present, he knew the patriarch's death would not improve his chances of marrying Jolie and saving himself from a life of drudgery on a Caribbean sugar plantation. But, his plan to kill the Grey Man would even the odds. Malcolm would have to see him in a favorable light if he proved himself a hero.

He had no choice but to go through with this plan now. Even though, if he was honest with himself, he wasn't sure he could pull it off.

For hours, Quentin watched as the creature listened to the conversations going on inside the house. As the moon reached its zenith in the night sky, it cast a last longing look through the window at Jolie a moment before it got up from the ground and started on its way to Château Hill, and Quentin knew the time had come.

Crouched on the knoll, he put up the spyglass one more time and watched the Grey Man as it left the village. It hung its head, its steps slow and plodding, and almost seemed unconcerned that it could be seen at any time.

Turning back toward the Babineaux house, he saw Jolie through the glass. She sat on the window seat in her bedroom, her head resting on her upraised knees, tears streaming down her face. Mireille came in the room and the two sisters held each other as they wept. After, they joined Malcolm in the only other room Quentin could see into from his position, the kitchen. They took turns talking to each other and the physician.

Quentin plopped down on the grass, watching the goings-on with renewed interest. A carriage was called for and something was brought out, wrapped in a white sheet, and Quentin knew for sure what had happened at last. Armand Babineaux had died while he waited for the opportunity to pursue the Grey Man. He could still go up the hill now, of course, but now he'd waited long enough that his nerves had gotten their chance to talk him out of it.

Tomorrow was another day, and now that he thought about it, it was the perfect day to enact his plan. Tomorrow was the prince's birthday, the anniversary of the day his parents had been killed. That gave Quentin a full day to steel himself for his plan.

How appropriate would it be if Quentin ended his life on such a tragic and significant day, saving the village from the Grey Man's reign in the process?

Chapter 15

Jolie and Mireille stayed up most of the night, listening to the eerie silence that filled the house now that Armand was gone. The carriage took their father's body to the undertaker, where it would be prepared for his funeral. Henrietta helped both women change into their mourning gowns, swathing them in black from head to foot. Malcolm changed his clothes, as well, and stayed up with his wife throughout the long night.

Jolie spent most of the night in her room, already missing her father. She felt such immense guilt for not being here for him while he was so ill. It may have been selfish, but she felt like the worst part of losing her father was that she had to suffer his loss alone. Mireille had Malcolm and her children to surround her with love now and after their father was buried. Jolie would have to endure her loss on her own, with no one to comfort her.

Naturally, her thoughts turned to Leo, wondering where he was right now. Would he learn of her father's death? Rosalie and Willard came into town at least once a week for food and other necessities. Surely they would hear the news and take it back to their master. What would she feel right now if he walked through the front door and held his arms out for her? Why did she think that would be the way he would react to the news of such a personal loss?

Jolie thought about how much hurt she'd seen in his eyes when he spoke of his own parents' deaths, and knew that the man she knew would understand. If anyone in this village knew what she was feeling, it was Leo. Not for the first time since she'd left, she missed him, a heaviness in her chest she couldn't attribute to her father's death alone.

If Leo were here, she would have someone to commiserate with, another person who knew what she was feeling. More than anything, she wanted him to just be there. Having him near would mitigate all the turmoil inside her right now. She'd been at the château only hours ago, but it already felt like she'd been gone for days, and she missed Leo.

It was tempting to go get Garnet and return, if only for a few hours. She wanted to see Willard and Rosalie again, and know she was safe once more. Even with Malcolm in the house, she felt exposed. Malcolm had a duty to protect her sister and their children first, and with no one else here, Jolie knew she might be in danger if Quentin showed up. With no concrete reason to think he would show up here, she had to believe he would leave her alone or she'd lose her mind in anxiety.

Looking out the window, she saw lights flicker in the palace windows, and even though she knew Leo couldn't see her from there, she lay down on the window seat, keeping her eyes on the château and imagining him watching over her. The thought was comforting, so she let her imagination run with the idea. Thinking of being under Leo's protection again brought her a feeling of security that washed over her like a warm bath. She rested her head on her arm and closed her eyes. Sleep didn't come easily, but it did come.

She was standing in the middle of Château Villeneuve's Great Hall. Dressed in her funeral gown, she was alone at first. The hall was silent. No music, no ticking clock, no guests, just her and one other person.

In front of her, the shadowy intruder appeared, his garb eerily similar to her own. All black, his face masked like last time, he held a dagger loosely in one hand. As she watched, he began to circle her, his steps slow, methodical. She turned with him, keeping her eyes on the mask.

The giant crow flew in through the transom and landed on the piano seat again. Its beak opened, but no sound came out this time. A door banged open behind Jolie, and she turned toward the sound.

Leo was coming through the southwest entrance to the Great Hall, dressed in rags that looked like they were rotting off his body as he walked toward her. She tried to move, to meet him halfway, but her shoes were stuck to the floor. When she yanked a leg forward, she fell to her knees, the toe of her shoe holding her down.

Leo reached for her, but the intruder in black jumped into action, lunging forward with his dagger at his hip. The knife plunged into Leo's chest, and he shattered like a pâpier-maché sculpture of himself, pieces scattering like torn newsprint all over the floor. In his place was the handsome stranger, his eyes wide, hair falling over his shoulders, mouth open in shock.

The handsome stranger had taken the knife wound, and as the intruder backed away, he left the dagger stuck in the handsome man's side, just beneath the ribs. The handle protruded at a downward angle, and Jolie realized the blade was deep in the stranger's lung. The stranger jerked the knife out and tossed it aside.

Jolie pulled on her feet with both hands, trying anything she could to move toward the stranger. Her feet slipped free of the shoes and she crawled across the floor. The intruder fled, his feet carrying him across the Great Hall and out the front entrance. She reached the stranger and took his face in her hands. He pulled her to him, his arms squeezing her body against his. He gasped in her ear, his breaths labored.

"Do you love me, Jolie?" the handsome stranger asked, his voice cracking and weak.

Jolie jerked awake, the man's broken voice echoing in her ears. She was still curled up on the window seat, and could tell it hadn't been long since she'd drifted off. For a moment, she couldn't remember where she was and when she saw the furnishings for her old bedroom at her father's house, she thought she must still be dreaming.

Reality is a cruel mistress, though, and came flooding back to her all at once, the memory of the previous day exploding in her chest. She turned away from the window and let the tears come. Sobs tore out of her like they were on fire. Today was the day she would have to start learning how to navigate a world without her father, and knowing she would have to do it alone only made the world around her seem that much worse.

****

Leo woke later than he meant to that morning, still half-sitting in his big bed in the south tower. He'd spend a long time last night watching out the window, knowing how Jolie was feeling. That there was nothing he could do for her now hurt him more than he cared to admit. If he could go to the village without being killed by some paranoid villager, he would already be on his way to the Babineaux house. He knew, though, that he'd never be allowed in the door. She needed her sister right now, maybe even more than he imagined she might need him.

The clock on the writing desk told him it was past nine o'clock, and the bright winter sun streamed in the balcony doors, making the room appear cheerful. He knew what day it was, though, and that there would be no joy found in it. It was his birthday, and he would know at midnight whether he had become a good enough man to break the curse. He felt different than he had even a month ago, but the condition of the curse he couldn't count on, and never had, was whether he had earned a woman's love.

As much as he loved Jolie, there was no guarantee that she loved him in return. Without her love, he would stay just as he was for the rest of his life. He wasn't afraid anymore, though, just resigned to his fate. If she came back, he would be elated. If she didn't, though, he would understand. If the curse didn't break there was no future for them together, anyway.

Out there, she could have any life she wanted. He would make sure she could travel anywhere she wanted to, and she could marry the man of her choice when she was ready. She deserved that much.

What would he do with all his remaining years if she didn't come back to him?

If the curse doesn't break after tonight, you'll have plenty of time to figure out your life afterward.

For now, he just had to survive today. Which brought him to the other conundrum he had to focus on. He had no doubt that Quentin was planning on coming back, and he imagined the boy's sense of drama might be getting the better of him, in consideration of what day it was.

Leo was no fool, knew who would win this fight once it started. Something about Quentin had him wondering, though. The man seemed confident in a way that made Leo more afraid than the situation should have warranted.

The Garamondes were known as avid hunters, and before Leo's transformation he had heard that the youngest of the family— only eleven at that time— was their most skilled. If Quentin was confident he could hold his own against Leo, there was more for the prince to be concerned about than was obvious. And, Quentin wanted Jolie for his bride. There was something to be said for a man who was willing to fight for the honor of winning a woman's hand. Leo himself was ready and able to do the same.

Leo would do well to be on his guard today. He got out of bed and dressed himself in simple clothes, just a white tunic and his most comfortable fawn breeches, white hose, and his familiar Hessians. Willard came up the stairs to greet him for the morning and he decided to join his valet for breakfast. A long day was ahead of all of them, and an empty stomach wouldn't do.

****

Before Jolie knew it, half the day was gone in making Armand's funeral arrangements. Henrietta and Desmond cleaned the old man's room, readying it for guests who visited. Dishes of food arrived, the neighbors reaching out to the family with whatever form of comfort they could provide. People trickled in and out of the house throughout the day, staying long enough to pay their respects and offer condolences before they left the family to their grief.

Mireille and Malcolm began to ready themselves to return to their home, as well. In just a few days, the house would be empty, and Jolie would truly be on her own. It was all happening so fast and Jolie couldn't stop her head from spinning. She could hardly believe that only a month ago, she had thought her life was complete, even simple. Now, in a short time, every part of her life felt like it had either fallen apart or been flipped upside down.

Just after noon, a coach pulled away from the house full of some of Mireille's things, taking it to their home in Compiegne ahead of them. Jolie let her take a few of Armand's things, as well, as mementos. Armand had left a will, and considering Jolie's position had changed since it was drafted, his belongings were divided equally between them. Armand's funeral was in a week's time in the churchyard across town. Beyond knowing the date and time of his funeral, Jolie didn't have room in her head for anything else. Just getting out of bed to help Malcolm to make the arrangements was difficult enough, and all she wanted to do once that bit of business was done was go back to bed. Mireille took a sleeping draught and Jolie was considering following suit when Henrietta tried to tempt her with luncheon.

"You must eat, child," the old maid said, loading a plate with food.

Jolie picked at it, eating without seeing or tasting anything she took. She didn't eat much, and when she was done Henrietta left it on the table in case she came back to it.

As she sat at her father's table, an odd feeling came over her. She couldn't identify it at first, just a strange thing that made her think of walking in on someone in the privy. Like she didn't belong where she was. It didn't make sense, because she was sitting in the kitchen she'd taken meals in for most of her life. The only time she'd ever been away from this house was during her time with Leo.

She should be happy to be home, but without Papa here the house felt empty, foreign. Without him, she wondered if it would ever feel like home again. Once Mireille and Malcolm left for home next week, she wasn't sure she would ever feel at home here again. This was Papa's house, not hers.

The idea of looking for a home of her own was daunting, and her mind kept turning back. To the château, and of course Leo, over and over again. She wondered at why she was so drawn to a place that should have frightened her. Perhaps it was because she'd seen the old building's secrets, including the biggest secret of all, Prince Leopold himself. Once a place's mysteries were solved, it wasn't nearly as frightening.

Jolie supposed that was why she felt the way she did about Leo. She hadn't put a word to her feelings for him yet, but she knew she cared for him. She worried about him, up on that hill alone.

Today was not a day he should spend alone with his thoughts. She didn't think there was anything she could do about it— she needed to be here. But she thought about him nonetheless.

Midnight would come and go and she would be right here. And in a week's time, she would still be right here. What about in a month? Or a year? Where would she be then? As hard as it was right now to think even a moment ahead, the time would come when she had to think of her future.

Cared for by a wealthy benefactor, who would no doubt allow her to live her life as she saw fit, the years could stretch on interminably without someone to share them with. She could travel as she'd always dreamed, spend time in foreign lands, meet thousands of new people, but would she always come back to this place, just to be alone all over again?

She supposed she might meet someone in her travels, or even in the village, that would befriend her. She might even marry someday, when she was ready. That thought was even more repellent than it used to be, and this time she knew the problem was: unfinished business. If she walked away from Leo, she would regret it. Maybe not until after her father's death faded to a dull ache rather than the sharp stab it was right now, but someday she would look back on the moment she chose to leave him in her past and be ashamed of herself.

Jolie cared for him, more than she was willing to admit. Even if there was no future for them, she wanted to run to him more than anything. Before midnight, before the curse ended, before anything else happened, she wanted to see Leo's face.

As if in answer to her thoughts, a knock came to the door and reminded her of why she was needed here. At least for now, there were doors to be answered and so many things to plan she didn't see how she would find time today to take a ride by herself. She shot one more glance toward Château Hill and went to answer the door.

A man bearing huge bouquets of flowers of every kind stood on the stoop. He introduced himself and she recognized the name as one of the Babineaux's neighbors. She let him in and as he walked past, caught the heady perfume of roses. Such an innocent scent, it sent her back three weeks to the night her father had fallen ill in the first place. All because she'd asked for a rose. Guilt boiled in the pit of her stomach and she had to sit down, falling into a chair in the foyer with a thud. Her breath hitched and tears stung her eyes.

This wouldn't do. She had to help her neighbor with the flowers, and there were still many things that needed tending to. She forced herself to take several deep breaths, then stood and headed toward the sitting room.

It was hours before she could return to the kitchen, and by then the sun was setting on the horizon. She looked at the clock and noted the time with a growing sense of foreboding. As time crept on, ever closer to that witching hour of midnight, she wondered what would happen. She made her way to her bedroom and sat at the window.

Up on top of Château Hill, torches were lit all the way around the stronghold. Through the window, Jolie could hear how quiet the whole village was. There was a thick feeling of apprehension in the air that permeated the land. The whole village seemed to be holding its breath.

Every window in the keep glowed with light from within. It looked much as it had ten years ago, as if a party was being held. It fooled only the few in the village too young to know the story.

No one was celebrating the prince's birthday tonight. Least of all the prince himself.

****

Leo felt more exposed than usual as he made his way toward Fontainbleu. It seemed like the whole village was watching for him tonight, waiting for the prince to show himself, or the Grey Man to come out from his hiding spot. As darkness fell, few stayed outdoors, but he still took a path that kept him outside the village until he reached the Babineaux property. He hunkered down behind a huge oak and watched through the windows.

From this vantage point, he could watch Jolie without being seen. She was looking up the hill again, like she had last night, and Leo wondered, or maybe hoped, she was thinking of him.

If tonight was the night Garamonde chose to make his stand, Leo wanted to make it worth his while. He didn't doubt his ability to beat Quentin in a fight, but he knew that there was still a chance he would be hurt or killed regardless. A man should never enter a fight with the idea in his head that he will come out of it unscathed.

Before long, he stood and started back toward home. He could only allow himself a short look at the woman in the window. A moment more and he might still be sitting there come midnight. If he left now, no matter what else happened tonight, at least he would have a memory of her looking up toward his home like this.

As he mounted Château Hill, he felt the hairs on the back of his neck stand on end. As he walked the path up the hill, he heard sounds most would miss. Twigs snapped and leaves rustled under someone's feet. Leo kept up his pace and gave no sign that he knew about his pursuer. The two would meet soon enough.

****

Quentin cut through the woods, parallel to path the monster took. His position was uphill from the road, so he could see the monster as it negotiated the winding path without it seeing him. His soft-soled boots made little noise on the dead leaves and castoff twigs on the forest floor as he matched the beast's pace. It was two feet taller than Quentin and most of its height was in its legs so for every step it took, he had to take two.

He let the Grey Man round the corners before him, staying a few paces behind as they drew closer. The only way the creature would see him would be to turn and look right at him. The final corner was coming up and the trees and brush that had been so thick on the bottom of the hill started to thin out, leaving Quentin exposed.

This is it, he thought. No matter what happened tonight, he was going to take on the monster of Château Villeneuve. Prince Leopold or not, the creature would die and it would be at Quentin Garamonde's hand.

****

Knowing he'd been caught looking in on Jolie, Leo tried to make his path away from her home as convoluted as possible but there were only two easily navigable routes up the hill. He had to either take the road that led to the front gate or the trail that Armand stumbled upon that brought him to the back courtyard and through the incomplete wall. The longer he was away, the bigger risk he took of being seen.

When he hadn't been able to shake off Jolie's suitor before reaching the foot of the hill, he had chosen the most direct route to his home. If Leo couldn't lead him astray, maybe he could reason with Quentin.

Leo entered the keep and wound his way to the south tower. Walking this floor for what might be the last time, he looked at pink and ivory rose that had started this journey. He grasped the hollow glass ball in his hand, his fingers gentle on its fragile surface, and plucked it from its sconce. The rose's light had gone out, leaving it looking like any other withered old rose in the world. Only three petals remained on the head of the flower, all of them dry and puckered.

There was a knock on the doorjamb and Leo turned. Willard stood in the doorway, looking uncomfortable. "My Lord—"

"—don't call me that," Leo interrupted, his voice soft. "I am not your Prince any longer." He settled the globe back in its mooring, then slipped off the cloak.

"Leo, Quentin Garamonde has returned and is circling the property. I believe he is trying to make his way in again," Willard said. His hands wrung together and he danced from one foot to the other.

"I know," Leopold said, tossing the cloak onto the bed. "He followed me from Jolie's home in the village."

"Why has he followed you? Jolie has gone home. Surely he can speak with her there."

"Because I am the Grey Man."

"That silly story again?" Willard stood up straighter, rolling his eyes.

"So it appears." Leo moved to the balcony, looking out over the south end of his property. The dark sky was like a fresh bruise, purple and black and blue behind the trees. "He saw me outside Jolie's bedroom. I was watching her."

Willard saw the blush that crept over the prince's face and smiled. They both chuckled.

"It appears he still wishes to marry her, but that's not enough anymore," Leo said, sobering. "Unless tonight goes very well, I will be in no position to stop it from happening."

Willard closed his eyes at the prince's words. "What shall we do about him?"

"Let him in, treat him as a guest. Perhaps I can reason with him." He opened his mouth to continue, then shook his head as if he thought better of it. He looked unsure, his eyes flicking to Willard's, searching for the old man's opinion.

"What if he saw your actions at Mademoiselle Babineaux's home as threatening? What if you can't reason with him?" Willard was nervous again, scraping his hands through his hair and that left-to-right dance starting again.

Looking again at the wilting rose, Leo sighed. A petal fell the bottom of the globe, leaving only two more. He'd rather be killed than live the rest of his life in this hell, and by midnight, just hours from now, the curse would come to fruition. Life without Jolie or death, those were his options. "I will accept whatever comes, Willard. You and the others should go. You are not safe here anymore."

Willard entered the room, even though he wanted to do anything but. His stomach twisted and he pressed a hand to it, but he held his head high. There was something he needed to tell his master and there might not be another chance to do it. "Prince Leopold, I am honored to have served you these past ten years."

Leo turned to his valet. The old man was screwing up his courage, rubbing the pad of his thumb against the insides of his fingers and holding his head up so high it looked painful. "You are not the boy you once were. The old woman's curse changed you in more ways than one, and all of them for the better."

Leo felt the old rage simmering against his spine, but he thought of Jolie and was able to calm himself.

"Hear me out, Master," Willard said, holding a hand out with an authority Leo had never seen in the man before. He stopped in his tracks and relaxed. "Your curse was a gift, Leopold. You are a changed man, which is what that old witch wanted. I'm just sorry you— "

"I love Jolie, Willard," Leo admitted, confirming his valet's suspicions. From the look on his face, so earnest, Willard knew he meant the words. The younger man turned away, gazing again out the window. "She just doesn't love me."

The master gave his servant a sheepish, regretful look, his eyes so sad the valet wished to go to him.

"I got halfway there," Leo said.

There was nothing more to say to that. "I'll get that meal laid out for our guest, Master."

"Then gather everyone up and leave this place. Take the coach. This is no home for anyone, not anymore." Quentin passed under the window, the top of his head lit by the torch light from inside. Leo watched as he crept by, not knowing his quarry was so close. It was only a matter of time before he made his way to the rear entrance.

Willard placed a hand on Leo's arm and the prince turned to face him. "Your parents would be proud of their son today."

Leo nodded and watched Willard as he left. Moments later, dishes rattled downstairs, the sound carrying through the otherwise silent fortress. Then, he heard a door shut. The coach house and stables were far enough away that he couldn't hear them leave but knowing how alone and isolated he was here, he wished he could see that his servants were safely away. Just one last time, he wanted to do his job as their master, to let his last act toward his employees be one of kindness and protection.

The door that led from the rear courtyard slammed open, banging against the stone wall. Leo looked at the pink-and-ivory rose in its globe, then braced himself for whatever was coming.

****

Henrietta had laid the children down for the night and was just untying the laces on Jolie's gown when there was a knock on the door. Desmond answered it, and Jolie heard him turn away whoever was there. The next sound she heard, muffled as the door was closing, was a man's voice shouting, "I must speak to Mademoiselle Jolie! Quentin Garamonde is on his way to the château!"

Jolie leapt away from Henrietta, running down the hall to the front door at full speed. "Hold the door, Desmond!" she called, and the old man jumped out of her way in the nick of time as she ran.

The man on the other side of the door, a shabby-looking man too young to be in such a sad state of health, spoke in cultured tones. "My name is Thomas Brilliande, Mademoiselle. I have some things to tell you about your fiancé that you need to know. I think he is about to do something terrible."

"If it is of Quentin you speak, that man was never my fiancé, as much as he desired to be," Jolie said, her eyes narrowed in suspicion.

"Pardon me, mademoiselle, a slip of the tongue," Thomas said, a small smile on his lips. "Be that as it may, I need to speak to you."

"What are you talking about?" Jolie asked. "And why should I believe what you have to tell me?"

"I saw Quentin as I was on my way to warn you about his plan. He is on his way right now to kill the Grey Man," Thomas explained.

Jolie's heart thudded against her breastbone, a sick feeling rising in her stomach. It was all too clear now, the purpose of all of Quentin's clandestine trips up the Hill. This was his plan all along, and neither she nor Leo had figured it out until it was too late. She had to do something; she couldn't just leave Leo up there all alone.

Thomas wasn't done, though. He hung his head, his shoulders slumping in shame, and said, "The worst part is, I'm to blame for this plan."

"How could you be?" Jolie was as bewildered as she'd ever been.

"I drew him a map and told him which room the Grey Man slept in."

Realization dawned and Jolie took a step back, her eyes wide. She didn't have time to come up with a plan. If Quentin knew where Leo slept, and was already on his way, she might already be too late. Thomas had given him the exact route he would need to take.

Jolie swore, then hauled up her skirts and took off for the stables, leaving Desmond staring after her, aghast at her language.

She ran to Garnet's stall and slapped the latch open, then grabbed handfuls of mane and pulled herself onto the horse's back. The gelding didn't have a bit in his bridle, but at least there were reins for Jolie to hold on to.

Once they were safely beyond the barn and paddock, she drove Garnet to a hard gallop. It was a long ride, the horse would tire, but there wasn't time to think about that. Midnight was only a couple of hours away, and if Quentin fulfilled his plan she would never forgive herself. She wasn't sure what she would do once she got there, either, but had to hold on to the hope that she would not be too late.

Jolie drove the horse as hard as she could, forcing him to jump over the boulders. More than once, she came close to upending them both as she cut corners. And still, she snapped the reins and urged the animal on. When she came to the old Tremonde Road, she let the horse pick its way up the narrow path. The torches cast a flickering orange glow over the grounds.

When she reached the wall, she left her father's horse at the gap and ran through the courtyard, ignoring scratches and cuts as she ran through the rose bushes, their thorns whipping against her skin as she held her skirts aloft.

The back door was hanging open, chill winter air blowing through it into the corridor. Walking through that portal felt like crossing the threshold into a strange new world, and she knew she may never come back out.

****

The Grey Man was even larger than Quentin had thought from a distance. Now, as he stood so close, he began to realize his folly. He'd come with too much confidence to a fight he didn't think he could win. All his planning had been for naught, and no amount of confidence in his plan would save him once this creature got hold of him.

With shoulders that wouldn't fit through a doorway in an average home and so tall it would have to duck to keep from scraping its head on the ceiling, this creature was the biggest thing Quentin had ever seen. When it breathed, its barrel chest took in more air than a blacksmith's bellows needed to run for a day. On an average man, such as himself, the beast's monstrous arms would drag on the floor, and its legs were as big around as Quentin's waist.

Frightened to the core of his soul, Quentin tried his best not to show it, puffing out his chest and straightening his spine. Perhaps if he projected a self-assured air, the beast would believe he was a worthy adversary and present Quentin with an easy opportunity to end this fight without hurting himself in the process.

"What is your business with my fiancée?" Quentin asked, pleased with how bold his voice sounded. "I saw you outside her home, watching her through her window."

"You are Quentin Garamonde, yes?" the monster said as it turned to face Quentin.

Quentin's eyes widened as he took in the appearance of the creature's face. Hairy from hairline to throat, it looked like no man Quentin had ever heard of. It might have walked out of some exotic jungle and stolen a nobleman's clothes. Panic threatened, and he forced himself to swallow several times before he spoke. "I am," was all he could manage.

The Grey Man stayed on the balcony. Quentin watched the thing's eyes, how they darted all over the room, assuring itself of its surroundings.

"I welcome you to my home," it said. "There is a meal laid below, if you would like. We can discuss our situation like men, if that pleases you."

Quentin's screwed his face up in a look of pure disgust. The thought of dining with this beast turned his stomach. The very idea that this monstrosity compared itself to a man infuriated him.

"There is nothing to discuss." To prove his point, he crouched and slid a dagger out of the shaft of his boot, the only weapon he had on his person. All his plans to lay in weapons had come to naught and all he had was a knife whose blade the beast could hide in its fist.

Any hope Leo had of civil discourse between the two of them disappeared at the sight of that knife. This wasn't a man bent on avenging his fiancée's honor, but one determined to slay the village dragon.

A flicker of movement in the corner of his eye drew his attention away from Quentin and he trained his eyes on a horse that was now wandering the grounds, illuminated in the torch light. It wasn't a familiar animal, but he knew of only one person who would risk life and limb to come to him at a time like this. His chest tightened and he turned away from Quentin to hide the emotion. Any moment now, Jolie would burst through the door behind Quentin and all he could hope was that this would all be over before she could get herself hurt.

Chapter 16

Jolie lunged up the stairs, taking them two at a time. She held handfuls of her skirt up, the weight of the material making her biceps burn with exertion. Water drops from the rain that started during the ride to the castle cooled her skin and raised goosebumps all over her body. Shivering, she pulled in great heaving breaths as she climbed.

Halfway up the stairs, her arms gave out and she couldn't hold the skirt anymore. She let the fabric fall, crawling up the stairs on her hands and feet as fast as they would carry her. "Leo!" she called as she mounted the last stair.

Quentin stood with his back to her just inside the doors to the balcony, a dagger in his hand, its blade coated with blood. He was dressed in black from head to toe, reminding her of the shadowy intruder she'd seen in her dream the night Quentin had broken in the second time. He danced from one foot to the other, nerves making his hands shake.

Leo fell against the jamb to the French doors that led to the balcony, clutching a wound in the lower right side of his chest. The knife had plunged between two ribs. Air whistled through his mouth and the open wound with a sick sucking sound. Jolie's mind flashed with a memory of the bizarre dream she'd had a few nights ago, of her handsome stranger and the wound he'd suffered.

Leo's eyes found Jolie's and softened, his cheeks lifting in an inexplicable smile. Blood poured from between his fingers and that horrible sucking sound carried on as Quentin stepped closer. Raising the dagger over his head in both hands, he moved to make the killing blow.

Jolie only had a moment to act. She charged forward and slammed into Quentin's back, propelling him forward until his thighs hit the railing on the balcony. Quentin gasped and reached for the rail, letting the dagger fall to the cobblestone path below with a metallic clatter.

Jolie strained against Quentin's body, trying to send him over his tipping point without going over herself. If she got his upper body over the edge, he wouldn't be able to stop himself.

He turned against her and grabbed her shoulders, every muscle in his body fighting against momentum and gravity to stay upright. He dug a hand into her hair and on instinctive reaction to the pain her hands went to his to try and free herself. He yanked against the back of her neck and pulled her toward the railing, twisting his body into safety.

Leo struggled forward, one big hand still covering the wound in his chest as if trying to hold the blood from gushing out of his body. He grabbed one of Quentin's shoulders and squeezed, the bones cracking and grinding against one another as they broke. The younger man screamed and let go of Jolie, clutching his injured shoulder as he stumbled backward toward the railing.

Leo pushed Jolie out of the way, his hand dragging across her chest as he moved between her and Quentin. She looked down at her chest where Leo's hand had been and saw a smear of his dark blood on her skin. She looked back up, ready to pounce if she saw any opportunity to help.

Quentin was screaming, a deep guttural sound from deep within his body, his hands clawing at his shoulder. Leo reached out for his hand and Quentin's grey eyes latched onto his, suspicious and angry, narrowed to little more than slits.

"I will take you to the village and get you help," Leo said. Doing so would expose him as everything the village held in their worst fever dreams, but the man needed a physician. Shock registered on Quentin's face, his eyes widening and his brow furrowing even as he took Leo's proffered hand.

As Leo was pulling him up, Quentin set his heels into the stones and used the monster's height and weight against him, pulling with all he had. Leo, so much weaker with the gaping wound in his side and lack of oxygen preventing him from thinking clearly, was caught off guard.

Jolie screamed and leapt forward as both men tumbled over the railing. Half a breath later she heard a sickening thud, and then nothing. She bolted down the stairs and through the Great Hall to the rear courtyard, slipping on the icy ground as she made her way to the overgrown path that led to the ground below the south tower.

She found them both sprawled on the worn cobbles of the path, several feet apart. Quentin was staring up at the mottled grey sky, his eyes unfocused and unseeing. Without pausing, she ran to Leo's side, dropping to her knees next to him. His torso didn't look right, his chest at the wrong angle to his hips and one side flatter than the other. The horrid sucking sound had become a thin whistle and she knew he was broken on the inside, his lungs damaged by the stab wound and the fall. He could only take short, shallow breaths, his body rocking with the effort.

Not knowing what to say or where she could touch him that wouldn't hurt, she fluttered her hands everywhere they could find purchase, finally reaching his face and turning it to her. Blood ran from one corner of his mouth and into the hair that covered his face.

At the touch of her hands, he forced himself to open his eyes. Unable to take a breath deep enough to speak, he tried to show her everything he wanted to say with his eyes. Lifting a hand to her face, he threaded his fingers into her hair.

He'd never seen her curly mass of red ringlets lay so flat and missed its usual volume. Her eyes were red from her tears; those drops of water lost in the ones the sky was dropping on them. Understanding of the magic bearer's purpose washed over him as he wished with all his will for just one more moment, then another, and another. The true cruelty of her curse made him want to weep. To find Jolie just days before he was to breathe his last was the most painful fact of his entire life. And the damnable irony of it all was, if he had grown up a good man, he may never have met her at all.

If given the choice he would do it all over again, just the same. He would rather live in love with Jolie for a few moments than live to old age without her. He just hoped she could see how he felt, even if she didn't return his affections.

Leo's eyes were so warm on hers she thought they could bring back the summer sun. Lying on his courtyard dying with no hope of help, he looked at her as if she were the most beautiful creature he'd ever seen. Clutching his hand against her skin, she had nothing but her own will to keep him alive. His lips moved and it took her a moment to understand what he was trying to say.

I'm sorry, he mouthed. *Forgive me.*

"Don't be silly," she started but his body convulsed, his back lifting off the ground as he tried to catch his breath.

Leo opened his mouth once more, his lips forming the words '*I love you*' over and over again as she stared back at him, speechless at his admission. Then, his hand broke free from hers and clenched into a fist before it fell to the ground.

An emptiness stole over him and black edges impinged on his field of vision, reminding him how short his time was. His whole body felt cold, even colder than the weather warranted.

Along the path, something glinted in the bleak stormy light and he turned his head. The globe containing his rose rolled itself down the path toward them, lit by the weakening torch light, another grim reminder that he'd lost. At least he wouldn't have to live much longer trapped in this body. And he would die looking to the eyes of his beloved.

As it drew closer, the globe began to glow with an unearthly white light. The rose lost another petal to the floor of the globe as it came to rest near his left hand. Only one left.

"Tell me what to do, Leo," Jolie said, breathless. His eyes found hers again and he took both her hands in his.

There was no room in his body for air anymore and he locked his eyes on hers as he took one last shuddering breath. His eyes rolled and his head fell back as the life slipped from his body.

For a moment she sat still, looking at his motionless body on the stone path, disbelieving. "Leo?" she called. She shook her head side to side as if the movement would take it all back.

With both hands, she shoved against his chest, knowing as his body rocked back and forth without resistance that her efforts were in vain. Realization crashed over her as the skies opened, pouring freezing water and bits of ice down on her as if the whole world was weeping with her. Her mouth went dry and her stomach clenched on what felt like a cannon ball.

"You can't leave me!" she cried, coming up on her knees. A bright flash of light from the edge of the forest caught her eye and she looked to see what it was.

From out of the trees stepped the same stooped old figure from her dream, clutching a crooked walking stick in her hands. She hobbled her way up to the path and as she drew closer Jolie realized she could see through the old woman. A misty, weak glow surrounded her, and Jolie's eyes latched onto the soft light as it trailed through the forest and toward her and Leo.

As she drew closer, the hag lifted a gnarled hand and the globe of glass rose from the ground, bathing them all in its eerie white light.

"No!" Jolie cried, reaching for the glass. Her fingers slipped along the surface as it continued to rise. "You can't have him, witch!" Desperate, she closed her eyes against a fresh bloom of pain in her chest. She didn't think she could survive another death so close to her father's, especially not Leo's.

The magic bearer just smiled and stopped. The globe carried the rose further away from Jolie and as it got closer to the old crone, panic set in, gripping her stomach tight and setting her legs to shaking.

The old woman was long dead, beyond reasoning with. Jolie closed her eyes, knowing she would walk away from this place alone, back to her father's house and to a life she was no longer sure was enough. She closed her eyes and lay her head on Leo's chest, still warm but so still. From the corner of her eye she saw the rose's last petal break free from the stem and start to fall. Closing her eyes again, she whispered the only words she had left to say.

"I love you."

The petal hit the bottom of the globe and the glass shattered, crackling in a pattern like a spider's web, then exploding in all directions. The shards formed an enormous sphere that surrounded the three of them; Leopold, the old magic bearer, and Jolie, in a glowing white orb. The rain within that circle stopped falling and hung in the air, fat drops suspended in the old woman's thrall. Nothing happened for a moment and Jolie reached out with trembling fingers and touched one of the drops of rain as it hung before her eyes. It bent and formed around her finger, then held that crescent-moon shape after she dropped her hand.

A blanket of shimmering white swallowed the hag whole, releasing her as the raven-haired beauty Prince Leopold had told her about.

The witch's smile was angelic and more than a little arrogant as she stepped toward where Leopold lay. The water drops splashed against her green dress, rolling off the fabric as if it were oil cloth, leaving no marks on the silk.

Jolie stood as she approached, unsure of what the woman was about to do. The woman knelt and kissed Leo's hairy cheek. When she stood, she raised her arms above her head and his body rose as easily as if he were weightless, his legs and arms dangling toward the ground.

A cloud of dazzling white, as brilliant as a million sparkling diamonds, formed above his head and as it fell, his shape started to change. The cloud sank, obscuring her view, and Jolie took a step forward to try and see what was happening. When it began to sink back to the ground she stepped back again.

The magic bearer breathed hard, her chest rising and falling and her stomach working to pull air into her lungs. The blanket of white

216

still hid Leo's body and Jolie looked at her, the questions she was too afraid to ask in her eyes.

The raven witch smiled and moved toward Quentin. Just as she had for Leo, she knelt and kissed him on the cheek, but this time there was no magic blanket, no bright flashes of light to hide his body from view. This man was not hers to heal.

When she turned back to Jolie, the magic bearer held her hands up, a sphere of white light forming between them. As she held it aloft it grew and ran down her body like water. Her back stooped and her skin sagged, her eyes dulled and grew watery in their deep sockets.

The beautiful witch shrunk back into the old woman, her haggard appearance alarming after her true beauty had been so clear. From under her robe, she produced a rose, this one as red as blood. With a toothless grin, she held out the flower. When Jolie took it from her without hesitation, her grin widened and she brought her ghostly hand to the younger woman's cheek. Her skin felt as light as gossamer, cool as ice water against Jolie's skin.

The old woman patted Jolie's cheek one last time, then walked toward the trees, disappearing into the thick undergrowth without a sound. The light that had heralded her journey dissipated, leaving the old woman to make the last leg of her trip in darkness.

As Jolie watched the old woman melt into the forest from whence she came, a hand fell on her shoulder and she gasped. The hand was warm and heavy, the touch gentle, and she closed her eyes. Without looking, she knew who the hand belonged to, but she was afraid to look at him now. Hope filled her chest, and not a little apprehension. The fingers pressed into her skin, turning her around. She kept her eyes closed as the rain began to patter around them again.

Leo's other hand lit on her other shoulder, then trailed down her arm. Twining her fingers in his, he pulled her close. When his forehead touched hers, all she felt was warm skin, and the hand on hers was smooth and warm. His hand was shaking in hers, his body trembling, and she realized he must be as scared as she.

"Open your eyes, Jolie."

Leo's voice was the same, still a deep, gentle rumble, and that gave her confidence that he was still the same man on the inside, no matter what he looked like now. She opened her eyes and looked into his, still the same dark eyes she'd grown so familiar with. They weren't as far away from her own anymore, she realized with a smile. Still taller

217

than her, he was shorter than he had been, and with that she needed to see him, head to foot.

"My goodness!" she said, stepping back. His hand held tight to hers as she looked him over. No more a Beast, he was a man once again. No one had seen Prince Leopold in ten years in this form. Propriety be damned, Jolie was thrilled that she was the first person to see him this way, and looked her fill.

The witch hadn't just turned him back into a man, she'd left him resplendent in a brocaded dark green cutaway coat over a matching waistcoat, white lawn shirt, fawn breeches, and the tall Hessian boots he favored. The very image of a true prince stood before her, and Jolie would have felt inadequate if he hadn't been looking at her like she raised and set the sun.

Gone was the thick hair that had obscured his features and the gross oversizing that had distorted his good looks. She realized something else, too. He was the man she had dreamt of almost every night since she'd arrived, the handsome stranger in the Great Hall.

"You're beautiful, Leo."

Leo closed his eyes and smiled, only now able to believe it had really happened. He hadn't heard her say it; his heart had stopped before she'd said the words, but she must love him for this to have happened. The weight of what all this meant crashed over him and a laugh bubbled up in his chest.

Jolie watched as he laughed, the sound like a song in her heart. When he pulled her to him, she wrapped her arms around his waist and looked up at him. His happiness was infectious and when his eyes met hers, they were warm and bright. Without warning, he dipped his face to hers and pressed a kiss to her lips. Surprised, her instinct was to pull away but his kiss felt so good that she let his lips linger on hers.

When he pulled away, Leo ducked his head, a flush creeping up his throat all the way to his hairline. "I've wanted to do that for weeks."

Jolie blinked a few times, absorbing what he'd said. "Weeks?"

Leo nodded, his eyes trained on his boots. At her stunned look, he continued, taking one of her hands in his and twining their fingers together. "I hoped, even then, that you could be the one to break the curse."

"But you never told me how," Jolie whispered, wonder in her tone and her big green eyes.

Leo stepped closer, dropping his forehead onto hers and

threading the fingers of his free hand into her hair. "I knew you would never fall in love with me."

So, that was what he'd needed, Jolie thought. She closed her eyes and put a hand on Leo's cheek. He wrapped his arms around her and pulled her close, a deep sound of satisfaction in his chest rumbling against her ear. Realizing how much they'd needed each other all along, she pressed her lips to his once more, her own happiness leaving her breathless.

Author's Note

I borrowed from real medical conditions like acromegaly and gigantism for Leo's height and exaggerated facial features. For the body hair, of course I was inspired by Ambras Syndrome, a medical condition that causes hair growth over a large percentage of the body. It is also known as hypertrichosis, and colloquially as Wolfman Syndrome.

I paid homage to the writer of the earliest version of this story in Prince Leopold and his family. Gabrielle-Suzanne Barbot de Villeneuve wrote *La Belle et la Bête* in 1742.

I also tried to include a few nods to the 1991 Disney version. Cogsworth was a Comtoise clock, a type of clock common in Age of Enlightenment France, where the story is set. The clock Jolie sees in the Great Hall during her dreams is also a Comtoise, albeit a gigantic version.

I read just about every adaptation of this story that I come across and thought it would be fun to write one of my own. Beauty and the Beast is one of my favorite stories, beginning in childhood, and I hope I have done it justice.

I need to give a HUGE thanks to my sister Beth for all her help with the research. She was extra handy!

About the Author

Sarah Winter lives in western Wyoming with her husband, two sons, and two lazy salamanders. A lifelong geek and movie fanatic, she can usually be found with a computer in her lap and the TV on in the background.

She makes up silly songs, speaks in foreign accents for no reason, and dances badly all day long. She's also fluent in movie quotes and can sing 'Bohemian Rhapsody' word for word. It's a valuable skill.

Sarah is also the author of *Snowbound*, a contemporary Western romance set in Wyoming, which was a Quarter Finalist in the 2014 Amazon Breakthrough Novel Award Contest. Her second novel, *Over the Line*, was selected for a publishing contract from Kindle Press in Amazon's Kindle Scout program.

Connect with Sarah online:

Pinterest, Instagram - @SisterSadieJ
Facebook - sarahwinterbooks

Check out my website at https://www.sarahjwinter.net/

About the Editor

Annamarie Ahlfs resides in a small town with no stoplights in northern Wisconsin where she was born and raised. She grew up reading *The Boxcar Children* and *Goosebumps* series, but has since turned to authors such as Jodi Picoult, Stephen King, Mitch Albom, and John Green to refine her writing skill. In 2014, Annamarie decided to go pro and enroll in Southern New Hampshire University to obtain a Bachelor's Degree in Creative Writing and English. Since her enrollment, Annamarie became an active member of the National Society of Leadership and Success, Sigma Tau Delta, and Alpha Sigma Lambda honor societies.

Annamarie writes nonfiction too, including tribal ordinances and clickbait free content articles. She currently serves as Lead Editor for Wyoming author Sarah Winter, and is working on her own debut young adult novel, *The Mysteries of Life and Death*.

Made in the USA
Las Vegas, NV
21 June 2021

25151954R10134